WALLOOMSAC
A ROMAN FLEUVE

DAVID R. SLAVITT

ANAPHORA LITERARY PRESS

ATLANTA, GEORGIA

ANAPHORA LITERARY PRESS
1803 Treehills Parkway
Stone Mountain, GA 30088
http://anaphoraliterary.com

Book design by Anna Faktorovich, Ph.D.

Cover Images: Franz Kafka, James Joyce, Elizabeth I: Rainbow Portrait, James Fenimore Cooper by Jarvis, Oscar Wilde.

Cover Photo of the Walloomsac River by David R. Slavitt.

Published in 2014 by Anaphora Literary Press

Walloomsac: A Roman Fleuve
David R. Slavitt—1st edition.

ISBN-13: 978-1-937536-90-9
ISBN-10: 1-937536-90-4

Library of Congress Control Number: 2014952145

WALLOOMSAC
A ROMAN FLEUVE

DAVID R. SLAVITT

ACKNOWLEDGEMENTS

The first part of this novel was previously released as a chapbook with Black Scat Press.

A short selection from Part 3 is forthcoming with the Per Contra, an e-magazine.

No difficulties occur in what has never been tried.
Criticism is almost baffled in discovering the defects
of what has not existed;
and eager enthusiasm and cheating hope
have all the wide field of imagination
in which they may expatiate with little or no opposition.
—*Edmund Burke*

CONTENTS

I

WALOOMSAC

There is a river. I don't know the name of it although I'm sure it has one (I could look it up and discover that it is the Walloomsac, but why bother?). In its bed there are innumerable round stones over which the current rushes. I've driven past it many times, and now and then have wondered what it would be like to try to write about it. What would be the subject? The water rushing by, looking the same but always different? Or one of the stones, maybe? But how does one pick? Or, worse, having picked, how does one keep track of which it was, because although they're not identical they are still pretty much the same? Indistinguishable, one from another. Or maybe it's neither the water nor the stones but the course of the river from source to where it ends, flowing, I'm sure, into some larger river, the Hudson, I suppose. That's what it is on a map. But that's not right either, because the line on the map is still and the essence of this river is motion, the current that glints in the sun and, probably, the moonlight, although this isn't a road I've ever wanted to drive at night.

The difficulty, I realized eventually, was that I was analyzing too much, separating inseparable aspects as if that clarified or helped in any way. Not only is it moving all the time but it is also all those things at once, the water, the banks, the stones, the glints of sunlight and the sound the water makes as it negotiates its way down through those rocks. Well, of course, but to defend myself a little (against whom?) we have been trained to think this way. We consider ourselves as individuals and even insist on that as if it were the most important thing in the world. (As if we were the most important things in the world.) That is the central idea of western civilization although it is almost certainly wrong.

Look at a swarm of midges or an astonishing wheeling of a flock of birds and try to choose one. Look at an anthill (vade ad formicam, o piger, as Jesus quipped, but in Aramaic most likely) and think of how they digest their food collectively, the stomach of one disgorging its minuscule tidbit into the stomach of another. The organism is the whole colony. But you get the point.

Stories should be like that, or informed by that. Characters may emerge for a moment, but should then morph into other versions of themselves, probably with other names, other memories and hopes. Me, me, me? Your tiny hand is frozen. An eminent physician gave a lecture I happened to hear about the doctor patient relationship and said to a room full of earnest colleagues, "You have to make a 'we!'"

Nobody laughed. Many of them thought of wee-wee but then repressed the idea, blaming themselves for silliness. I swear by silliness. It is more reliable than wisdom and, in extremis, more useful. So let us make a wee. (Oui, oui!) Let us create out of this awkwardness a character, one M. La Trine. (First name? Jacques, perhaps) and wonder what his parents were thinking of. Or theirs. A defiant gesture, not to change the name, to maintain the La Trine honor. Admirable, if dumb. The family's reaction to the giggles of boors was to pronounce it "Tryne" for a while, but that didn't last more than a generation or two. Jean-Jacques de la Trine was not the inventor of the flush toilet.

That would have been nice. The word is a contraction of "lavatrina" which is the Latin for washbasin or washroom. I haven't the faintest idea what that would be in Aramaic.

The flush toilet was invented by John Harington, a son of an illegitimate son of VIII and a troublesome member of Elizabeth's court. He is remembered for his having translated *Orlando Furioso* into English, but his fame is the toilet, to which we still refer as a John. Elizabeth banished him for some peccadillo or other, not for life but only until he had translated the Ariosto epic. And off he went to some remote fastness (aren't all fastnesses remote?) with an Italian *dizionario* and a large supply of goose quills. His good friend La Trine sent him encouraging letters from Paris. French letters, those would have been, which is to say Condoms. That was of course the English word for them, because young men on the grand tour would send them back to friends at home enclosed with their letters. The French called them English coats. (They were made, after all, of sheep gut) Madame de Sevigne called them "armor against enjoyment and a spider's web against danger." It was Casanova who popularized their use. It was Sir Thomas Crapper who popularized the use of the flush toilet, and his name is also attached to the device, but one wonders what the difficulty was in persuading people to use flush toilets rather then chamber pots and privies.

"*Mon chère ami,*" La Trine wrote to his friend Harington...

You didn't know, did you, that Cher Ami was the name of a carrier pigeon of the United States Signal Corps in World War I? Shot in the breast, he managed nevertheless to flutter home to his roost with his message capsule intact carrying word from the Lost Battalion (of the 77th Infantry Division) that they needed help. The French awarded the bird a Croix de Guerre. Posthumously.

"*Alouette, gentille alouette, Alouette, je te plumerai.*" Jean-Jacques probably didn't write that but he would have written something in French. And that's French. It's even about a bird, but a lark rather than a pigeon. Still, in an imaginary letter from a fictive character to a real one (or one with an actual historical presence) are we obliged to pay attention to such details? Cui bono? Q. E. D. QE2.

So Harington scribbles away, following the arduous rhyme scheme of the Italian (a language in which almost everything rhymes with everything else) in English, which is nowhere near so generous. And he manages to produce one of the great translations into our language. Dryden was as good, maybe, but no better. And his correspondence with La Trine was diverting from this arduous work in that it was full of court gossip—not Elizabeth's court but Charles IX, a Valois king, so there were lots of scandals and plenty of catastrophes, the Massacre of Vassy, the St. Bartholomew's Day Massacre, and the siege of Rochelle, *par exemple*. The thing about distant fastnesses is that almost nothing happens in them. Out in the fields, peasants plow, staring at their oxen's assholes. Up in the tower, Harington, who has just completed another stanza, looks out at the paysage and the only moving thing is that ploughman and an occasional bird crossing the sky, a lark maybe.

The letters they exchange are being examined on both sides of the channel. Or, what is almost as good, they have to assume that there are censors going over what they say and looking for thoughts that are reportable. Insurrection is not the worry of either court, but religious heterodoxy. They may not have been religious in those days, but they couldn't help believing in religion, which could kill you if you put a foot wrong. The only safe subject was literature, in which they were both legitimately interested. (Can an illegitimate person have a legitimate interest?) The arguably excessive spread of literacy has forced more recent tyrants to include literature among the grounds for imprisonment and even death. Or, in Dostoyevsky's case, (yes, actually a legal case) that mock execution. Think of Mandelstam. Or, more difficult, try not to think of Mandelstam. Many people are able to do this with little effort, but now that the name has come up it will be a while before the immunity returns. And I do not make it any easier by alluding to Mandelstam variables, which are numerical quantities that encode the energy, momentum, and angles of particles in a scattering process in a Lorentz-invariant fashion. That was Stanley's idea. The other one, Osip, was the one who pissed off Stalin, which gets us back albeit circuitously to M. La Trine, doesn't it, and his accounts of refinement and scandal in the mess Paris had become.

They wrote about women. Of course, their communications were not altogether transparent. We learn to write to make ourselves clear and then, as we get better at it, we learn to eschew clarity, preferring ambiguity, subtlety, suggestion, allusion, and all the elegant forms of obfuscation that protect us from brutes—the censors or the mob. The woman about whom Harington complained was Elizabeth, and La Trine's belle dame sans merci was Catherine de Médicis, who dictated to Francis II, her fifteen-year-old son, what he should do and how and when and to whom. Then, on his death, she became the regent for her ten-year-old son, Charles IX. La Trine felt himself to be probably in greater danger than Harington, so he signed his communications simply with the number 3, which is a "trine." (A men's room with three urinals would be a trine latrine, even though few people say that.)

The discussion, as I conceive it, would have been quite grand, literary and wise (these adjectives are not necessarily adjacent). But also playful. John observes that the tradition of love poetry often represents the woman as being cruel and capricious, but nobody seems to imagine that those qualities do not follow the females from the boudoir or salon into the conference room or throne room. Jean-Jacques replies, ever so tactfully, that it isn't necessarily a matter of gender. There are maniacs and monsters in both sexes and the correlation is probably random, although it is true that we are unused to rulers who are women and therefore more uncertain of how we expect them to behave. But all that means is that the sample (Elizabeth and Catherine) is too small to speculate about. "*Mère, d'ailleurs*," he writes (mother, anyway.) This sounds very much like "*merde, d'ailleurs*" (shit anyway). It is always comforting to have a correspondent upon whom one can rely to notice such *jeux* and smile at them.

Charles IX was not, himself, a bad hat, as Jean-Jacques observes. Aside from the unfortunate events of St. Bartholomew's day and his chagrin and rage at his mother about it, he is perhaps remembered best for his Edict of Roussillon, which established that the year begins on January 1. Not Christmas, or Easter, or March 1, as it did in various dioceses but January 1. April 1 would have been good, too, but you can't have everything. For his part, Harington makes observations about Ariosto, whom he has been translating day after day. An epic, yes, but very funny. Either Ariosto is making jokes or else it is Harington, playing games, inventing an absurd version of the poem. Taking liberties, which is the very thing that banishment is supposed to prevent. He can appeal to the text, of course, and have other Italian speakers verify that, sì, this is actually what Ariosto wrote. But will the queen be patient enough to consider such testimony. She could very well shake her head and signal that his be removed. (Considering that despite his illegitimacy he was still related to Elizabeth, his family connection would entitle him to be beheaded rather than hanged.)

Mostly a quick death, the procedure could go wrong. On 27th May 1541, the 68-year-old Margaret Pole, Countess of Salisbury was dragged to the block, but she refused to lay her head on the block. Forced down, she struggled. The inexperienced executioner missed her neck entirely and made a gash in her shoulder. She leapt from the block and was chased by the executioner with his axe. She was struck eleven times before she died. It is not impossible to imagine that there were several executioners and officials could chose an accomplished one or a bungler as they thought appropriate to the crimes of the condemned.

Harington puts the quill down in its holder, rises from his writing table, and returns to the window, not to look out but only to stretch and breathe some fresh air. He needs a rest. The quill needs a rest. (I do, too.)

Sir Walter Scott refers in *Waverly* to the writer Francisco de Ubeda, who wrote his history of *La Picara Justina Diez* and who complained of his pen having caught a hair, whereupon "with more eloquence than common sense," he commences "an affectionate expostulation with that useful implement, upbraiding it with being the quill of a goose—a bird inconstant by nature, as frequenting the three elements of water, earth, and air indifferently, and being, of course, 'to one thing constant never.'" Then on his own divagation, he says he "entirely dissent(s) from Francisco de Ubeda in this matter, and hold(s) it the most useful quality of (his) pen, that it can speedily change from grave to gay, and from description and dialogue to narrative and character. So that if (his) quill display no other properties of its mother-goose than her mutability it resembled a smiling summer's day, in which, notwithstanding, we are made sensible by certain, although slight signs that it may thunder and lighten before the close of evening."

Isn't that lovely? What speaks to me most directly is Scott's ease of intruding himself into his story to perform the flight about the goose feather. It is no mere violation of the decorum of narration but rather is the essence of the novel. Scott and the readers are conspirators in the telling of Captain Waverly's adventures. Waverly in his handsome uniform is a conceit; Scott at his writing table is real as the book keeps reminding us. That is the fresh air Harington is inhaling through the open window of his room in the turret of his banishment.

Harington will complete the translation, appear at court to present the manuscript to the astonished queen, and be welcomed back, although her majesty warns him that it would be a good idea for him to watch his step and leave the ladies- in-waiting alone. In Paris, La Trine dies during the course of an operation in which the surgeon was trying to remove a kidney stone that was blocking his urethra. (Wouldn't you know?)

His papers and effects are bundled up and shipped to Klaus Wasserman, a cousin in Mainz. The sheaf of Harington's letters would be of great interest to scholars both of history and literature, but they were destroyed in a fire in the early nineteenth century. Klaus Wasserman's great grandson was August Paul von Wassermann. (When was the "von" added? In 1910, actually, when August's father, a Bavarian banker, was elevated to the nobility, which wasn't easy for a Jew.) In 1906, when he was still a mere Wassermann, he developed the complement fixation test for syphilis antibodies. It wasn't an absolutely reliable test, because it couldn't distinguish between syphilis, systemic lupus erythematosus, malaria, and tuberculosis and it sometimes failed to indicate anything whatever in a patient who was infected with one or more of these diseases, but still it was better than nothing.

Or was it? Let us imagine a responsible and conscientious young man, a captain, say (we can give him the same rank as Waverly) who is about to return to Berlin from a posting in a barracks somewhere in the east (Letschin? Zechin? Does it make any difference?) where the Russians might attack if the Bosnian Crisis is not peacefully resolved. He has visited the local brothel a few times (where there are barracks there are brothels) and he wants to be sure that he is disease-free and in no danger of infecting Greta, his beautiful fiancée. We cannot fault him for such thoughtfulness. He goes to the Kaiser-Wilhelm-Gesellschaft for the Advancement of Science, where Dr. Wasserman is Director of the Department of Experimental Therapy and he is one of the doctor's very early patients. (Or subjects, because the therapy is, as the sign on the door proclaims in bold, gold, Gothic letters, experimental.) One wonders how the captain heard about Wasserman's work. Barracks gossip? A friend in Berlin who met Wasserman at a party? There are many possibilities among which it would be tedious to choose. But there he sits in the examining room and the distinguished, rather severe-looking physician with a formidable mustache courteously knocks on the door and enters. Symptoms? None whatever. The captain explains the reason for his visit and the doctor is pleased. To diagnose syphilis in someone who is obviously syphilitic is no great achievement. But to determine whether an apparently healthy person is afflicted is, after all, what the test is for. The public health implications will be nothing less than splendid.

You have a reason to be concerned? The captain (let us call him Gustav—Gustav Schäuble, which has that decorative umlaut in it) confesses to his patronization of prostitutes. This, too, is satisfactory for von Wasserman's purpose. He explains to the officer that, contrary to popular belief, one cannot acquire the naughty spirochetes in a latrine. (Him again? Nice that he should drop by.) Dr. Wasserman's assistant draws the blood and he tells the captain that they will have the results in two or three days. Gustav thanks him. He doesn't salute—Wasserman is not an officer—but he does a crisp, slight bow, a brief inclination of the head actually, and departs.

The results are not what he'd hoped for. The results of the test are positive.

So for Greta's sake the wedding must be postponed. Or cancelled actually, because she is likely to be angry with him. Gone are his dreams of domestic bliss, a family, and respectable comfort. The usual treatment for the disease is mercury salts, which are not reliably effective. Paul Erlich's Magic Bullet, his *magische Kugel*, has yet to be discovered. (This was Salvarsan, of course, which has arsenic in it.) The captain's life, as he has imagined it, is over. He is now disgraced, an outcast like Charles Baudelaire, Karen Blixen, Napoleon Bonaparte, Beau Brummell, Al Capone, Gaetano Donizetti, Bedřich Smetana, Paul Gauguin, Heinrich Heine, Henry VIII, Ivan the Terrible, Scott Joplin, John Keats, Édouard Manet, Guy de Maupassant, Friedrich Nietzsche, Leo Tolstoy, Vincent van Gogh, and Oscar Wilde. Franz Schubert, Henri de Toulouse-Lautrec, John Wilmot, Earl of Rochester, Lord Randolph Churchill, and Adolf Hitler.

Those are all famous syphilitics, or better say they are all famous people who had syphilis. They certainly weren't famous as syphilitics. But if some contrarian decided to establish a Syphilitic Hall of Fame, in Camden, NY, maybe, East St. Louis, or, no, in Las Vegas, these are some of the people who would almost certainly be included.

But the thing is that Gustav's thing is fine. He doesn't have syphilis at all. The test results are a mistake, a false positive. (Dare one say a fiction?). If he had married Greta, he would almost certainly have infected her but with a different disease than the one he feared. By 1910, when Paul Ehrlich's Salvarsan came onto the market (and quickly became the best selling pharmaceutical of its time), Greta had married someone else, a lawyer let us suppose. And by 1913, the captain had died of a hemorrhage from the TB, which was a death not much worse than what he would have faced in the trenches in 1914. Ehrlich got a Nobel Prize for his work. There was a movie about him with Edward G. Robinson playing the eponymous part. There was a German stamp with his picture on it. There is a crater of the moon named after him.

It's a novel, isn't it? Rather old fashioned but with some great scenes in it, and uplifting, because science is good and we want the young people to aspire (and also perhaps study chemistry). But what would be the import of it. You can't just say that syphilis is bad and that therefore a cure is good. There was controversy about that, because without STDs (sexually transmitted diseases that is, not Doctorates in Sacred Theology) there will be promiscuity and immorality. The very basis of our civilization will be threatened, etc., etc. One could even make an argument that Salvarsan, and then penicillin, and the birth control pills have had that effect and that civilization has collapsed without anyone noticing. Or it could just be the triumph over adversity because work in the lab is arduous and frustrating. Or it could be about anti-Semitism, because both Wasserman and Ehrlich were Jews and the Reich tried to erase their names from memory. The name of the street in Frankfurt-Sachsenhausen was changed to something else and, only after the war was it restored to honor the good doctor. Sachsenhausen's name, the House of Saxons, was not changed, but there is a memorial to those who died in the concentration camp there.

But let us get back to our story. (What story?) Gustav's, I think. The others, the biggies, only come in for brief scenes. That was Walter Scott's secret, to save the emperor for the denouement. (Tolstoy breaks this rule.) So Gustav's life in Panavision and Technicolor with wonderful recreations of Berlin in the early twentieth century. But it is nonetheless absurd. Utterly ridiculous. (Uttarly Pradesh, as they might say in Lucknow.) Not only did Gustav not understand it, but I don't understand it. (He is only a captain; I am the author and therefore outrank him.) What are any of us to think?

Ah ha! My point exactly. (You take my point? I've got your nose.) The purpose of these fitful gestures of babouinisme is to get rid of the wrong kind of reader. Readers with the wrong kind of expectations. Have you ever left a newspaper on a table only to see the cat jump up and sit on it, as though she were reading it anally? That's the image I have in mind for most readers. (The people who don't read at all are like cats sitting on the rug from which no information of any kind can arise.) Half the literate adults in America read fewer than one book a year. Many of them read none at all. I admire them. These are the people who know their place. It's the literate illiterates who bother me, the ones who presume, thinking that they can read. They have distorted the literary marketplace, which now depends less on excellence than on the potential of some books to sell in the hundreds of thousands. Wal-Mart and Costco determine winners and losers. And Amazon and Barnes and Noble. And what are those novels like? They have plots for one thing. This happens and then that, and there is cause and effect, and there is some kind of rough justice in the outcome. The reader is satisfied by a story that makes sense—even though his or, more often her, life makes no sense whatever. What do you expect such readers to make of Gustav's aggressively nonsensical life? The best medical care in the world, and they screw up his life. Or not. "First do no harm," says Hypocrites, but if that were the rule most of us wouldn't dare to get out of bed in the morning.

Gustav goes back to the barracks in Zechin to maintain his men in good order and prepared for an attack by the Russians. Which never comes. This time the Bosnian Crisis has been resolved by the politicians. It is the Serbian Crisis that has not yet arisen, which they won't be able to figure out how to address, but by then Gustav is *gestorben*. On the wrong side of the grass and pushing up daisies.

(Do you know that there is a magazine called *Gun and Garden*? And that, more often than not, gardenias grow in gardens?)

When Greta hears belatedly about the death of her former fiancée, is she saddened, if only for a moment? Is she pleased, perhaps, that the sonofabitch no longer troubles the world with his faithless and objectionable existence? Perhaps we should tell the story from her point of view, departing only now and then to demonstrate her mis-understanding of what's going on. She is an epitome of misprision.

Is that what Oscar Wilde had in mind when he created Miss Prism in *The Importance of Being Earnest*? Miss Prision? Or, considering how a prism refracts light, is that unnecessary? (It is painful to re-port that there are masters' essays and doctoral dissertations about Miss Prism that were written and approved at Stanford, Harvard, and Berkeley—as if there were anything complicated about her character. Or, worse, how about Miss Prism and Edward Casaubon—write for three or four months?)

We recall that it was Gustav's concern for Greta's health and his reluctance to infect her with this loathsome disease that brought him to Dr. Wasserman's offices in the first place. For this he is relentless-ly pursued by a vengeful fury and he winds up an impoverished and drunken officer in the barracks east of nowhere, gambling away his money, seeking solace in the tavern and the brothel, and whiling away the boring hours when the soldiers are not on parade (there's noth-ing else for them to do) reading. Goethe, perhaps. "*Das Ewig Weibli-che Zieht Uns Hinan,*" he says. The eternal feminine draws us upward. Ja, Ja, Gustav thinks. And then, like a seagull with a large clam in its talons, the old *Weibliche* lets us fall to smash on the rocks so she can devour our soft innards. "A bottle of schnapps, *Schankkellner.*"

Do not feel sorry for him. It is a sign of his refinement that he is unwilling to settle for the imperfect world in which he finds himself. He is beyond disappointment and has reached an acme of philosophi-cal disgust. If we think about it from the right point of view, it is an achievement. He has seen through the nonsense that we exchange to reassure one another and, having reached a truth, embraces it. He could commit suicide, but that would be too easy. (Especially for a fictional character, it is easy indeed.) Better to sit and brood, drinking and dwindling. That would be the honest response and the brave one.

But to reconsider, is it not the case that most suicides are sorties into the world of imagination? Think how they'll miss me, he tells himself. Think how they'll regret having driven me to this extremity. It's all fiction, because it is in the future that the act of suicide will obliterate. Even if his faithless friends and fickle women do suffer some twinge of regret, it won't do him any good because he will have abdicated from the world in which such things matter only to an unimaginable condition of non-being, a darkness beyond all darknesses, a silence more profound than anything we have in the real world. And what is beyond the real world? Fiction! But not the orderly kind to which we have grown accustomed. This is chaotic like the dreams of a drug addict. (Has it ever been considered that God might well be a drug addict? Or even a pusher? That would explain a lot that has been happening on earth.)

So, far better than suicide is the idea of it. Gustav sits in the gloomy bar and imagines that he isn't in the bar or anywhere else for that matter. He is no longer thinking of Greta and her husband who is, even at this very moment, likely to be fondling the breasts that should have been his to caress. His *Weltschmerz* has ascended to a far higher plane in which he can consider the many defects not only of his own life but of all men's lives. As cavalrymen might jest, "Who will say him neigh?"

In the beguiling cartoon world in which most novels are set, there is a come-uppance. Gustav doesn't even have to know about it. It's better, maybe, if he doesn't. That way the reader can feel like one of the gods, looking down on the characters with an understanding none of them can possibly imagine. (Unless, of course, they read the novel, too, but can a character in a book read the book? Can he then pick up his quill--or, all right, fountain pen—and write the author or perhaps the editor of the *Times Literary Supplement* to protest about the factual mistakes and the errors of interpretation? I could have just said the TLS and assumed that anyone reading this piece of persiflage would know what those letters stood for. (Surely not Transport Layer Security, which has to do with cryptography.) But it's a habit hard to break even though it seems painfully condescending.

Would it be possible for Dr. Wassermann to discover, through some coincidence we might contrive, what a bad time Gustav has had because of him? Is that at all probable in the real world? That's for novels. And movies. A shrink and a hooker are standing in line one behind the other at the complaint department of a large department store and they discover that her garish boudoir chaise has been delivered, mistakenly, to him, while his much more staid consulting room couch has been delivered to her. A cute meet, that's called. Could we do something like that? Of course. But would we want to? That would be beyond condescending. That would be pimping.

The evening he has announced the results of the test to Gustav, Dr. Wassermann goes to hear Mahler (another Gustav entirely) who is to appear as the guest conductor of the *Berliner Philharmoniker* (which is not, alas, a group of harmoniker players). Is that cheating, going from the captain to the composer in that abrupt way? It seems perfectly stochastic but that is what makes it natural. It could have been Hans von Bülow, the regular conductor, but it wasn't. No rhyme or reason. (What rhymes with von Bülow anyway?)

The program probably omits an account of the founding of the orchestra, which is one of the great cautionary tales in performance history. The ensemble was originally called *Frühere Bilsesche Kapelle* (literally, "Former Bilse's Band" when the 52 musicians founded it, breaking away from Bilse's Band because he had taken them to play in Warsaw and the train tickets were for fourth class. Not third. Fourth! Did they have seats? Windows? Floor, for God's sake? These were cars for migrant workers who had mud on their shoes and spoke no known languages. And among these wretched of the earth, the musicians were to travel with instruments in their handsome cases that proclaimed their worth and therefore invited theft from the glinty-eyed, horny-handed farmworkers. What kind of *Scheiße* was that? Did the musicians board the train? I do hope not. I prefer to imagine that they decided there on the platform that this was intolerable, the last straw (der letzte Strohhalm?) and that they would return to their homes to meet later in the week and form a new orchestra.

For Dr. Wassermann it was a grand evening of music. There was a Schubert symphony first, and then the new Mahler piece. Mahler took the Schubert slightly slower than most conductors would, bringing out a quiet sadness that lurks under its sublime lyricism. Syphilitics (Schubert, not Mahler) have reason to be melancholy, after all. But it was the Mahler that Wassermann had come to hear, the spaciousness of it, the sense that world-weariness was rousing itself to sing, even though there was every reason not to. Except will. And heroism. Schopenhauer and Nietzsche could have been sitting in the auditorium, both of them nodding agreement with the sweet heartbreak of the cellos and then the yearning of the woodwinds.

There is reason for the gloom. Mahler has never recovered from the death of his daughter, Maria, from diphtheria. His physician's discovery of his defective heart was a further blow. His wife Alma began taking lovers, although she continued to live with Gustav. We may even imagine that she made up some plausible story to tell Gustav that for him to have sex with her would be a strain on his heart. In other words, she was claiming that she was fucking around for reasons of

Gustav's health. (To argue with her would also have strained his heart almost as much as she was straining all reason. Even Dr. Freud, whom he consulted for his unbearable depression, seemed impressed by the composer's troubles, not that he actually said so, but with his long oval face and trim beard, Freud could nod eloquently in delicate assent.

Never mind the theories. Most psychiatrists don't pay much attention to them anymore. It was the occasional, barely perceptible nod that was his great therapeutic instrumentality. The elongated oval face, the beard, the glasses... it's Daddy. Or God. Or whatever you need. And if he nods, his patients have the feeling, at least for the instant, of being understood. Sympathy can be comforting, but true understanding is what dissolves loneliness. That dismal sense of isolation from the rest of mankind doesn't disappear but it diminishes perceptibly at least for a while, and that is the comfort, or at least a vision of it. What Dr. Wasserman was feeling in the concert hall, Mahler had been feeling in Freud's cluttered consulting room. Or something very like. At least for the time being (and what in hell else is there?), one can breathe. The heaviness lifts. The mood brightens. Freud was perfectly well aware of this, of course, but how could he have written it down. All that theoretical stuff with the ego and the id, and the Oedipus complex is decorative to be sure but nodding is always good. With the lips ever so slightly pursed as if in concentration on what the patient has been saying. Nod? It doesn't even have to be sincere but it projects empathy, suggests understanding and compassion. Basically that's what gypsies do at carnivals. (It works for them, too.) Wynken and Blynken were assiduous medical students, but out in practice it was Nod who had the gift. (You think I am making foolishness? Not so. It is an undeniable fact that Wynken, Blynken, and Nod appeared briefly as gas-mask-wearing, tricycle-riding villains in *Doom Patrol* comics. With that as a precedent, how can I dedicate, how can I consecrate, how can I hallow this ground?)

But the question (what question?) is not about Freud's practice. More intricately, who beside ourselves can connect Freud and Mahler with the troubles and momentary exaltation of Dr. Wassermann, never mind the miseries of Captain Schäuble? Schopenhauer perhaps, and Nietzsche, who may or may not be in the hall, but their views are too lofty, too abstract. Still, there is a connection or the chance for one as our eyes roam this way and that. Outside, flittering about the gas lamps on the street, there are tiny flying insects, among which one can suppose, if only for an instant, such connections. What holds them together this way is the light from the lamp, of course. And what holds our oddly assorted group of figments together is the light of our attention.

What? Is this what it's going to be? More of the same until the book stops? Yes, as I have already warned. When will we know it's over? Well, you can, of course, stop at any time, and in that case it will be over for you. Or you can go on until there are no more pages on the right hand side (left hand side for the Hebrew translation). For me? It will be over when there is no more energy, when the pieces come together. Or turn out to be impossible to bring together. How did Jackson Pollock know that his painting was finished? (He had the advantage of the canvas on the floor, the dimensions of which were his ((only?)) constraints. Here, the canvas is whatever size feels right. So if it feels right to stop, do. I shall not hold it against you. Most people in the world will not have glanced even at these introductory pages. You are one of the elite, an enthusiast, and almost impossibly raffiné. In a limited way, you are one of my friends.

But if we are friends, why do I not show greater consideration for you, cater to your tastes, give you what you're used to, and try to ingratiate myself? Because that would be insulting to both of us. I am typing away, sometimes imagining a short excursion, another goddam (i.e. difficult to sell) novella, but now and again I have the amusing thought that it could go on and on, growing like a kudzu vine to take over all of North Carolina, not to mention the rest of my life. A thousand pages of this word salad? Three thousand, to match Musil or Proust? Might this not grow into one of those imposing works that are published in two or three volumes boxed? I have learned to dread finishing anything because that puts me out of a job. It is depressing. I am, yet again, a former writer. Or even a non-writer, like all the other people in the subway car who always look stunned. (Who is to say that they are not? And if they were off their medications, the subway would be even more dangerous than it is. The MBTA has signs up telling riders: "If you see something, say something." But there is nobody in the station to whom to say anything. And by the time you've got your cellphone out and are dialing the emergency number, you and everyone else in the car could have been blown to smithereens (from "smiodar," which means "fragments" in Irish Gaelic. 'Een' is a commonplace diminutive). The MBTA sign could be meant only for me. "If you see something, say something."
What about people who don't write?

Or, for writers, the sign could read the other way. If you want to say something, see something. Look at something. Stare at it until meaning arises from it. And it's better if you don't entirely understand the meaning, because that is what you will discover in the course of writing. (That was badly phrased: I hate writing courses, and I imagine Flaubert taking one and grin.)

Harington wasn't writing just to keep himself occupied. He wanted to finish his work so he could leave the grim tower (abolie? as in the sixteenth card in the Tarot Major Arcana?) and return to London and life. He was working as fast as he could but paying close attention to what he was doing. Out of pride? Probably. But also because he couldn't help enjoying it. It is very good and he was aware of that. One can misjudge an original work, but with a translation, there is a yardstick against which to measure what is on the manuscript page. Wine, women, song, and civilization are also enjoyable and he was good at all of these. You'd think that his being Elizabeth's godson would give him more leeway than most courtiers had, but in fact Elizabeth was more likely to be embarrassed by his louche behavior and not entirely jocular satires and more angry about his deportment. Still, she did have 101 other godchildren. (Dalmatians?) I'd have liked it there in his cell, I think. Books to read. Music to play (I've always wanted to learn the lute). A quiet, repetitive life, which is what the Muse finds comfortable. Or, anyway, I do.

Worst case, which is often entertaining to imagine, is that there are no readers and that this can't be done. There can't be a novel without a story, without characters that persist through the pages, without some development. There should be an enlightenment somewhere, an adjustment. Not this but that. Very satisfying, or it can appear so. But is life like that? Are there characters who stay with us for more than a few years? Wives, husbands, parents, children, sure (or so you hope), but other than them? You move from city to city, shedding friends each time. People whom you saw fairly frequently are now a thousand miles away and you have lost touch. (Or, as we get older, they may be dead.) You have an experience and then you may discover something about the world or yourself, but the probability is that you'll just forget it and move on. Self-consciousness is not such a great gift. It allows you to shave, maybe, recognizing as you look in the mirror that, yes, it's your face. But it doesn't lead to wisdom. It doesn't improve your life. Mostly it weighs you down. It is a defect to be self-satisfied, but if you are not satisfied, then what the hell is the point of living? And you get older and decrepit, hard of hearing, more shortsighted, with less and less energy. You are now the whingeing being that wakes up from naps that are longer and more frequent. You? I! Or, more accurately, I, you, he, she, we, you (plural) and they nap. Or take a nap. Nap, of a nap, to or for a nap, nap, from a nap, O nap. Can

I make it any more clear? I nap, I have napped, I napped, I shall nap, I shall have napped, and so on, endlessly, through all the conjugations and declensions. These and Euclid's theorems are reliable, although not often useful these days. But you can trust them. You can take a nap as you can take a breath but you can't keep one or give one. Much of life is like that. (Or maybe not.)

Even so, do I need readers at this age and condition of life? An author imagines an audience and, even if it is fictional, that's what he's good at, isn't it? Imagining. Fictions. We tell ourselves stories all the time, knowing they are untrue but taking comfort from them. Even if these readers were to become real, they would remain figments, unless they write, as a few of them will, to ask for explanations or autographs. (Or worse, they ask that you "don't inscribe it, please, but just sign it." As if it isn't clear that the autograph seeker is going to resell the book. Legally, I don't have to return it. Anything that comes in the mail that you haven't asked for is yours to keep. The return address labels from the SPCA with dogs and cats and rabbits on them? (Who else would want them, with your name and address on them?) Even copies of your own book. And you can use the return envelope for its postage, covering the address with a new label. Nasty? But what do these scroungers deserve? And it isn't the scrounging so much as the insult to my intelligence. Don't inscribe it? How could he declare any more clearly that he hasn't read it and doesn't intend to but plans to resell it instantly? What, upon mine honor, does that require of me?

In Harington's time and La Trine's, it wasn't so bad. Very few people knew how to read even in London and Paris, and it was likely that most of them knew each other. To have a fictive audience, it helps if you can supply names and faces for at least a few of them. It wasn't a club, really, but a culture, a civilization. Go and catch a falling civilization.

You flip a few pages ahead, looking for a section break, a good place to pause in this ebullition of *dreckerai*. But there aren't any. That's not an accident. One of the few things I had in mind as I commenced this was that there should be no sections, no chapters. I do not go so far as Thomas Bernhard (I don't have his nerve) and do the entire thing (whatever it is) in one paragraph. An uninterrupted column of type. Exhilarating? Impish? Sadistic? Are these mutually exclusive? (In any event, Bernhard is a great writer and you should put his name on your list. Or return this to the library and instead take out one of his. Or send this book to me without any expectation of seeing it again.)

Like the unhappy Hauptman, Bernhard was diagnosed as having tuberculosis. But that was an error and one with catastrophic consequences, for he was sent off to a sanatorium. (Or is it sanitorium? It turns out that these are the same word and that only Americans and Australians make any distinction, one of them being a long term facility mostly for tuberculosis and the other a hospital, often a psychiatric one, but with the advent of antibiotics the sanitaria have mostly disappeared.) Anyway, Bernhard is shipped off to this TB facility, even though he doesn't have the disease and of course he contracts it there from all those tubercular people by whom he is now surrounded. Small wonder that he was *un petit peu* grumpy. About everything. And having been so wronged, he had every right.

Manuel Bandiera, one of Brazil's greatest (and funniest) poets of the twentieth century, really did have TB. They send him across the ocean to Davos in Switzerland for the healthy air of the mountains offered by the sanitarium. And there he contracts surrealism. (Is that a disease? Or a mere symptom?) He meets a gang of European poets, painters, and intellectuals there, Paul Éluard for one, and learns what has been happening in the twentieth century in intellectual circles in Europe, which he takes back to Brazil. It is a cultural watershed, as La Trine would claim. Did they do cultures back then? Did some Brazilian doctor put some of the poet's sputum in a petri dish to see whether any tuberculosis germs grew? No, that's not right. It's a skin test, to see whether the patient has developed an antibody to the TB bacterium. In 72 hours the doctor looks to see the degree of induration (swelling, for God's sake, but "induration" sounds more impressive) around the area where the tuberculin units were injected, usually the forearm. (Forearmed is forewarned?) A positive result doesn't actually mean that the patient has tuberculosis but only that he has been exposed to it. And a negative result doesn't mean that the person doesn't have tuberculosis. Some test! It is called the Mantoux test because Charles Mantoux invented it. He read his paper to the French Academy of Sciences in 1910. Too late to do our poor Captain Schäuble any good. Better late than never, people say, but he would take exception. As drunk and depressed as he was, he approved of disease, TB and all others. He had been trained to contemplate mass death with a certain sang froid (or, as he might have put it, *Kaltblütigkeit*) and as between being cut in half by a cannon ball and coughing one's lungs out into the crachoir next to his sick bed, what's to choose? The disease, probably, because it strikes civilians, too, who didn't enlist and therefore suppose that they are safe.

Davos, by the way, is where Herr Mann sends Hans Castorp to visit his tubercular cousin, but it turns out that he has the disease, too. That's the plot of *Der Zauberberg*. The air is cold and thin there and Castorp perceives that the passage of time is quite different from down in the lowlands of Hamburg. It is an elegant metaphor that does not insist upon itself. There are antibiotics now, usually a number of them that the patient has to take at specified times of the day for six months or so. Screw that up or feel better and stop taking the drugs and the beasty bugs become immune to the Isoniazid, Rifampin, Pyrazinamide, Ethambutol, and whatever else your druggist has sent over and you are as doomed as the good soldier Schäuble and will die sooner rather than later. Does it make much difference? Is existence such a good thing?

Castorp intends to visit for only a few weeks but as it turns out he stays on for seven years until, at the end, he goes off to fight in World War I—which he does not expect to survive. I could have let Gustav Schäuble do that, but readers would suppose I was imitating Mann, so, to be my own man, I have him die before the first shots are fired.

Come to think of it Schäuble doesn't die because he never lived. Best of all, Sophocles says somewhere, is never to be born. Well the captain wasn't. I dreamed him up, as you will no doubt recall, conjuring the shadow of a shadow out of phonemes, out of pure nothing and he can float on forever, sitting in that putative bar with the Captain from Köpenick, Wilhelm Voigt, who was, you will recall, an impostor. And also fictional. He puts on a uniform and poses as a captain, which is, for the purpose of the play, sufficient. The uniform is real but the wearer is not. (This may have been the case with General MacArthur.) Schäuble is also fictional but he is not posing, except to us, which us not a crime. It is his purpose in life. Voigt, however, an ex-convict, seems to have no other aim in life either, so it is his purpose, too. They swap stories and buy each other schnapps—from which they never get drunk unless I say so. Nicht wahr? (Nick is the bartender or--what the hell was it? --*der Schankkellner.*) And Wahr? Wahrheit is whatever Dichtung says it is. (Otto von Dichtung, chief librarian of Magdeburg for some years in the late nineteenth century, fought against the Dewey decimal system and had the books in his library arranged chronologically according to the year of their publication. The books were more difficult to find but one developed a sense of history walking along the time-machine shelves while, with Dewey, it was all simultaneous.)

Schäuble, by this time a sodden wreck of what he had been only a few years earlier, says impressive things about having understood the purpose of his life. "This is what I am," he says, speaking slowly and enunciating very carefully as drunks often do in the misguided belief that no one will notice that they are sozzled.

"This is what I was meant to be. It was my destiny from the beginning, from before I was born, but it took me a long time to discover that. And the world has gone to great lengths to explain it to me."

"Nonsense," says Voigt, who may be a criminal and an imposter but is not a fool. "Look at me! If there were predestination, I could never have been convicted of anything. No criminal could even be tried, because we could all plead predestination. It wasn't our fault. We were fated to do whatever it was. Blame God. Morality goes out the window. Or, better, say that our pretensions to morality are defenestrated. With the baby, the bathwater, and the contents of the chamber pot."

"Scheiss," says Schäuble.

"Exactly," says Voigt.

"For a criminal and an impostor, you take a high tone, sir."

"That's why it's fun," says Voigt. "But which comes first, the character or the costume? The words or the music? The chicken salad or the egg salad?"

"I don't follow you."

"Is that my fault or yours?"

And so forth. But where were we? We were talking (as they were also) about TB and syphilis. Why? It's understandable if you are puzzled. But you have to keep in mind that TB and syphilis were the great subjects of a lot of nineteenth century fiction and opera. The TB was a metaphor for the other, to which it was almost as inelegant to refer to as to contract. This is why Violetta dies in *La Traviata*. What Dumas and then Piave were relying on was that the audience would make the substitution. What sense does it make otherwise to have the courtesan come down with tuberculosis? The disease has to be a punishment that God or nature inflicts upon her for fucking around. Could she die of diphtheria (hard to sing) or appendicitis? Pneumonia? Shingles? None of those would make sense. Some would be so discordant as to be funny. Let's imagine her with psoriasis, scratching herself to death in that closing but now not-quite-so-touching scene. No? No! I am not dismissing her. Actually, I think she was impressively bold for those times. Even now it would be cheeky for Madonna or one of the Kardashians to wear white camellias most of the time but red ones on the days she was having her period to épater la bourgeoisie and pretty much everyone else. Even Colette would blink.

In the twentieth century, AIDS was the incurable (and therefore sad) disease to which was attached a soupçon of culpability. (How many smidges to the soupçon? How many crotchets to the minim?) But AIDS is now under control, or it would be if those who suffer from it would take their medicine. As it is a million people die every year.

Or is it three million? Is there a difference? TB survives mostly in the third world; and syphilis has been vanquished (or nearly) by antibiotics. What is a novelist or a librettist now to do? Assume that all is well? (At least in the sense of not sick?) People now march "against breast cancer," wearing pink bows. (Does that make them feel better?) How about marching against Crohn's disease (brown ribbons) or eczema (shreddy red ones)? The implication in any of these marches is that progress can be made, the disease can be cured or even conquered, and that heaven's perfection is just around the corner, if only they keep marching. The logical extension of this is the march against death (black ribbons, perhaps?) in which all of us are involved. Maybe marching isn't enough. We must fight them, as in the war against poverty, the war against terror, the war against [your nomination here]. We will fight them in the produce sections, we will fight them in the hedgerows (or would if we had hedgerows), and we will fight them at the hairdressers', who do at least try to make their customers look younger and more attractive than they would otherwise.

Did Freud help Mahler at all? The evidence of *Kindertotenlieder* is ambiguous. Mahler was still heartbroken but he was able to function well enough to write this beautiful and moving piece, setting Friedrich Rückert's poems to music. It was an outcome that may not have been entirely happy but was better than what the composer had expected. "Now the sun wants to rise as brightly / as if nothing terrible had occurred during the night. / The calamity had happened only to me, / but the sun shines equally on everyone." Compared to that kind of suffering, Captain Schäuble's complaint diminishes a bit. He didn't get the girl. He and Greta didn't have a life together. And they never had children, who are always hostages to fate, particularly back then when there were no immunizations or antibiotics with which to prevent or treat childhood diseases. Many died. The bereaved parents either hardened their hearts and became robots or they disintegrated. The best of them, I think, were ruined and ended up in bars, not necessarily the same one as the captains patronized, but which of them would have been particularly aware of his surroundings when it was oblivion itself that he was seeking?

It's sad about the Mahler girl, and the music, as I've just said, is gorgeous, but this is no invitation to the sentimental connection of art with hurt. Art—writing, painting, or composing—is better than that, and only the vulgar turn away from the art (which is demanding) to focus on the hurt, which is simple enough to understand (is it?) and an occasion for expressions of cheap compassion. It gets even crazier than that. There are some who think it was a Good Thing that Maria died because look at the masterpiece her death produced. No, it didn't. Mahler produced it, and if he was grieving and the grief comes through in the music, okay. But if the doctors had known anything at all about disease and she had lived, the father, in a better mood, might have composed music that was just as good but maybe more cheerful.

Happy music, even, like Papa Haydn's. Don't cry for Maria Mahler. (Or Argentina.) Even if she had recovered, she'd have died by now. And more likely than not, she'd have been forgotten like her sister Anna, who got better. Who remembers her or even knows her name? The dying itself wasn't unusual. Gustav's reaction was understandable. But we are seduced by the story, in which Maria did not participate at all, and Gustav, only reluctantly. These stories—all stories--are a betrayal of the truth of life, which isn't coherent and doesn't have meaning. Can you deal with that? Or shall we go back to Peter Rabbit and his dimwitted brothers scampering about in farmer MacGregor's garden? Yes, we all yearn for justice, or at least some rudimentary order that we might understand after much study and contemplation. That's what historians do and they fail miserably, because it can't be done. So we bid a brusque farewell to reality and escape to the fantasies of poets and novelists. In their work we can discern patterns, but they are all artifactual. And illusory.

Poor Maria! But did she suffer as much as her father? (The mother was so self-absorbed that she would hardly have noticed Maria's death or, if she did, would have shrugged it off in a brutally brief time, thinking instead about Alexander Zemlinsky, Oskar Kokoschka, Walter Gropius, Franz Werfel, and most of the other male names in the Vienna phone book.) In the favelas of Rio where the infant mortality rate is unbelievably high, the mothers believe in angels. Their babies that are born alive but then sicken and die from disease or malnutrition they think of as having departed voluntarily as angels might if they were demoted to an earthly existence. The reason for these deaths, then, is the children's superior refinement and disinclination to be subjected to years of the squalor and suffering they find around them. They look about and decide, quite reasonably, to re-ascend. The mothers take comfort in this idea. And perhaps they even disapprove a bit of those children who are willing to live and grow up, satisfied enough to accept the world's hideous imperfections.

No!

You think I could make that up? That's the other problem with fiction. It has no anchor and yet seems to be stuck on the sandbars of convention. What kind of monster could invent what I have just written? Or what we read in the newspapers every morning? Journalists pretend to keep us informed so as to enable an enlightened democracy, but they don't for a minute believe that or suppose that we do. It's the pornography of violence that they peddle. "If it bleeds, it leads," as some crusty, old, eye-shaded, cigar-chomping editor is said to have said, and schools of journalism have to pretend to themselves and their students that he never said any such thing and that, even if he did, it isn't true.

Freud nods, this time with his eyes closed for a moment for emphasis.

The truth is just another seasoning to be added (sparingly) to the stew of existence. Those favelas, for instance, however depressing and outrageous, are on offer to tourists who are coming down for the World Cup. There are organized tours with police protection units, the justification for which is that the money (some of it, anyway) will be used to improve conditions there. But if they are too much improved, they will no longer be sufficiently picturesque to attract enough customers to fill the seats of the buses with the bulletproof windows. Not even Bandiera could have imagined such a wrinkle in the unmade bed of civilization.

I mentioned that he met Éluard there in Davos, but I neglected to adduce the French poet's sad tale. He married Elena Ivanovna Diakonova at the sanitarium in 1917. In point of fact, they were both seventeen. And even though you may never have heard of Diakonova, you probably know her as Gala Dalì. For three years or so she, Éluard, and Max Ernst maintained a ménage à trois, until she met Dalì for whom she left the other two even though (or perhaps because?) he (Dalì) was ten years younger than she. Considering these domestic arrangements, their invention of Surrealism seems unremarkable.

But back to the favelas. These tours would be depressing if they didn't pipe in Carmen Miranda music to remind the tourists that Brazil, indeed all of South America, is a fantasy. (Compared to Europe, Africa, and Asia, those bastions of earnestness and reason?) Well, no, but in Europe the plumbing is a little better. Northern Europe, anyway. One of the great magnets for tourists in Paris is the sewer system, through which people travel on small boats with guides, and as they leave they are provided with brochures in five languages written by Jacques La Fontaine, a great-great-grand nephew, perhaps, of Harington's epissstolary friend.)

Il faut vivre, after all. But why? To cultivate one's *jardin*? To eat one's ton of dirt? To harass the lower animals? But there is also the *faux vivre*, the artificial life of fiction with its interplay of imaginary characters with a contrived simulacrum of fate. And we drag our eyeballs across the lines of type if only to avoid looking at what is going on just outside the window.

"But what if it is real?" La Fontaine asks.

How can it be? I'm making it up, paragraph by paragraph.

"Suppose that that's what you think but that God is doing it. It is his *métier, n'est-ce pas*. He is eternal, which means he's very old. And probably forgetful. He's telling a story and loses track of what he's saying. Old people do that. But he is God. 'One is One and all alone and ever more shall be so,' and so on. There is nobody to prompt him and remind him where he was. Even assuming that there are angels, which of them would be so bold as to correct him or criticize? Whatever he says goes, even if he's not quite sure where it is going. Have you thought of that?"

I must have. You're saying it, after all.

"Very droll. But tiresome."

Watch your mouth. I can omit you at any time and your existence, no matter how shadowy, will disappear into the bits and bytes of which we are all made.

"Jesus! Epicurus?"

We must choose. Jesus or Epicurus.

"*Donnez moi une fracture.*"

That's not worthy of us.

"Speak for yourself. I rather like it. And I am a character, so I am entitled to have preferences, tastes, idiosyncrasies. Characteristics. Not necessarily the same as yours, assuming that you are any good at all and can imagine things. You want to run a puppet theater? Go ahead. But there is an integrity to novels, and whether you like it or not, you have to respect it. You do outrank me, but I, too, have rights."

Like a Zen master illustrating his point to a dim novice in the monastery courtyard, the author turns La Fontaine into a bug on the surface of his desk and crushes it with the ball of his right thumb. Rights? What rights?

Reconstituting himself as La Latrine, he replies, "You'll discover that as we go along."

And then he asks, "But God never revises, does he?"

Why not?

"We'd know."

Would we? There's a philosophical conundrum that says God remakes the world every Thursday. Just the way it was, or maybe with some differences but none that we notice. And our memories are accordingly adjusted. And our libraries. The truth is PRAVDA, which is to say that it's whatever the government finds convenient. The news.

History. Everything.

"Giddying."

Isn't it? Chaotic, in fact, but there's no way for any of us to know. Those anti-evolutionists are wrong, crazy in fact, but that doesn't mean God couldn't have scattered million-year-old dinosaurs around in the 6,000-year-old earth. There is no way to disprove that, except that it's silly and it's hard enough to believe in any God, let alone a ridiculous one.

La Trine covers his ears and shouts, "Lalalala," at the top of his voice in order not to hear any more.

Harington's ghost rouses itself to chide me. Even such a rapscallion as he finds this undignified and says I can't do this to one of my characters. The answer is that they're my characters and I can do as I please. As the gods can do with us whatever they want. The only answer is humility, submission, and, if you can manage it, indifference. Want nothing and fear nothing. Think of Raskolnikov under the Bodhi tree, or Anna Karenina, or Emma Bovary. Those novels would be quite different. Great expectations? There shouldn't be any at all, great or terrible. The genre depends on them, of course. (What will happen? Will it come out all right?) But it is the assumptions of the genre that are wrong. If nothing has significance, then nothing significant can happen. Just random events, but no plots. "Plotz!" In German, it's the command to dogs to sit.

"Oh, come on."

That would be *kum*.

When I was a kid, we went to the movies. We didn't specify or even care much which movie it was. The movies. Like watching television. (It doesn't matter what show is on.) There were double features. We came in at any time, sat through the end of one movie, watched the other from beginning to end, and then watched the beginning of the first picture until we came to a scene we recognized with dialogue we'd heard before. That was when we left the darkness of the theater to emerge into the improbable dazzle of daylight. I mention this because I have wondered, not very seriously I confess, about the extremely unlikely possibility of selling the movie rights to this. In any faithful adaptation, it would just keep going, looping along (literally) without making any particular sense and without any familiar scene to signal to the patrons that they can leave now. And that, *messieurs dames* is life, of which this is supposed to be a simulacrum.

The theatergoers could sit there forever, giving up their own lives and investing their identities in the characters on the screen. Impossible? Yes, of course, but isn't that what most of us are trying to do?

It's only in the restrooms and the food stand in the lobby that we return briefly and reluctantly to reality. These lives we lead can't be real.
They are too boring and tedious. Out here, nobody says, "A man's gotta
do what a man's gotta do," or "Play it, Sam."

That last line is from Casablanca, but the other? I don't remember.
Probably many films, and sometimes as a joke. To such an existential-
ist observation, Charles IX, would have objected: he thought a man's
gotta do what his mama tells him--although Catherine de Médicis had
to go to a great deal of trouble on occasion to get him to obey. It is not
that the son was obstreperous. He was absolutely deranged. When
he could no longer stand her importuning, he told her to go ahead
and kill Coligny, who had been his good friend and then, while the
soldiers were at it, kill all the Huguenots. (Seven thousand, it turned
out.) Some French historians suggest that he felt remorse about this
massacre, but he seems to have made no mention of it on his death-
bed confession. His disease, tuberculosis, took a spectacular form in
which he was covered with bloody perspiration. Difficult to resist
finding meaning in that, as the Huguenots did, but to do so would be
wrong. Unless, of course, you can think of two other mass murderers
who succumbed in the same way. Or even one so that doctors could
nod and say, "We see that."

The Valois kings are to France what cowboys and Indians are to
Americans. Good versus evil, except that with the cowboy stories, as
with the Valois tales, it's hard to pick out the good guys. Charles was
only 22 at the time of the massacre. *Vingt-deux.* Mispronounce it just
a little and you can say it as God comes (*Vient dieu*).

This was on the continent that holds itself out as the acme of civil-
ity for the Africans, South Americans, and Asians to emulate. I have
to assume that Bandiera, who encountered this posturing when he
came over from Brazil and was an extraordinarily intelligent fellow,
understood immediately the looniness of the claim. Perhaps that was
what appealed to him about it. And impelled him to surrealism. After
all, seminars in European history and comparative literature should
properly be held in classrooms in abattoirs that stink with the smell of
offal and drying blood. Growing up in Pernambuco where the jungle
is no mere metaphor, he was nonetheless impressed by the European
savagery of tribe with tribe, religion with religion, and language with
language. To assert one is to deny all the others, in which event it
becomes necessary to kill to maintain one's primacy and excellence.
Cougars behave the same way about their hunting grounds. Their in-
stincts are ours.

Obrigado.

De nada.

Many of Bandeira's poems are jokes, but very bitter. As is, one could argue, the world. But even that is a misrepresentation. The whole idea of a joke is that there is, somewhere or other, a point to it. To experience there is no point. Only at the most abstract level is existence itself a joke. Therefore, when a writer picks up his stylo, he does so with his fingers crossed—which makes it difficult to hold the writing instrument. He scribbles away as if he had something to say to an audience that is mostly imaginary and, insofar as it is real is likely to misunderstand anything he puts down on the paper. All those monkeys typing away to try to reproduce the works of Charles Dickens or William Shakespeare? As far as they are concerned, that's exactly what they have done. If we don't see it, that's on us. "It was the best of times; it was the worst of times. It was xrtdoddwlah." Yes, it certainly was.

Pernambuco was, very briefly, an independent country. Or, if not quite a country, then a captaincy. Brazil is where the nuts come from, but Pernambuco is where the jacaranda comes from. Now that Pernambuco is no longer independent, the jacaranda is often called Brazilwood. John III of Portugal granted the region to Duarte Coelho Pereira in 1534 who drove off the Indians (the Tupi-Guarani) and es-tablished sugar plantations, greedy for what they used to call white gold. John in Portuguese is João and the diminutive is Joãozinho. But if you Google it, what you first get is *banheiro*, which sounds rather like Bandiera but means john in the sense of bathroom. As in Haring-ton. Or La Trine.

Aha! A connection! It all fits. But does it? And if it does, what does it mean? Nada. (Portugal is the land of fado but also nada.) Believe me. I didn't exactly think it up but I did stumble upon this similarity between *banheiro* and Bandiera and considered it for a bit and I can-not see that it is, in any way whatsoever, significant. I know, I know. It isn't satisfactory for me, either, but it may be that satisfaction, itself, is the ultimate delusion, the final fiction, and that there is no such thing in the lives we have to lead. How do we get out of this? There isn't any escape, although some of us believe there must be a way, somehow, of emerging from these menacing, foreign shadows into the daylight outside. Or venturing farther in. What do you suppose they were do-ing in Plato's cave?

In Pernambuco, where Bandiera grew up, the alternative is all around, with the whispering, buzzing, screaming jungle that en-croaches on all sides as if it wanted to squeeze the small settlement back into the sea. Plants with huge leaves, monkeys with prehensile tails (except of course for the marmosets) and rustling noises that the wind makes in the canopy of the trees many feet overhead serve to put the not very impressive streets in their place. (A street should know its place, or we would all be lost.) Even the braggadocio of the Nannai Resort & Spa seems absurd. You can, if you have the taste for it and the money, lie on a chaise on the beach or sit on the veranda of your *bangalô super luxo*, drinking rum punch and looking out at the sea, but this is not exactly relaxing because you can never forget how temporary it all is. You will check out, but so will the hotel and the city. All of Brazil will be resorbed into the primitive, devoured by the voraciousness of nature.

It keeps you... not humble but balanced. You are less likely to lose your perspective. You take a longer view as Bandiera learned to do from boyhood. You learn to pay attention to curious, small facts that are pleasant to consider but otherwise useless (and all the better for that). Did you know for example that marmosets have claws on all their fingers except their thumbs, which have fingernails? I daresay not. Not even the marmosets have considered the implications of this evolutionary compromise that is as plain as their hands before their faces. The oldest and most intelligent of them (they can live for as long as twenty years) do not bother themselves about such matters. Indeed, the wisest (*un singe sage*) would disdain such a subject as unworthy even of the common marmoset. Typing out the works of Dickens? Sure. But contemplating one's fingernails? That is not legitimately a monkey's quadranimous business. (Marmosetisme, perhaps?)

Aside from the common marmosets there are also buffy-tufted ones with the white ears. These are unimaginably cute, can curl up in one of your pockets, and peep out with the huge eyes of their adorable faces to astonish your friends at Le Cirque. They are, therefore, in demand as pets, but I'd as soon not go there (nor would they, I do believe).

It does strike me as odd that Bandiera had to go to Switzerland to learn about surrealism when it was ubiquitous in Pernambuco, the indolent gestures of the residents in the direction of reason and order being so implausible and to seem funny. "Ordem e Progresso" are the words on the Brazilian flag, expressing the most forlorn of hopes. The phrase isn't even local but comes from Auguste Comte's motto of positivism: "*L'amour pour principe et l'ordre pour base; le progrès pour but.*" ("Love as a principle and order as the basis; progress as the goal"). After a while, the joke wears thin and one is drawn to a more realistic negativism: "Chaos and Entropy," which is what the screeching birds and animals in the jungle have been proclaiming from pre-historic times. And history seems to have confirmed their dim view of life on the planet.

At the very least, when Bandiera heard the odd remarks of Éluard, he was able to respond not only intellectually but viscerally, recognizing their truth immediately, having grown up with it. (Or the truth of the remarks' modesty, which is almost the same thing.) After all, what were the claims of Isidore Auguste Marie François Xavier Comte but an attempt to remedy the disorder of the French Revolution (which was over before he was born)? The very idea of bloodthirsty mobs roaming the streets and killing people was abhorrent, although, if truth be told, his reaction was not unusual. Bakhunin had not yet announced that "to destroy is also a creative act." Comte had a vision of something better, the order and progress that could be achieved scientifically. It was like trying to persuade lions to become vegetarians so they could lie down with lambs, but unless you are very smart or very stupid, you might miss that. The lions are unlikely to be persuaded. Karl Marx and John Stuart Mill also had batty ideas about the improvement of humanity. (It is always for the improvement of humanity that people will do ghastly things, having a fine pretext for their innate bloodthirstiness.)

Hey, you know what? You could stop here. Just stop reading. It's going to go on like this. I have no idea for how long. You have the advantage over me because you (putatively) have the book (again putatively) in your hand and, riffling the pages with your thumbnail, you can see how many remain. But I tell you in more candor than most writers allow themselves that it will be more of the same. So if you wish to stop, stop. If you wish to press two, press two. If you want a directory of employees, push three. If you wish to obliterate the memory of Auguste Compte from the minds of men, push four. If you are calling after business hours, push five and leave your message at the tone. For Spanish *aprima el número nueve*.

The notion of a thousand-page tome was just to scare you. And myself. If it does go on for a thousand pages, I will no doubt have been committed to a mental hospital where I am allowed only crayons to write with because they are implements with which I cannot hurt myself or other patients. (Reviewers may allude to my commitment and even praise it.) But what is reasonable (as if reasonableness counted for anything in this sublunary, sublunatic world)? A hundred pages? Maybe 80? Less than that, and it won't be a book but a mere feuilleton. (A possible title? No, that's like calling it A Book, which isn't bad either. And has been used.) Do we want to be classy and call it *Une Écriture*?

That turns out, however, to be a scripture and would be misleadingly biblical. Or a feminist tract, more often than not by Hélène Cixious. Google it, or look at Amazon and what you get is a lot of Cixious frou-frou and a reference to Nancy K. Miller, a social scientist who asks "Is *écriture* feminine lesbian cunnilingus?" (These people take the fun out of everything, don't they? They are all the heiresses of Auguste Compte, you see, so it can happen. What is most bothersome about the question is that it's pleonastic. All feminine cunnilingus is likely to be lesbian, and vice versa.) Dr. Miller is Distinguished Professor of English and Comparative Literature at the Graduate Center, CUNY. Cunylingus? Or is that a pleonasm, too? Is Nancy Miller possibly related to Henry? I fear not. (Or Arthur? Or Joe?)

One of the advantages Harington enjoyed was that he didn't have to deal with all this bumf (short for bum-fodder, or toilet paper). People who got the idea into their heads that there was a better way to govern England than Elizabeth's weren't likely to keep their heads for long. The shadow of the axe loomed over everything the courtiers did and said, so you can see that the few jokers in that pack had real nerve. Harington? Walter Ralegh? Henry Howard, the Earl of Surrey? They were witty guys, surely, but beyond and before it they were brave. Or perhaps wise. They understood the vagaries of fortune and accepted them, as some large souls are able to do. They demonstrated commitment. It is people like Compte who are restless and want to improve things, who have dreams and plans...

There must have been a few prescient Frenchmen who laughed at him, not for errors in his philosophical expositions but for their irrelevance to the ground they all lived on, where too much rain or too little can wipe out a crop, a year's earnings, a lifetime's plans. You want to rationalize that? La Trine laughs until the tears run down his legs, and that is without having to imagine the mass murders that were bound to come from Compte's misapprehensions. And hubris. "The Religion of Humanity" was one of his books and the title is not (intentionally) a joke. Take the ditsiest dame you can imagine, dressed by some first-line fashionista, bejeweled like a Christmas tree, and with a marmoset nestled in her pocket. The marmoset knows more than Compte ever did. And more than she does. (I have been thinking about these beasts and I realize that, of course, the claws are for climbing trees and the thumbnails are for peeling fruit and riffling pages in books.)

Are you positive about that?

No. Not at all. I am not positive about anything. After all, there are limits to positivism. Heisenberg says, "The positivists have a simple solution: the world must be divided into that which we can say clearly and the rest, which we had better pass over in silence. But can any one conceive of a more pointless philosophy, seeing that what we can say clearly amounts to next to nothing? If we omitted all that is unclear we would probably be left with completely uninteresting and trivial tautologies."

Really? One could reply that uninteresting and trivial tautologies are probably true, too, but that no particles of truth, however tiny, should be ignored or spurned.

What am I talking about? The world we live in and the lives we lead. We are like those farmers on the slopes of volcanoes. They know what can happen when the mountain erupts. It has happened before. But the soil is rich because of those past eruptions and the chances are fair to good that the volcano won't do anything tomorrow or the day after. Each thinks it won't happen in his lifetime. And he goes out every morning to tend his vines, hoping that he and they will not be destroyed that night in a river of molten lava. He is "living in the moment," as the self-help people tell us to do. A bunch of dumb peasants on a dangerous hillside like those poor sods in *Stromboli*? What have they to do with us? But it's us on that hillside of another Zauberberg. The indigent indigenes do not understand geology or volcanology, but whatever is important for them to know, they know. And we know, too, that every step we take is on eggshells. In which event, the only way to proceed is by dancing strenuously.

Stromboli are also those rolled-up things with meat and cheese, essentially pizzas (pizze?) that have been made into spirals. The probability that the people on the volcanic Aeolian island eat these is minuscule. Those people—Strombolieri? Stromboligni? Strombolitani? Strombolesi?—cling to their mountainside, subsisting mostly on fish, but they also have olives, lemons, capers, and prickly pears. Its juice tastes like something between bubblegum and watermelon if you can imagine such a thing. They have to be harvested before the sun comes up, at least according to T. S. Eliot, who says, "Here we go round the prickly-pear/ at five o'clock in the morning." He also says, "Do I dare to eat a prickly-pear?" or something close to that. (Would you care to pare a pair of prickly pears?) The natives are restless, however, and are usually awake before dawn. They are poor and terrified, as in Rossellini's splendid movie, and tourists come to see their desperation. (Perhaps the same company that operates these tours runs the favela tours in Rio). There were ten thousand of these Strombolestichi a few years ago, but the latest eruptions discouraged (or killed?) a lot of them so there are only a few hundred left now. Strombolicchio is a sea stack of very hard basalt a little more than a mile from the volcano, a tiny island that is off limits to visitors because a very rare lizard lives there. The Italians are admirably solicitous of endangered species about which they care a lot. But what would they have done for Jewish lizards? You furrow your brow but think at last of the Tegu lizards that have come up from Brazil, exhausted from all that Order and Progress and hoping to retire to Florida, which strives less. They grow up to four feet in length, weigh as much as thirty pounds, and have extremely sharp teeth. It has not been reported that they wear polo shirts with Jewish golfers embroidered on them but neither it has it been reported that they don't.

As a *Gedankenexperiment,* let us put M. Compte there on Stromboli, setting him down in San Bartolo or San Vincenzo or, better yet, the smaller village of Ginostra in the southwest part of the island. Once he has recovered from his first moments of astonishment, let him look up at the three active craters of the volcano and try to explain positivism to the hard-bitten natives who cannot afford to worry about life and death or good and evil and social justice but think only about dinner. They would have much to teach the Parisian *philosophe.* (Whether or not he'd be willing to learn is another question.) Do I exaggerate for dramatic effect? ("God help me, but can do no other!" Luther quipped perhaps not realizing that this could serve as an excuse for anything— including his hatred of Jews and, for all I know, lizards.) But it is the simple truth that the Strombolesqueñoes only got electricity in 2004. Anyway, there he is, M. Compte, the foggy, froggy Frenchman, trying to persuade these people that "the progress of the individual mind is not only an illustration, but an indirect evidence of that of the general mind." (If he were a "real" Comte, he would be Mons. le Compte, but inasmuch as that's merely his name, he doesn't get any such fancy treatment. People often call their dogs Prince or Duke, or even Rex, but rarely Compte.)

They are not rude, these people of Stromboli. (Or they are rude, but not unmannerly, living as they do in rude huts and putting to sea in their rude boats.) Surely they do not want to offend the foreigner who may, at the end of his incomprehensible disquisition want to take their photographs, which would mean a tip. But they keep looking up, over their shoulders. A nervous tick, perhaps? No, no, it is their habit: they are just checking the sky for falling balls of flame and molten rock. It happens, not every day but often enough. They'd tell this fellow but their French is not good enough and he seems to have very little Sicilian Italian, which is what they speak on those rare occasions when they resort to words.

As he explains about logical positivism and his theories of social science, they nod as people would do if they were interested in what they were hearing or as if they at least understood what the words meant, and he is encouraged enough to continue (he would probably continue even without encouragement): "Now, the existing disorder is abundantly accounted for by the existence, all at once, of three incompatible philosophies--the theological, the metaphysical, and the positive. Any one of these might alone secure some sort of social order; but while the three coexist, it is impossible for us to understand one another upon any essential point whatever." Is that his problem? (Or one of his problems?) They back away. He follows them. Should they throw stones at him? Donkey turds? What does it take to get a guy like this to dumb down and wise up? Can't he look up at the craters and understand that thinking about them won't make a damned bit of difference? The improvement of the world is an absurd idea. Simply to make this island livable (also an absurd idea) would be an extravagant undertaking beyond the powers of any government or army. The Italians understand that outside of opera there are no cures for reality.

We pluck him up from that forbidding shore. There are no beaches anywhere: it's a volcano. (Which a just and merciful God has put there to keep us humble?) So we may as well put him back into his time and place. The Parisians are not much more receptive to his theories but the food is better. He is perched now on a barstool, chatting with his friends, ideally *des brèves de comptoir,* at which he would presumably be very good. As Archimedes' smarter brother said, "Give me a place to stand and I'd rather sit down." Auguste is happy to be on home ground again where he knows his way around the complicated streets and alleys at least of his own arrondissement.

Let us leave him there in the bar while we go for a stroll around Paris. Most of you have revisited great cities—Paris, of course, but Rome or London would do—and you can recognize some of the prominent landmarks. But once you take a wrong turn, you are lost. In New York, which is a numbered grid, you can pretty much figure out where you are, in Manhattan anyway. But Brooklyn? The Bronx? Your sense of direction muddles, especially at night or on a cloudy day where you can't figure out directions from the sun's place in the sky. This is how life is for old people who lose track. Not just of their the physical location but their intellectual one as well. Where do we stand? How did we get here? Where had we wanted to go? There are maps, but how can we orient them. (Orient is the wrong word: we want to figure out which way is north.) Where is the boutique, the gallery, the museum, the police station, the restaurant? Eventually, the men's room. "Do you know the geography?" is the Brits' way of asking where the bathroom is. (M. La Trine makes another of his ridiculous, Hitchcockian appearances, entering a pissoir or disappearing down into the Metro where the faces are seldom "petals on a wet, black bough.") The longer one spends tramping the streets, the less vague is his internal map of where he is in relation to his hotel. But no city, no matter how familiar, is entirely clear. They keep tearing down buildings and putting up new ones. Sometimes they rename the streets (as with Erlichstrasse, remember? Or The Avenue of the Americas, which is still Sixth Avenue, no matter what the street signs say). Different cities present different degrees of difficulty. "Only the Dead Know Brooklyn" is the title of a Thomas Wolfe short story. By extension, only the dying know Naples; only the young know Paris; only the smug know Greenwich; only the desperate know Camden; only the bored know Lubbock, and so on.

The questions you keep asking yourself are the fundamental ones: is this familiar? Have you been here before? Could you find it again? Not as goddamned metaphors but as straightforward inquiries. Serendipity has its rewards but also its costs as darkness falls and you begin to worry that this may not be a safe neighborhood. (Are there any safe neighborhoods where birds of prey are not making attentive circles overhead?) To intensify those feeling of anxiety, let it be cold and raining. Let the dancing glow of gas-lamps reflect menace from the wet asphalt of the curved street. How to get out of here? At last when you do arrive at a familiar corner, along with the relief you feel stupid and helpless because you should have been able to figure out where you were. There is a warm, golden light coming from the rain-smeared windows of a café, but you cannot decide whether it is a reward or an indictment.

Those lapses of memory, of context, of position are intermittent but frequent enough to be unsettling. "It happened before?" Dr. Krankheit asks. "Well, it's happened again." It isn't just foolish wordplay but a symptom of time's passing—fast enough to dizzy a Castorp high in the Swiss Alps. And, as his doctors tell him, his condition is serious although, from the right point of view, it is also absurd—like the corpses from the even higher sanitarium they have to bring down the mountain by bobsled. (How many live men in the bobsled? Can they do it with a two-man luge, the corpse on top and then, on the bottom, the undertaker who actually steers? Does the *Fédération International de Luge de Course* sanction this practice (authorizing or forbidding)? Do they have this on YouTube along with the sneezing panda?)

We are approaching the fiftieth manuscript page. There are, I expect, rather fewer of us now than at the start, but *tant pis.* (Again, M. La Trine?) The question arises in my mind and surely in yours as to how much longer this can go on. Indeed, even before that, we wonder what it is. A novel? Not quite. An essay? Ravings? Free association? Screed? Not quite any of those, either. There are associations but they are by no means free. Perhaps we can relax and think of it as an extended prose poem, the advantage of that category being that it has no rules and therefore raises no expectations. Or an impossibly long stand-up routine. It is what it is, or whatever you think it is. It is a Rorschach test. Rorschach, whether you are aware of this or not, is a municipality in the canton of St. Gallen in Switzerland on the south side of Lake Constance. It is about 75 miles from Davos. It pleases me to imagine that when hops crops are in the peasant women there make woolen coverlets and sofa throws with the famous test blots as their designs. But perhaps it would be well to think of this convolution of sentences as a randomly evolving pattern like that of frost upon a windowpane that can sometimes appear to the believers in the parking lot below to be an image of the Blessed Virgin. (Or any other virgin with similar features.) She shows up sometimes on potato chips, too. And the people who see her are not wiseacres like us but devout believers. This is interesting because the devout and the irreverent join together at such moments, each sure of the rightness of his attitude and yet sharing the same image up there on the second-floor window. Pray for us now and at the hour of our death, would you? Or, if not now, then just at the hour of our death when, as Pascal argues, it can do no harm. ("Premium non knockere" could be a slogan of a gasoline company if more motorists knew Latin.)

You're not convinced. Neither am I, if I may say so. This undertaking (albeit not on a bobsled) requires a bit of nerve, just to write without any plan except where the sentences lead, or the whorls of the cerebrum. Nerve, I should say, and disgust. A writer in my position (sitting, actually) needs to have written enough novels to be tired of them and even annoyed. Guilty, perhaps, because of their generic falsity. Even the simplest slice of life betrays what it pretends to serve up on the plate, raw and bloody. We know better and so does he, unless he is dismayingly stupid. (Many novelists are, but not all.) I admire those writers who do one novel and then give it up. Philip Larkin, Lionel Trilling, Harper Lee, Alan Tate (I think), J. D. Salinger, Margaret Mitchell, and (add names here). [You, not me.]

Recidivists and repeat offenders need some excuse, to themselves more than to us. Think here of Ronald Firbank and his outrageous fripperies. His altitude—in the loftier sanitarium--is beyond my imagination. Or tolerance. Because there is no air there at all. Just a deadly crystalline chill. So where does this leave us? Intelligence is yearning for a sanctuary in foolishness, where it is unlikely that many people will be looking for it.

What were we talking about? In a general way, I mean. Disease, I think. Spectacular ruin of grand victims who deserved better. (Actually, it was the notion of deserving and the more deeply underlying idea of reason that we were considering.) Do you remember *A Song to Remember*? (Now there's a title, the whole seven words!) It was a 1945 movie about Frédéric Chopin with Cornel Wilde as the Polish composer. It was a more or less standard biopic but it had one scene of astonishing vividness I shall never forget—with Wilde playing some rousing Polonaise on a grand piano and coughing up dark red blood that splashes impressively on the white ivory keys. In time to the music, actually, although later on, out in the daylight, one realized that this would have been unlikely. Still, very impressive. In most movies, when somebody coughs, it means that he or she will die in the next ten minutes. (A real cough would have been a reason to reshoot the scene, because reality cannot be allowed to intrude on fiction, especially at these prices.) So they could have just had Frédéric cough a couple of times and then lie down. But they wanted it to be bigger more spectacular and shocking. So this bravura gesture with blood on the piano keys, which might have been Charles Vidor's idea (he was the director) or Sid Buchman's (he was the writer).

Buchman was my pediatrician's brother, although I had no idea of this when I was a pediatric patient sitting on his examination table. Sid Buchman was famous in Hollywood for getting fired off a Rin Tin Tin movie by writing a scene in which the dog carries a baby into a burning building. A breathtaking idea, at least as good as the hematological polonaise in the movie. (If he'd quit, the studio would have stopped paying him, which meant that he had to get the producer to fire him so as to keep the money coming in.) If I were an Indian or an Eskimo and had a totem animal spirit to guide my life, I guess mine would be Rin Tin Tin--not the real dog of course or even the movie version, but Dr. Buchman's brother's mannerist variation of that. I am only now realizing this, but that may be because as a younger man I couldn't have accepted such an idea. I'd have dismissed it as ridiculous. Now I cling to ridiculousness, knowing that it is by no means a disqualification for credibility. *Au contraire.* Or, saving M. La Trine's persistent presence, *eau contraire.*

So, Rin Tin Tin, in a Dadaist fiction carries the baby into the conflagration. Or in the producer's more conventional and even banal version, he carries the baby out and to safety. It doesn't matter because, in another building, there is a press agent, cigar chomping I imagine, who is writing the "true" biography of the dog, the significance of the punctuation being that it isn't true at all. The dog's story was that he'd been rescued from a bombed kennel in World War I by Lee Duncan, an American Soldier, who brought him to Hollywood after the war, trained him, and found parts for him in silent films hoping that he (the dog, but Duncan, too) could cash in a little on the success of Strong-heart, an earlier canine star. That business about the dog having been found by the kindly American soldier is too full of human-interest appeal for us to credit it. Even if it's true, it isn't true. When do the press releases of film companies pretend to correspond with any reality outside the studio gates?

Nonsense converges with nonsense, but we may attempt to sort it out by putting on white coats (stethoscopes and head-mirrors, optional) and distinguishing among genres. The farce of Buchman, the treacle of Vidor, and the baroque invention of the press agent appeal to different parts of our mental equipment. (Slide.) There was, somewhere in that yeasty nexus, a real dog. (Slide.) At least for a while. Rinny died in 1932 and wasn't an animal anymore. He had become an industry. The studio found other German Shepherds that looked like him and, yielding only a little to the real world, claimed that these other dogs were his sons or grandsons, great nephews, or second cousins twice removed. There's someone in Texas who had a Rin Tin Tin museum in Latexo (Slide.) that is now closed and who claims to own Rin Tin Tin XII, with whom she makes public appearances "to maintain the legacy" and also, if we may indulge in vulgar realism, to make a few dollars for dog and human chow. This is why the muse of Satire shakes her head in despair. She has descended from Helicon and now lives in a cave; the other muses claim not to know her.

There were a number of Lassies, too, all of them looking pretty much the same. (One can no longer say this of Chinese waiters, but all collies do look a lot alike.) It was easier and faster to train different dogs to do different tricks, (*sitz, plotz, kum*, and so on). With the collies, then, there was never a Lassie; they were all supposititious, authenticated and united only in the minds of their millions of fans. This is, I do believe, reception theory. (Reception theory tells us that if someone is giving a reception and the drinks are free, you should by all means go, even if it's to celebrate an anniversary issue of *Gun and Garden*.)

We seem to have blundered into another difficulty—the first person pronoun. When I write and you read "I," the temptation is to suppose that I am saying something about myself. Or in my own voice. (Vouching, lawyers call it, and it is forbidden in courtrooms.) Perhaps, but perhaps not. Who am I to tell you about myself? I have only a fuzzy idea of who I am, what I have been and done, and what my life has been like. The truth is that I have forgotten the truth, and what I have done to compensate is what we all do, which is to invent the filler. I make up stuff in which I soon come to believe, so that it is as real as anything that might have happened. "Why, oh why, oh why-o/ why did I ever leave the bayou." There are dots I am sure about--jobs, girls, women, children—but who was the actor between this and that and what happened to him from Kindergarten to near senility? What I can attest to is a severe toothache when I was seven, although even an experience as vivid as that blurs so that I can't remember now which tooth it was. What follows from this quirk in human behavior is that none of us is real. We are all self-generated fictions into which we settle and which our friends and associates (who are also fictions) are obliged to accept. Do not let your guard down. I am, to the best of my knowledge and belief, not under oath, and even if I were the chances are that any truth I told would be partial and distorted. Even acciden-tal. Eyewitnesses are mostly famous for making mistakes.

Tout le monde! Et tu, *Le Monde*! The most serious and earnest people, therefore, are the ones who are the least trustworthy because they refuse to recognize the basic truth of untruthfulness. They are willingly ignorant. Invincibly ignorant—as Catholics said of the Jews. They meant it as an insult but we take it as a badge of honor. "What weighs 12,000 pounds, is gray, and has a long trunk." "That's irrel-evant!" "That'sa right!" That'sa the only kind of courtroom I might not mistrust.

Mons. le Comte (having thought of him, I am reluctant to dismiss him) descends the sweeping stone staircase of his chateau carrying one of his *chats*. A kitten. Unlike Richelieu, who liked kittens but then gave them away when they grew out of that cute stage, le Comte de Quelquepart keeps them all. And he spends much of his time decid-ing on outré names for them, like Gregory IX, Vsevolod, or Pedro the Cruel (a king of Portugal). It is a shame that Rin Tin Tin XII will never get to gambol on the greensward with Gregory IX, but such a scene is not inconceivable. Think of it. Somebody throws a stick. (The count or one of his footmen?) Rin Tin Tin bounds after it with great ener-gy. Gregory, meanwhile, sits sedately at the count's feet and watches, wondering why the dog is doing that.

To be a count is to have a low-end title. Tolstoy was one, as was Dracula. Monte Cristo pretended to be one. They rule over coun-

ties, or used to. Portugal, for instance, was once a county, but it pro-
moted itself to a kingdom somewhere along the line. Count Basie?
Of course not. And Leconte de Lisle wasn't either. That was just his
name. Countess Lucilla Mara de Vescovi Whitman also comes to mind,
of course, the lady who made ties (or, at those prices cravats) for Sina-
tra and other such luminaries. Her firm is still in business, I guess.
All her ties, except Frank's maybe, have a little coronet on the front,
which seems a bit vainglorious. The label on the outside is a relatively
new thing. L. L. Bean and Northface turn all their customers into bill-
boards. Lacoste (who was not a count but merely a tennis player)
relied on those little crocodiles embroidered on the front of his tee
shirts. Steinway's name used to be over the keyboards of their pianos
where the pianist could see it, but now, on the concert grands at least,
they put it on the side where the audience stares at it.

All of this is after Quelquepart's time. He is spared the indignity his
great grandson has to endure of having to turn down offers to license
condoms, say, that would bear the family name and coat of arms. Or
the box would. The condoms, themselves, would not have any print-
ing on them. (Not even, "Sold only for the diminution of pleasure.")

"It's big money, Count," the businessman tells him. "Are you sure
you can afford to turn it down? You don't even want time to think
about it?"

The distinguished silver-haired gentleman does not bother to reply. He merely shakes his head silently, saddened that the world has
come to this. (Perhaps the businessman should have applied for the
Wurlitzer Company for the right to use their name on condoms—the
organ people.) I can understand the count's distaste. Not that I'd be
so quick to turn down an offer like that, but I do regret that even those
few representatives who are left of refinement, taste, and judgment
are so woefully and frequently assailed. The Earl of Sandwich has
a chain of airport sandwich shops, which, profitable or not, must be
humiliating. We should protect these people, perhaps establishing a
reservation for them on one of those tiny sea-stack islands that poke
up from the depths to break the surface near active volcanoes. There
would be butlers and valets and embroidered bell-pulls with which
they could summon other servants and they could live carefree, indolent lives basking in the sunshine like those lizards on Strombolicchio.

Consider for a moment: I have not been lying to you, which is a
great accomplishment in any book. The mood of the entire work is
more or less the *subjonctif* in which it is permissible to woolgather but
impossible to assert a falsity—because it does not deign to assert anything. If there were a Comte du Subjonctif, his shield would be blank

except for the family motto: "*Il aurait pu être.*"

Yes, it's an absurd idea, but it is no more ridiculous than the Duca di Verdura, the duke of vegetables, who is an actual Sicilian nobleman. Did he grow them? Was he the first to take vegetables to the opera house in Palermo to fling at unsatisfactory performers who had, before him, been assailed mostly with fruit? We don't do this in America but perhaps we should. It would enlarge the audience for opera, with the added excitement of stock-car races where the speed of the cars may be impressive but people really come to see the debacles. The soprano's tremolo is excessive? Throw overripe peaches and tomatoes. She is off key? Throw under-ripe cantaloupes. Or prickly pears.

Where were we? Anywhere! Quelquepart! I remember, Davos, where the luges with corpses come hurtling down the mountainside from time to time to encourage the patient to follow their regimens, take their medicines, and try to get well. Éluard, Bandiera, and a third man. Not the Third Man, the one played by Orson Welles (Harry Lime, who says, "five hundred years of democracy and peace – and what did that produce? The cuckoo clock.") That would make the scene silly. Another man, then. Maybe Mann, who must have visited now and then when his wife was a patient. Or perhaps Castorp. (Why not?) They have been sitting on a balcony, playing pinochle, discussing life and art, and drinking bullion. Éluard has been reciting one of his poems:

> The transparency of men passing among them by chance
> And passing women breathed by your elegant obstinacies
> Your obsessions in a heart of lead on virgin lips
> The vices the virtues so imperfect

Bandiera likes it well enough, but then his French is not yet very good and he is untroubled by not understanding it. What he seizes upon are the striking locutions. Elegant obstinacies? Virgin lips? The girl has never sucked anyone off? Or is there a loftier significance, as of a poet yet to pronounce, with his lips, the verses he hopes (vainly) will change the world? It's hard to tell with Éluard. (He will soon abandon surrealism and become a Communist, which, as he may discover, is merely another form of surrealism.) "The vices the virtues so imperfect" is encouraging, really. Rather Catholic. If the vices are imperfect, then there is a chance that the virtues, however imperfect, may be sufficient to deserve forgiveness. Bandiera is a quirky Catholic, with a great poem about Santa Rita of the Impossibilities to whom he prays for a good death. He does not try to recite it because Éluard's

Portuguese is notional at best and Bandiera's French, although somewhat better, is not adequate to his purpose.

A luge comes shooting down and, because of a slight miscalcula-
tion, hits a large rock. Bang! Now there are two corpses and someone
will have to telephone. But none of them moves. They hardly react.
Death is everywhere, in the heights above Davos so that one becomes
accustomed to it. Castorp reflects upon this without bothering to
commit the thought to speech. They all know this, although they learn
it one at a time and it is a difficult journey for each. And each thinks
only of himself, at least at the beginning. Then the self begins to dis-
solve as if in a heat shimmer that arises, paradoxically, from the cold.

The process is mildly interesting. One starts by thinking of himself
as one thing and his disease as another. He is fighting his disease. After a time, however, the relationship changes, and he and the disease
ally themselves, so that he is it and it is he. (And all the patients are
it, and it is them.) After that, there is no more fighting, only pinochle
and bouillon. (And, given the location, probably a cuckoo clock.) It
follows then, that there is a disease sitting at the table embodied by
a trinity of its sufferers who, whether they have realized it nor not,
are all the same being. Does the Holy Trinity ever play pinochle with
itself? Does the Son ever avail himself of his knowledge of the Holy
Ghost's cards? Can he help it? That would make cards very difficult
for him/them. Except solitaire, but that would cause theological dis-
putation here below. Also jokes would be impossible. A joke depends
on surprise, after all, but each of them would anticipate the others'
punch lines. Nothing to do up there but enjoy the view and perhaps
the pleasant feeling of cold on one's/their face(s).

The celestial pinochle business is ridiculous but it does raise the
question of identity. If I am my disease or my diseases, am I not also
my death? And is it in that regard that all men can be said to be brothers? I'lla mention "Alle Menschen," which is interesting because even
Schiller decided that was too sappy and flabby and changed it to "*Bet-
tler werden Fürstenbrüder*," which is less abstract, with beggars becoming princes' brothers. That is perhaps too cute and too leftist but
at least there's a germ of thought in it.

What the three men out there on the solarium balcony share is
that sensation of cold, which is supposed to be good for them. Who
knows why? If one of the symptoms of tuberculosis is a low-grade fe-
ver, then conceivably the low temperatures of the high altitudes might
be a way to compensate for that, might even have some fundamental
benefit. It would also save the sanitaria a lot of money for coal. For
Bandeira, the constant chill is exotic, altogether different from hot,

muggy Rio or perspiring Pernambuco. Here one goes for a walk and
feels his face sting in the wind and then go numb, which is worrisome
because it means that the nerves have given up sending signals to a
brain that refuses to pay attention. That change from pain to numb-
ness could, perhaps, make a poem. Not a serious poem, because the
observation is too simple (minded) to bear weight, but even the most
delicate glass bauble can glitter in the right light. Sensation and then
its exhaustion. A metaphor for life? No doubt, but which is the vehicle
and which is the tenor? (And who is the baritone? No, Who's on first!
Have we learned nothing in all these years?)

Okay, okay. We all die, and then we get to face that card-playing
trio in the sky and they feed us lines from vaudeville to which we are
supposed to respond. "I'm dubious," says the Holy Ghost (which is,
theologically correct) and you have to say, "How do you do, Mr. Dubious?" or you get sent away--not to translate Ariosto but to memorize
The Magic Mountain or some such text. (And you have to do this in
German, but you can pick that up in three or four years, and then you'll
be *Gut zu gehen*.) Once you've got that down pat, Castorp will live as
long as you do. And then after you, which he would have done anyway,
the cold wind stinging his cheeks and the bullion cooling in the China
cup in his hand. "Down pat," comes from a card-player's expression,
which means that he's satisfied with his cards and does not need any
new ones from the dealer, but I don't believe that this happens in pinochle.

Castorp does not say much to his companions. They are all fictional (now) but the other two had lives once. Castorp, another man's
character, is therefore a fiction of a fiction, which is why he is so wan
and listless. (It could also be his disease, of which this could be an ex-
acerbation.) Sometimes it seems as if he is barely there. You can see
him but you can also see through him, as if he were an ectoplasmic being. Or one of the undead. But then everyone in the sanitarium can be
described as undead. And the rest of us, down here in the lowlands?
Us, too.

Do not feel sorry for Castorp. He has his place in a very good conventional novel, which helps us to know him, to learn the mediocrity
that Mann assigns him, to imagine what he remembers, and to guess
what he may be thinking. The others have memories, too, but they
are private people, even if their writings are efforts to communicate
something from that dark core of selfhood. (They are poets, though,
and with them even when we see what they mean we cannot be sure
how they mean it. Or whether. The muse of Irony is hunkered down
in that cave with the muse of Satire, and they have both given up won-

dering why they don't get the respect they deserve. (They might, if people were smarter and my grandmother were a trolley car.) To hell with it. Let them play pinochle, too.

One would think that such eminent figures as Paul, Manuel, and Hans would have profound things to say and that it is my fault for not conveying adequately the richness of their observations. The point is that, as with the Holy Trinity, everything important has been said or can be assumed to have been said. Can be taken for granted. Or for granite. They exchange comments about the weather, their companions in the dining room, their doctors, the headlines in the newspapers, but that can be likened to the conversations we have every day. "Good morning. How are you?" "Fine, and you?" "Couldn't be better!" We're not simply wasting each other's time but are maintaining a surface below which we both understand that more is going on. "You're looking well at the moment, but you're going to die anyway." "What other way can there ever be?" "None, except that I am going to die also." Those things, too, are true but it is unnecessary to say them. In the sanitarium or anywhere else, where le Comte de Quelquepart keeps a hunting lodge, to refer too directly to such things is considered bad form. To complicate further an already vertiginous situation, there is also a descant of conscious thought that floats in and out that nobody expresses, flimsiness that we take for granite but don't even find remarkable. It's just the mind's motor idling. The soft clicking of the gears inside the cuckoo clock. (Wouldn't it be satisfactory to have a cuckoo clock with Orson Welles popping out of the little door to announce the hour in that sarcastic voice of his?)

Indeed, the silences that lovers sometimes share, or parents enjoy with children, sitting together without the need of saying a word are communicative but do not lend themselves to drama or fiction. Look at two cats, litter sisters, lying next to each other on the coverlet. One licks the other's head for a moment and then settles down to snuggle with her. If they could speak, words would only get in the way.

Mann was a part of the *Exilliteratur*, the German literature of exile during the time of the Nazis. It' an impressive list, including, among others, Theodor Adorno, Hannah Arendt, Walter Benjamin, Bertolt Brecht, Hermann Broch, Ernst Bloch, Alfred Döblin, Lion Feuchtwanger, Bruno Frank, Oskar Maria Graf, Hermann Hesse, Max Horkheimer, Heinrich Eduard Jacob, Hermann Kesten, Annette Kolb, Siegfried Kracauer, Emil Ludwig, Heinrich Mann, Klaus Mann, Erika Mann, Ludwig Marcuse, Robert Musil, Robert Neumann, Erich Maria Remarque, Ludwig Renn, Joseph Roth, Alice Rühle-Gerstel and Otto Rühle, Felix Salten, Anna Seghers, Franz Werfel, Bodo Uhse, Max Brod,

Arnold Zweig and Stefan Zweig. A serious bunch of guys. Of course, they had much to be serious about, Nazism, Fascism, Communism, and, eventually, nihilism, which is what it mostly adds up to although many of them tried heroically to avoid that slough of despond. Some of them found it impossible to avoid, however, and ended up committing suicide. But for reasons that seem disproportionately petty. Zweig (Stefan) had fled to Brazil where he had a house up in the hills near Rio and his agony had little to do, at least on the surface, with the havoc back in Europe. He felt cut off because there were no libraries and no *gemütlich* cafés. So he and his wife did themselves in. Roth was managing (barely) in Paris where he was slowly but determinedly drinking himself to death, but when he received news that his friend, Ernst Toller had hanged himself in New York, he gave up and killed himself, too. What people give as reasons are seldom the real reasons. About suicide or living or anything else.

Let us pull back a bit and, further down the wide solarium, take note of a solitary figure who is reading a book. Nothing spectacular in that, or even, at first glance, relevant, but the book in the silver-haired gentleman's elegantly manicured hands is Thucydides' *Peloponnesian Wars*, which he pores through and then starts again. He is somewhat tiresome in the dining hall because he is either silent or else he talks about how Thucydides is the only book one needs. Everything about human folly and pretension is there. One of the great moments in the history of civilization with some of the best minds the species has produced, and they messed it all up, miscalculating, misunderstanding one another, and ultimately destroying each other. The Athenians and the Spartans. After that, World War I shrinks in significance. The French, the Germans, the Russians, the English all had intelligent men in positions of power. They might as well have been monkeys. (The typing marmosets?) Now and again, he turns a page. Occasionally he consults a Greek-German dictionary on the table beside him to look up the meaning of a word. If we pay attention, we can see him rubbing his eyes occasionally, not in disbelief but to wipe away the tears he feels brimming up before they spill down his delicately lined cheeks. Oskar Schäuble, we may call him, a cousin of the Captain we imagined some time ago.

Not far beyond him, on a wickerwork chaise with a blanket over her lower body, a slender, well-dressed, middle-aged woman is consulting a guide to Davos. She is not much interested in the subject but it is her custom to learn about places she has visited in her travels, which she realizes may well end here. It is mildly diverting for her to learn that the model for the Davos sanitarium was in the Polish village of Görbersdorf, where the first such institution was established in 1854. (In 1945, the name will be changed to Sokołowsko in honor of the merits of the Polish internist Alfred SokołowskI who had been a close co-worker of Hermann Brehmer, brother-in-law of Countess Maria von Colomb, a niece of Prussian General Gebhard Leberecht von Blücher. It was that countess, delighted by the scenery there, who persuaded Brehmer, himself tubercular, to establish a health resort for consumptive patients.)

The woman's brow is ever so slightly wrinkled, as if she were concentrating, intent on remembering as many of these stupid details as she can. There will not be an examination. None of this is interesting enough to talk about at dinner. (Not that it will be any more tedious than details of the Peloponnesian Wars.) But the solidity of facts is something she has always clung to. Belief in God may be difficult, but belief in the existence of Countess Maria von Colomb is not particularly demanding. Or in General Blucher, for whom, incidentally, the shoe is named. He was the man who commissioned a boot with side pieces lapped over the front in an effort to provide his troops with better footwear. Napoleon is reported to have said that an army marches on its belly, but the feet are also involved, and it was to these that the Prussian officer devoted his attention, even though to assert that an army marches on its feet is to lose the point of the emperor's epigram. (That, too, would be a plausible title.)

Facts. Do they, in the long run, make any difference? Is it reassuring to know that bouillon comes from Belgium and that Godfrey of Bouillon was a leader of the First Crusade and the first ruler of the Kingdom of Jerusalem? Or that court bouillon is the especially rich variety that was served at court? But then is it unsettling to learn that the Godfrey and his Belgian town had nothing to do with the beef broth, the name of which comes from *boullir*, the French word meaning to boil? The truth of the assertion hardly matters. It is the specificity that we find tasty.

Has anyone ever made this observation before? I must suppose so. Whether it got written down or not is another question. But one could attribute it to Isidore of Seville who said pretty much everything. At least it seems that way because of his *Etymologiae,* an encyclopedia, which assembled extracts of many books from classical antiquity that would have otherwise been lost. So there are all kinds of oddly assorted stuff in it. Or maybe it could have been Bernard of Clairvaux. He said (he really did): "There are those who seek knowledge for the sake of knowledge; that is Curiosity. There are those who seek knowledge to be known by others; that is Vanity. There are those who seek knowledge in order to serve; that is Love." And he might have added that there are those who do not seek knowledge at all and wouldn't know it if they stepped in it. Let us not think too badly, therefore, of the earnest woman in the chair with the guidebook in her lap. She is seeking knowledge merely out of habit, but it is a good habit and as good a way as any other to pass the time she has left. Shall I name her? What would be the point? You wouldn't believe me anyway, and sometimes it's better not to know the name. She should just be an image, a good-looking woman with the rosy cheeks the tubercular sometimes display.

Zauberberg, indeed! How far down do we have to go and how far away to get past the magic and back to a recognizable world? And why would we want to, even if we could?

That Bernie of Clairvaux had a droll sense of humor. He couldn't possibly have meant that observation to be taken straight, with that spurious uplift at the end. Love! "Love-a, love-a, love alone/that caused King Edward to lose his throne." That has a little sizzle to it. My kids were in a play many years ago, "The Mystery of the Ming Tree." (The Ming tree is the Polyscias fruticosa and its leaves are used as a tonic, anti-inflammatory, antitoxin, and an antibacterial ointment. They have been proven to be an aid in digestion. The root is also used as a diuretic and febrifuge and is employed for neuralgia and rheumatic pains. Beside its medicinal purposes, Polyscias fruticosa is also an ornamental plant and a spice.) The Ming tree played no part in the play, however, which was about a wizard who set three oriental-ish riddles for the young hero to answer. What was wind wrapped in paper? What was fire wrapped in paper? And what was love wrapped in paper? The answers were fairly obvious. A fan, a lantern, and then... A Bible? Oh, come on!

I'd have liked it better if the answer had been a condom, which would also work. That would be fun especially in a play for children. As Isidore of Seville said with a wink and a leer, "If they's big enough, they's old enough."

Of course this is tasteless. Tastelessness requires dedication, a disregard for conventional thinking, and a certain independence of mind, and no one is going to make any progress in life by obeying the strictures of Emily Post and taking her Mrs. Toplofty as his model. Mrs. Toplofty? She was an Emily Post character, more or less out of Sir Walter Scott, who liked to give such names to minor characters in his novels. Now that the curious cognomen has surfaced in my mind, shall we assign it to our lady with the guidebook? Or less coyly, shall we recognize her claim to it? Serena Toplofty, who, before she was stricken with TB, used to concern herself with the different monograms one uses for the dining room and the bathroom. Or how to address dignitaries—Your Excellency, Your Honor, Your Grace, Madam Secretary, or simply "sir," which is what you say to a king the second time you address him. If she needed that kind of information, we can imagine easily enough the elegant dinner parties she and Reginald used to have in palmier days. Reginald, and then, I think, Clarence.

Does anyone care about these rules anymore? Perhaps on one of those sea-stack island retreats with the embroidered bell pulls. You realize, don't you, that those pulls have to be commissioned. I don't imagine that you can just go into a shop, no matter how pretentious and pricey, and ask to see bell pulls. (No, that turns out to be wrong. My imagination has failed me yet again. I try to be cynical but apparently I need more practice. Amazon has them. They even have Downton Abbey bell pulls for the sincerely delusional. Or maybe for people like me who are looking for demented house presents. (The corresponding bells in the kitchen and the servants to respond to them are not supplied—not for thirteen dollars.)

How many can they sell? And to whom? I invite you to think of those people whose lives are so limited that they retreat into fantasy. Or ascend. To their own foggy Zauberberg where the air is cool and thin and there is, for a change, quiet. Surely, that is what they are shopping for, equipment for their dreams. Somebody will hang his pull on the wall and look at it from time to time, imagining a life in which a footman would answer the summons. Not "delusional" as I said before with a lack of charity. It would not be a terrible distortion to see it a kind of prayer. He could as easily drape Buddhist prayer flags around the room. Or install religious icons on the walls that he can explain are there because he is a connoisseur. But they are also for devotion, when no one is looking. There must be a purpose, a hope, an alternative to this life. And without even admitting to himself what he is doing, he uses these gewgaws to enable devotion or meditation or moments of abnegation.

Whatever works. Let us look again at Mrs. Toplofty who appears to be studying the guidebook in her lap. She is reading it but not reading it. She is passing her eyes over the words and, perhaps, parsing the sentences. But does she care about the names of the mountains she can see from her chaise? Why would she? The text is any text, and the activity of reading is a way of suppressing (somewhat) the thought of death that is always with her, like tinnitus in the ear of an afflicted person. She could be looking at railway schedules, which might serve her purpose better because she could engage with them more strenuously, setting herself various destinations and then figuring which connections would be least inefficient. Railroad stations are dismal, and she worries about encountering a Tolstoy (not the count, and not even necessarily Tolstoy) who has come to sit on one of the benches where he waits not for a train but a chariot, coming for to carry him home. Too dramatic. Too distracting.

When any character in a Dreiser novel takes a train, there was an actual train that that ran from Dep. to Arr. at the times specified in the book. He looked them up. He could not imagine that the schedules would ever change. (A novelist, yet.) So now only graduate students writing papers look up ancient timetables to prove that this was his practice. (So? So? Then what?_

But Serena isn't actually going anywhere. She is just plotting a route. From Oslo to, say, Košice in (then) Austria-Hungary, somewhere not on a main line. She would have to go through Vienna, or perhaps Innsbruck. I was in Košice once. It was the weekend of the Slovakian marathon, which is unlike other marathons in that, as I watched from the window of a bar on the main street, I could see the contestants running in both directions. What that had to mean was that there wasn't a route of 26 miles (and 385 yards) the officials could find any-where, so they had to make do with a thirteen-mile course on which the runners did laps, as in a swimming meet. Or a two-mile course on which they did thirteen laps. Confusing to watch. The bar I would have preferred was across the street, but one couldn't cross because there were *polícia* every twenty feet to protect the runners. Or in-timidate the non-runners. The *polícia* are criminals in black combat uniforms. Or, conceivably, like the runners, they periodically change direction and swap clothes and activities.

People come from all over Eastern Europe to see the marathon, which meant that there were no flights out that weekend. I was stuck there. But there are criminal organizations that smuggle refugees in and out. I had to go to one of their offices, which are not hard to find. *Pašeráci* is written on the windows in large gilt letters, and it is the Slovakian word for "smugglers." The man behind the counter was still wearing his police uniform. There was a routine in which they issued a false passport for which I had to dye my hair black. I looked a little younger, perhaps, but close-up the effect was unconvincing. I might as well have been wearing a large button proclaiming that I was an impostor, or a fugitive, or even a spy—but why would anyone spy on Slovakia?

No, no, almost none of that happened. There was a marathon, and the runners were running in both directions, but the rest is embroi-

dery. Nevertheless if the general sense of my experience is as I de-
scribe it, what is to inhibit our elaborating the silliness? As Isidore of
Seville may well have said, "See Košice and you have seen the world."
Meaning what? That the rest of the world is just like it? Or that if
you're visiting Košice you must have already been everywhere else.
Either is correct. I should warn Mrs. Toplofty that the chances of her
actually going there are slender. (Especially in that she is, herself, not
actual—as she has begun to suspect for some time now. But neither is
anyone else in the sanitarium, which is a kind of comfort.)

Those of you who have learned German and memorized *The Magic
Mountain* will recall (and be able to recite) the passage in which Mann
talks about Castorp's odd conviction that the painting on the wall of his
grandfather was more the man than the man himself. (*Mann ist Mann*,
which has nothing to do with Thomas or Erika or Klaus, is an early
play by Brecht.) The formality of the portrait, in which his grandfather is wearing his ceremonial senatorial costume, seems to the young
boy (Castorp is remembering this) more persuasive, more characteristic, than the flesh and bones grandfather who pottered about the
house and put in his false teeth only for meals. Still less real was his
grandfather's cadaver laid out among all those tuberoses with an ivory
crucifix in its hands, a life-sized waxworks of the deceased person to
which he could not feel any connection. This is part of the reason for
his equanimity about his disease and the prospect of his body's death.
As all of us should do but few manage, he has been schooling himself
in the art of dying since that boyhood moment. Éluard and Bandeira
think Castorp is something of a dullard because he doesn't talk much.
He will answer direct questions but only rarely does he volunteer his
views on any subject they happen to be discussing, however playfully.
In fact, Castorp is quite alert but doesn't care anymore. (In fact? A
fictional person making a cameo appearance in another fiction? What
fact could there possibly be?) He has thought about having his own
portrait painted in that same style, but for whom? The painting of
his grandfather was sufficient and remains so, especially in that the
grandfather's name was also Hans. (Castorp ist Castorp?) It seems to
be the world's judgment that one Hans Castorp is enough. Certainly
the one in the solarium would agree with it.

(Berthold Brecht's play is about brainwashing, the malleability of
the self, and the problem of human identity as Galy Gay (no kidding)
is transformed into a military man in British India. Brecht was quite
correct in his understanding of these psychological and philosophical
difficulties; his only lapse was to react to them with a puzzlement and
anger that were uncharacteristically naive. What else did he expect?)

I was kidding before. (When have I not been?) Nobody is going to memorize that long novel. That, perhaps, is the great difference between novels and poems. You can memorize a poem--even a long one. Think of those bards who committed *The Iliad* or *The Mahabharata* (parts of them, anyway) to memory so they could making a living by going around and reciting to their audiences at dinner parties and literary evenings. A novel, even one you have just finished, starts immediately to blur. You can go back and look, of course, if there is some detail to which you wish to refer. And for a while you will retain the plot and the characters (which are, as I have been maintaining all along, unimportant). It's the timbre that counts, the tessitura that stays with you, the subtle effects of sentence structure that you translate (all reading is translation) into a human being. A line may stay with you—"God Bless Captain Vere!" But it is the authorial voice you retain longest.

Hang it all, Ezra Pound, there are as many Sordellos as there are readers. My Faulkner and yours will be similar but not identical. We claim him. He claims us. It is as if we were all sitting in that solarium together, looking up at the mountains above Davos now and then, but with books in our laps as we wait for our mid-morning bouillon. Among other things.

In his tower, where the view is much less spectacular, Harington puts down his quill, stretches, yawns, and rereads the stanza he has just completed:

> Upon the sill and through the columns there,
> Ran young and wanton girls, in frolic sport;
> Who haply yet would have appeared more fair,
> Had they observed a woman's fitting port.
> All are arrayed in green, and garlands wear
> Of the fresh leaf. Him these in courteous sort,
> With many proffers and fair mien entice.
> And welcome to this opening Paradise :

Satisfactory. Better than satisfactory. But remember he is betting his life that Queen Elizabeth will like it enough not to have him beheaded. This is a condition in which many writers find themselves, but only in a metaphoric way. Still, metaphors can bite. Would it be worth writing a children's story about "The Boy who Cried Metaphor"?

But wait. Harington is four hundred years earlier! Is there no sequence to this? No order? Of course not. As T. S. Eliot said (he didn't write this but it is what one heard, listening as he read it aloud), "Dime present and dime bast are both perhaps present in dime future." The quirky elocution diminished its pomposity a bit, which was a good thing. Anyway, all he was saying is that everything is simultaneous. Which is true, because he's dead and he's still saying it, isn't he? In dime future.

And Harington, too, lives on, although faintly. Are they the two figures at the far end of the solarium? Has someone been reading something by one or the other of these poets? Or have they just dropped by for the bouillon? Not impossibly they have come in merely to use the john. (It is far too grand an establishment to have a latrine.) It is a prized piece of student folk-knowledge that one class passes on to the next that T. S. Eliot's name is an anagram of *toilets*, so that he and John have more in common than just the writing of poems.

On second thought, let it be 1924, the year of publication of *The Magic Mountain*. Coincidentally, Kafka, who also has tuberculosis, publishes "The Hunger Artist" in that year. He is in another sanitarium engaged in the business of dying, and also correcting proof of that short, terrifying piece. His small but pleasantly sunny room is at the end of a corridor near death's door. The story is about a hunger artist, who makes a living by fasting. Or more bluntly one could say that he makes a living by dying. (As which of us does not?) Students write papers about the meaning of this strange tale, forgetting that the first place to look is at what's in plain sight. Kafka's TB was not the usual pulmonary kind; he had laryngeal tuberculosis which may or may not have been the end-state of the pulmonary disease he probably also had or it could have developed quite independently. He had suffered from clinical depression and social anxiety throughout his entire life. His other complaints included migraines, insomnia, constipation, boils, et alia. (Alia is the one that will get most of us some time or other.) One of the symptoms of the laryngeal disease is an inability to swallow— so back before parenteral nutrition had been invented, he starved to death. He was, himself, the hunger artist. (Hunger + Artist, no?)

The eponymous hero, or victim, is on display in a cage on a bed of straw. There are watchers around the clock whose job it is to witness that he has ingested no food. He is allowed sips of water now and again, but he's not a thirst artist, after all. The story is brief. The hunger artist dies. (This is not O. Henry, and there are no O. Henry Bars for him to scarf.) As with any artist, he becomes his art, losing all identity but his hunger, which would be all but impossible to imagine for anyone who wasn't starving to death, himself. What we are reading, then, is not about hunger after all but is a speculation about identity. The closer the artist comes to death, the less he is an individual and the more he becomes the condition, the sensation, the agony of hunger. It is horrible, but perhaps, as Kafka implies, tolerable as a means of escape from the confines of self.

Kafka was working on proof when he finally gave up the ghost. Or let the ghost go. Or became the ghost and let himself go. What is there to say? As a young man, at the Charles Ferdinand University, he studied law and received a Doctor of Laws degree, so we can legitimately refer to him Franz Kafka, Esq. Had he not been an attorney he would merely have been Kafkaesque. Yes, yes, aggressively stupid, but it is the best I can come up with to suggest how he could infuse meanings into words or extract meanings from them. To him they were not individual Leibnitzian monads but living creatures in which thoughts can seed themselves and grow. Like mold in the refrigerator. Especially sour cream. It is a risky business to reopen a container of sour cream. (Cream cheese, too.) Will there be that greenish evidence of corruption or can I put a dollop onto my baked potato? With the steady stillicide of catastrophes raining down upon us from the newspapers, these are relatively minor worries, but we entertain them because we can. They are bearable or at last not overwhelming. Nothing to make a federal case about. If it were, would we consult *Rechtsanwalt* Kafka, sitting behind his desk with impressively buckram-bound sets of law books? And if we did, would he laugh? Kafka's laughter would be unbearable, I think. Almost as bad as God's. And a part of their joke is that there is no hope, no help, no remedy for us or for any of the panoply of maladies that afflict us. We can commiserate with Kafka. We do. That's why we read him. He says simple things that are shocking enough to soothe us: "I need solitude for my writing; not 'like a hermit' - that wouldn't be enough - but like a dead man."

It's like going to a Zen master who doesn't necessarily teach you anything but hits you a lot. It's painful. You think, at first, that it must mean something. But what do you know? You're a mere novice, suitable only for cleaning the latrines (Still?) and getting slapped. ["He Who Gets Slapped" is a play by Leonid Andreyev about a clown whose job it is (métier, one might say) to be slapped by the other clowns. Hohoho! He's in love with Consuelo, but that hardly matters. There was a movie of it with Lon Chaney as "He" and Norma Shearer as Consuelo. Socko in Chi. Boffo in Cleve. The point is that being slapped is . . . the human condition? Like TB or syphilis? Or Zen.] The idea of the Zen slap might be to shake the misconceptions out of the novice's head physically. Or to wake him up. Or, as he finally comes to understand with the eventual dawning of enlightenment, it is of no use whatever except as a way the master has of working out his frustrations. He likes to hit people. It is the fun part of his job. The best way to get him to stop is to laugh at each blow. A high, shrill, nearly hysterical laugh is best, but any energetic cachinnation has a good chance of being effective.

The strength of Kafka is that he sees things we don't see and has experiences we don't have. Or, suppressing the laughter, he claims to. And which of us is so sure of himself, so hyperperceptive, with such exquisitely attenuated nerves, that he can dismiss these claims? By good fortune, I have a life that he recommends, with nothing intruding upon me so that I am free, if I choose to do so, to spend all day at the desk. Not answering the phone (it takes messages). Not moving except to stretch or pee or get fresh coffee. But in the *Aphorisms*, Kafka says, "There is no need for you to leave the house. Stay at your table and listen. Don't even listen, just wait. Don't even wait, be completely quiet and alone. The world will offer itself to you to be unmasked; it can't do otherwise; in raptures it will writhe before you." Can that happen? I am alone and it is completely quiet, except for the heater that rumbles into life when bidden to do so by the thermostat, but I am used to that and hardly hear it. I sit. I wait. I don't wait. The world, if it is offering itself to me, is astonishingly shy. If it is writhing before me, it makes an heroic attempt to disguise it, like a woman at a dinner table who is having an orgasm and tries not to let the other guests notice anything unusual. Surely, if I were paying attention, I might suspect? No? Not even the telltale yawn that she covers, putting her hand up to her mouth? Unless I am alert to it, I will miss it. As I must miss, I suppose, a great deal of the excitement that goes on around me. But Kafka, sick unto death, starving, and with an aura announcing a migraine? There is a ringing in his ears. His vision has changed so that he sees zigzag lines that move like the neon lights on theater marquees. (He also has an abdominal cramp, but that is unrelated to the migraine.)

Is that the "writhing"? Is it not the world's but his? He is an eminent writher, as someone with impaired pronunciation might say with greater accuracy than those of us with perfect elocution can imagine. ("Writer/writher" is another word with an alternate meaning moving in an out on the brainwaves that break on the shingle. Joyce loved these.)

Shingle? I could have said "shore," and did at first, but shore is unspecific. It is, in my mind, sandy, a beach really. Shingle is stones and hard to walk on. The breaking of small waves would be more interesting to watch, wouldn't it? If the tide were coming in, one could pick out an individual stone and watch it to see whether the next wave would submerge it. Or the one after that. Or surely the seventh. Surely?

Scientists reject the idea that waves come in sets of seven and the seventh is usually the largest, even though, in the short run, that seems to be an observable phenomenon. (Check out Stewart's *Introduction to Physical Oceanography*.) But do you believe the oceanographers, then, or your own lying eyes?

Anything to get out of that little room in the sanatorium where the great, sad, greatly sad man is in his uncomfortable clinic chair reading proof. He would rather have stayed in bed but the doctors, who can't do much, at least can try to prevent bedsores by having him sit up from time to time. And he is willing, not that he thinks that it will do any good but because it is another trial, another torment. And those are familiar.

I don't think Mann had TB. But that raises the question of whether *Magic Mountain* is better or worse for having been imagined. It's a lovely metaphor and it's a good book. But he had to make up what Kafka had experienced at first hand. There are arguments on both sides. Kafka's misery is difficult to dismiss, but it is an awkward business to "privilege" (as the scholars now say) suffering over the art. The truth of fiction depends on its not being true. Otherwise, it is mere reportage dressed up a little. The fiction of truth, on the other hand, is not to be eschewed (and espat out). Melville brought actual experience of the sea to *Moby Dick*. We admire that. But would we not admire him even more if he had been sitting in a sod farmhouse in Nebraska just dreaming it all up? (I often think of Peter De Vries' opening line of *The Vale of Laughter* that starts, "Call me, Ishmael. Call me any time of the day or night.")

All those angry girls (deprived, scorned, and made to spend four years of their lives at expensive colleges with credit cards, iPhones and laptops) read Sylvia Plath's poems less for the poetry than for the odor of the gas of her oven into which she stuck her head. A suicide, she must have understood the great feminist issues. (Why?) And also, if she's dead, she isn't going to write any more (or anymore—here, both are correct). This means the assignments are not unreasonably lengthy. Also, her husband, Ted Hughes, had a mistress who also killed herself, which can't be a coincidence and must therefore prove beyond a reasonable doubt the vileness of his oppression of women. (Must it?) These filters are too dark to read through. But who cares? Poems are mainly occasions for essays these days and with the poet's suicide there's more juicy stuff to write about.

Kafka's troubles were less dramatic (were they?) but sufficient. (I cannot imagine writers whose troubles were not "sufficient unto the day.") His father, Hermann, was worse than Plath's, and Franz's *Let-*

ter to my Father is a better piece of writing than that famous poem of hers that says basically that her father was a Nazi. The bottom line? It doesn't make any difference. Suffering, real or imagined, is at the heart of existence and a writer has to do his best to look at it and not flinch if he is to portray it.

I have read some of his Zürnau aphorisms that he wanted destroyed. Max Brod, his friend and executor, refused to do this and we have them. They are, as you might guess, rather gloomy. "Can you know anything other than deception? If ever the deception is annihilated, you must not look in that direction or you will turn into a pillar of salt." The catch, I think, is that deception is never annihilated, so we don't have anything to worry about. But is that thought comforting? Or even bearable? The only thing that allows us to continue to live is our stupidity. Our denseness. Our ineptitude. Everything you were ashamed of is what keeps you going. It's the stuff you were proud of that turns out to be vain and absurd.

Surely we are supposed to think of Lot's wife, who was the first pillar of salt. Not for looking back at the cities of the plain, Kafka suggests, but for seeing through and annihilating their deception. Lot and the rest of the Jews were delusional, which is what allowed them to live. Another one of God's jokes, which are, I am afraid, tasteless but beyond our criticism.

The hunger artist is never named. It is difficult, then, to imagine scenes in which he and Castorp banter with each other about their predicaments and, conceivably, their authors. We can remedy this, of course, and call him Fringale. And a first name? But why? Hildegarde had only the one name. And Zazie. And Yanni. And Valli, whose first name was Alida but nobody used it. Colette had first names, Sidonie-Gabrielle, but who remembers them? The point is that she didn't need them. So let our character be Fringale tout court. (Those few of you who are still with me may scratch your heads for a moment but then remember it as the French word for hunger pangs, and if so, my chapeau is doffed to you.)

Mann and Kafka are merely authors. Castorp and Fringale are characters who have outlived their creators. As I have outlived mine. Not merely my parents, but God, too, who passed away sometime in the late nineteenth century, perhaps on a bed of straw in a cage in a carnival somewhere in Eastern Europe. Nietzsche announced this, although Hegel had said it earlier. It is better in German: *Gott is tot*, with the rhyme of the alveolar stops. (No, no, not dental, because the rear part of the tongue does not touch the teeth but the alveolar ridge.) Astonishingly nobody seemed to take notice. There is a panther in the empty cage now, and it draws more customers than God ever did.

There are, I ought to tell you, no such animals as panthers. They are black leopards, and if you look closely, preferably through the bars of a cage, you will see the leopard rosettes, which, as the proverb asserts, cannot change although they can be obscured for whatever competitive advantage that may afford. (You see leopard coats at le Cirque but very few panther coats, with or without marmosets peeking from the pockets.)

It would require an act of will to put Fringale in Zurich, where Mann died. It is easier to imagine Castorp paying a visit to the Kierling Sanatorium in Schelesen, just outside of Vienna, where Kafka died. We could imagine them, then, in the *Wiener Kaffeehaus*, which is, as the name suggests, a coffeehouse in Vienna. (There is another such establishment in Maryville, Tennessee, but that's not the one I had in mind.) So, put them in Vienna and sit them in comfy chairs in a quiet corner. The waiter comes to take their order and Fringale, characteristically, says, "Nothing for me, thank you." Castorp asks for an *Einspaenner* Coffee with the whipped cream on top and a *Millirahmstrudel*.

Characteristically? He's a character and we might expect him to behave like himself. But not necessarily, and surely not always. He could, if he is well enough imagined, surprise us, his author, and even us by doing something, some small innovative gesture that was within his range but never actualized. Or fictionalized. Part of the fun of writing a novel is to see what twitches of life the stick figures of the outline may exhibit, putting us to shame because, at least for that instant, they are smarter than we are. Or the book is. It is highly improbable, but Mann and Kafka could have sat in these very chairs discussing life and art. And tuberculosis, no doubt. I choose to imagine that Castorp and Fringale have thought of this but neither brings it up because where would it get them? Or us? Still, these very chairs? Why on earth not?

Fiction has a way of progressing and an experienced novelist will enjoy giving the characters as free a rein as he can manage. It occurs to me that the trouble with reality is that it doesn't do this and that from the events of today it is impossible to make any intelligent guesses about those of tomorrow. There is no rationale, there are no discernible tendencies. Only Gypsies and Greek Pythias presume to tell us about what impends and they are notoriously ambiguous and unreliable. Those kinds of discontinuities that we accept in life would never work in any fiction, even aggressively experimental fiction. (Auden said, I think, "I can't tell which one I hate worse:/ modernist novels or free verse." And of course he was posing, because he was very generous to a number of free-verse poets.)

Fringale and Castorp look at each other for a few moments in silence. Neither of them was at all prepared for anything like this. Their worlds are more plausible than ours after all. But neither is displeased. And both affect a sophistication that never betrays surprise. They have much in common. Oddly, or perhaps not, the first information they exchange is about the coincidence of their authors both having worked for insurance companies, Kafka for the Assicurazioni Generali, and Mann for the South German Fire Insurance Company. Generally, these are thought to be uncongenial jobs for writers, although Wallace Stevens worked for the Hartford Accident and Indemnity Company in Connecticut for many years and seems not to have been bothered much. (Is there PMLA paper in this? In the name of the dead God, I certainly hope not.)

The two fictional characters speculate that the monotony of such work might well have impelled the young writers to leave, strike out, and take up literature. Apparently, both of them were good at their jobs but bored out of their minds. Tedium, however, is not a bad nest for the fledgling talent. At the very least, it is not distracting. The daydreams of the desk may congeal to form the stories that are accumulating in the mind and spirit for the writing table in the evenings. Nobody has any idea about the genesis of writing, mostly because when the writer is typing or scribbling, he is unselfconscious. Can't remember a thing about his life away from the table, or even at the table but before he took up his pen. (For many of us, that is one of the attractions of an otherwise difficult and frustrating occupation, the promise not of fame but of oblivion.)

Castorp says that he is proud of his author for having arrived at many of Kafka's views merely from intuition, contemplation, philosophy and empathy. "The freedom that comes from having a terminal illness is not like anything else in human experience. He understood this wonder and expressed it through me, his creation."

"The tuberculosis Kafka had was not merely a disease but an enlightenment, a deepening of his understanding," Fringale says. "In those tranquil months at his sister's place in Zürnau he makes frighteningly shrewd comments about mortality. As fictional characters who do not die, we don't have to worry about that, but, if the author chooses, we may. There is a resistance among many readers to nihilism, but by art, or artifice, one can imply enough for them to accept it and, more or less, understand. In those aphorisms he wrote during that visit to the pleasant little Bohemian village, he wrote: 'The animal twists the whip out of its master's grip and whips itself to become its own master.'"

The waiter brings the coffee and the strudel. And two glasses of water, one of which Fringale picks up sips from.

Castorp stirs his coffee and looks around. "Do you notice that gray-haired fellow over there?" he asks, indicating a direction with a nod of his head. "He is taking notes. And although it may be my own fantasy, he may be eavesdropping on us and writing down what we say?"

Fringale smiles. "Is he writing down what we're saying or are we saying what he's writing down? Have you asked yourself that?"

"It's not an answerable question," Castorp replies.

"That doesn't mean that one can't ask it."

"Probably not."

"In ordinary circumstances, it would be rude," Fringale decides. "An invasion of privacy. But then, we have no secrets, do we?"

"Don't we? Any plausible character in a book has parts of himself or herself that the author doesn't bother to communicate but leaves the reader to infer. Those thoughts and actions have a kind of existence then, do they not?"

"But they are not secret" Fringale says. "At most, they are private."

"But consider our conversation here and now," Castorp replies with a self-satisfied smile. "Who could imagine this? Characters from two different books sitting together in a coffee house with a third man nearby, one who is not inconceivably the author of yet a third book in which we make a shadowy appearance? Would you not consider this as private?"

"Perhaps," Fringale concedes with a reciprocal smile. "But if that fellow is an author, the one imagining us, we cannot have secrets from him. At best, we can surprise him in minor ways."

Castorp puts his cup and saucer down on the table and gets up to seek the toilette, an action the author had no reason to expect. (In Flemish it would be *gemak,* or in Slovak, *záchod,* or Fijian, *vale-lailai-*-which sounds more like an oceanfront resort than a WC.) Thus, he surprises the author, whose riposte in those odd languages would have surprised him in turn, if he had been able to read this. It certainly surprised the author, who had no idea that M. La Trine was also in the coffeehouse, just out of sight but able to communicate by brain waves as some fictional characters seem able to do.

[That wouldn't be a bad title, would it? *The Reciprocal Smile*?

No, too kitsch-y. I' like *Vale-lailai* better.]

And anyway, what is all this potty talk about Johns and La Trines? Can there be any point to it? Certainly, there is. Characters in novels don't generally go to the can. In movies they have men talking at adjacent urinals to show how realistic they are. We saw Jane Fonda pee in *Klute*. But mostly Andrei, Pierre, Raskolnikov, Ahab, and all those other fictitious guys don't even excuse themselves. They just disappear for a few moments and it is the convention for us not to notice. But why put it in? Because it's irksome and boring, an interruption to whatever else is going on in our lives. And that's assuming that the going is going well. Our unpretentious physicality asserts itself and this ought to be a reminder of our limitations, even though we try as hard as the novelists do to ignore it (which means that their distortions are no worse than our own).

Castorp returns, sits down, and says to his companion that there is no particular advantage in having a terminal disease. If you think about it, mortality is, by definition, a fatal condition but people manage nonetheless to deny what they perfectly well know, think happy thoughts, and live tranquil lives. Or, in blunt terms, to become, even as the blood flows in their veins and the breath pumps in and out of their lungs, fictional characters.

"If real people are fictional and fictional people are fictional," Fringale asks in a pleasant, amused way, "who is real?"

"Real? What does 'real' mean?" Castorp asks. "These are metaphysical questions that have no place in our discussion. Neither we nor our authors have any interest in such subjects. Or him over there, I'd wager."

Fringale takes another small sip of water, very slowly, savoring it as if it were a fine wine. "It doesn't matter," he says. "The question is whether we have free will and, if you put it that way, it's too stupid even to ask. None of us has that. We do as our authors tell us. In the world that is off the pages, they are all going to die, whatever they think or want, and only when they accept that, even embrace it, can they have a glimpse of freedom. Or not freedom but its illusion, which is just as good."

"That's very gloomy."

"What do you expect? Kafka is gloomy. I am a Kafka creation. But that doesn't mean that we aren't correct."

"Would you like a taste of this *Millirahmstrudel*? It's very good."

"Sure, why not? Thank you," Fringale says, surprising himself, his companion and me, too. He takes a bit, using Castorp's fork. (They both have TB but what worse can happen to them?) "Very good. Very tasty."

The silvery haired man leaves a few coins on the table, puts his notebook into his pocket and leaves. He is not the author after all but a landlord's agent and has come in for a coffee and he has been making a list of those tenants who are behind in the rent and upon whom he

must call this afternoon with varying degrees of courtesy and firm-
ness. In other words, no matter what Castorp and Fringale may have
thought, I was not the man. Or I'd prefer not to be the man. Let there
be some distance between us. Actually, I've never been to Vienna.

Why? That's just how it has been. I did go once to Berlin not so
much to see the city but to discover what I might feel being in such a
place. Whatever I felt, it wasn't clear. Or even very powerful. Parts
of it were prettier than I had expected with many gardens full of flowers, bushes, and trees. The flowers were like any other flowers, but
I had the notion that they were being sarcastic. For such beauty to
grow in cursed earth was not an outrage but... cheeky, snide, and, as I
say, sarcastic. I had prepared myself for the visit by figuring out and
memorizing the German question, *Was war Ihr Großvater machen in
zweiundvierzig?* What was your grandfather doing in forty-two? I had
rejected the idea of sewing yellow six-pointed stars on my jacket and
overcoat. I didn't want to embarrass my wife. But the question could
nestle in my mind, comforting me even if I never had occasion to pose
it. It was like the postcards I have from Auschwitz (yes, they sell postcards there: the only requirement for respect and decorum being a
sign forbidding the eating of ice cream. Yoghurt, however, is not forbidden.). The postcards are now in a cabinet waiting for some affront
or insult that might distress me enough to let me to mail one.

There have been moments when I was tempted. There were people who were rude or annoying enough for me to imagine getting out
one of the cards. But I only have three of them and if I sent one, I'd be
down to two. It's better in some ways to have them here in my study
where they are potentialities than to put stamps on them and let them
go. In the same way, I never actually asked that question about the
Berliners' grandfathers, but it was nice to have it ready in case of need.
The key word here is "actually," which suggests a solidity, a common-
sense reality to which we can all refer and about which we must agree.
But must we?

Consider the possibility that the real world is just one option
among many. An opinion to which there are always alternatives. Disease—tuberculosis or cancer--legitimates the sufferers' option of
committing suicide but we all have that choice—to stay or to go, to
accept or reject the world around us. Many of us consider it from time
to time, the way I consider sending those Auschwitz postcards that
are always delightfully at hand. We don't have to die to find solace
in the thought of death. It is like walking along one of those European streets in the early evening when the whores are standing there,
making themselves available. You don't have to engage one to have a

milder but more various erotic experience of knowing that you could. That sullen looking one with the long black hair is appealing. Or that plumpish one, slightly older but still apparently cheerful is attractive partly for her body but partly too for her spirit, her willingness to put up with this life longer than she had planned to do. Mostly, these girls come up from the south, work the streets for a few years, and then go back home to use the money to open a shop of some kind. She has perhaps met a man who keeps her here? How would I know? The important thing isn't the action but the freedom to act, for me and for her too. "Our art," Kafka says in one of those aphorisms, "is an art that is dazzled by truth: the light shed on the rapidly fleeing grimace is true—nothing else is." To redefine truth in that way is to allow it to be important. (If it weren't for the adverb, *The Rapidly Fleeing Grimace* would be a thought for a title. Without the adverb, *The Fleeting Grimace*?) If you were sitting in your doctor's office and you happened to notice the disappearing trace of a facial expression steeled not to betray his discomfort at what he was about to say, you wouldn't need the words that he was about to pronounce. You would hear them, but they would already be redundant, pleonastic, superfluous, and almost insulting. Or they would if they registered, which is improbable because you would already have felt the shock of their import.

It is not easy to do. The doctors have trained themselves to be unemotional. They want to be supportive, and sometimes are, but beyond that they want not to upset their patients. So they do as much as they can to assume their expressions of unconcerned concern. To this degree, they are real doctors playing the role of doctor. You do not have an otoscope in your pocket that you can whip out to look into a patient's ear and try to peer past the drum and into the brain. You have to pay attention to subtle cues and clues—as he does, too. It is a game, then, but it is your money on the table, your life in the chair. It does you no good to remind yourself that his white coat is a costume in this comedy (or farce) and that under it his body is as vulnerable as yours. Maybe even as sick as yours, but he wouldn't want you to know that.

There are lectures these people go to on how to talk to patients. These are acting classes. "Won't you sit down, Mrs. Gundlefinger!" Say that with menace, with concern, with lust, with contempt, with indifference. (You can pass the time on trains and busses doing this if you don't say the words aloud.) They have scripts that they follow. No joke. (And, they are advised not to make jokes.) Reality, as we have been discussing it, is inadequate to the needs of the clinical encounter. It is unreliable, dangerous, and can be ugly. So they learn to circumvent it as much as they can.

With compassion this time: "Won't you sit down, Mrs. Gundlefinger."

Again, not so exaggerated.

Again. Better.

Castorp, of course, was beyond caring. As was his doctor. The large question had been asked and answered. Now there were merely the trivial inquiries about how he was sleeping, how much he was coughing, what color was his sputum and whether he was bringing up blood, the usual, banal exchanges, almost as routine for them as "How are you feeling?" when we say it to one another. "Oh, fine, thank you." (The person who asked doesn't really want to know.)

They used to call this "bedside manner," but how many doctors come to your bedside anymore—unless it's in a hospital? You're lucky if they're willing to meet you in the emergency room. They were better in the old days (before I was born), but then they couldn't do much to help you. No antibiotics. No fiber optics. No CAT scans or MRIs. No replacement-part surgery. They could diagnose and tell you whether you were probably going to live or not, but if you couldn't afford a doctor you'd find that out eventually, wouldn't you? With the modern armamentarium, a doctor could have helped Maria Mahler pull through. Gustav would have been grateful. And Anna? My guess is that she would have been relieved. Fucking her way through the Austrian *Who's Who*, she must have felt fleeting moments of doubt, if not guilt, and during these twinges of regret she might have viewed Maria's death as a judgment. It didn't bother her all that much, apparently, but now and then, briefly, a little. She might even have come to enjoy these passing emotional shadows, thinking of them as an indication that the universe was at least taking notice. Each of these pangs carried the perverse implication that she was—would have been—not so bad a mother. So she welcomed them: they were orgasms of guilt, some of them sharp enough to make her cry out.

I am being fanciful of course. But it is an agreeable conceit and, in any event, may be the plain truth of it. Surely it is the kindest thought I have ever had about that woman. Not enough to make me cry out, but worth one of Dr. Freud's possibly sympathetic but possibly staged nods.

The usual take on Anna Schindler Mahler Gropius Werfel is that she must have been a sensation. All those celebrities panting after her? Wow! But you look at the pictures online and you can't imagine what the fuss was about. The question should be posed exactly the opposite way: why couldn't she hold on to any of these guys? What prevented her from settling on one and staying with him? Was she just a ditsy dame? Or are we going to imagine her as a troubled soul unable to find rest and contentment in any bed in the world? She's dead so it doesn't matter to her. It's what appeals to us, whatever makes a better, more interesting story.

Attracting these people couldn't have been difficult for her. She was, there can be no doubt, flirtatious, sitting just a little closer than was necessary, leaning toward the guy, putting her hand on his forearm now and then ostensibly to emphasize whatever otherwise unimportant thing she happened to be saying. Many women are like that, but they don't mean it and it's at least partly an amusement, a joke. But she was available. To Alexander Zemlinsky first (he was her music teacher) but very soon thereafter to Gustav Klimt and Max Burkhard, the theater director. (Sounds like a lot, but ask your daughter or niece or grand-daughter about "hooking up" in colleges these days.) Then Mahler, who might have been a father figure (he was nineteen years her senior) or maybe not.

She and Mahler have what is a more or less conventional marriage, which is to say that it is utterly unknowable. Tolstoy tells us that happy families are all alike, while Nabokov says that unhappy families are all alike. Both are correct, although these assertions were made in novels, from which we do not require factual accuracy. It doesn't matter. The thing is that when Maria dies, Alma is beside herself or claims to be and goes to a spa for a rest cure. A spa is a sanitarium where the guests mostly do not have TB. Neurasthenia, maybe, although, according to the American Psychiatric Association's Diagnostic and Statistical Manual of Mental Disorders, that isn't a disease anymore. The World Health Organization still recognizes it (how difficult must it be to recognize?) as does the Chinese Society of Psychiatry, but then the problems of the Chinese may be more severe than ours and sufficient to bring it on still. (And think of all those years in which we didn't recognize China.) The symptoms were or are: fatigue, anxiety, headache, neuralgia and depression. If I had neuralgia, I'd think I might claim to be suffering from it. Or maybe one doesn't have to check off every item on the list to qualify. (It is a fine sounding ailment like catarrh, apoplexy, quinsy, and gleet.) She went to a spa, but probably not the spa at Spa (in Belgium). Maybe the baths at Baden Baden. (Or Bath?) All these places specialized in neurasthenia. (Some also offered high colonics.) They were resorts that claimed in some way to be good for your health.

So she is at Marienbad maybe. (Why not? This is where Renais set his movie.) There Alma meets Walter Gropius. (Gropy-ass?) (I do apologize for that.) He is younger than Gustav and happy to serve as a distraction for her. The spa offers deep massage and so does he. But it's merely a brief thing (one of those clocks that now and then chimes/ just one of those times) and they go their separate ways, not getting together again until years later when Gustav dies in New York (the heart, remember?). She is sad to have become a widow but not enough to prevent her from having a "tumultuous" affair with Oskar Kokoschka, the painter. (Tumultuous? Do neighbors complain about the noise they make in bed?) When the heat of this liaison cools, she leaves Oskar (or he, her) and marries Gropius. Good. A nice ending. Anyway, an ending. For a nice conventional novel, where there is a sense of cloture and we feel we have been instructed in the mysteries of life and love, although in what way we have been enlightened would be difficult to say, exactly. Knowledge is good, but the feeling of having knowledge is almost as good and requires less effort. "Tomorrow is another day," Scarlet says, and by gosh and by golly, who can argue with her?

Endings are tricky, but so are beginnings and middles. *Finis origine pendet* is Andover's motto, and it means the end depends on the beginning, which means in turn that if any of you little bastards ever make it in the world, remember that you owe it all to us, right? So give! (They have an endowment of the better part of a billion dollars and they're a high school.)

Alma has no idea that the appropriate place for an ending has come and gone. She goes right on eating and drinking, having sex, and even going to the bathroom sometimes. She has a kid by Gropius. And then another kid Gropius wants to believe is his (why?) but she tells him the truth, the actual *emes*, which may be admirable but has its downside. (Did she let the information slip or hurl it at his head as if it were a piece of crockery? Did she vomit it out—in an emesis of *emes*? Has anyone ever written an ms about that emesis?) It's Franz Werfel's, she tells him.

D-i-v-o-r-c-e, and not an amicable one. (Amicable divorces are probably unnecessary.) She is at least exercised enough to drop Gropius' name from her notepaper and become Anna Mahler-Werfel. Neurasthenia? I'd call it Attention Deficit Disorder. But as Francis said, "Who am I to judge?" (The pope, I mean.)

What connection has any of this with Alma, you may ask? What can I tell you—that I am afraid I neglected to put in some casual encounter at Marienbad in which Gropius has breakfast with Erich Castorp, a cousin of Hans' but a character whom Mann never mentions in his novel? (Those of you who have memorized the novel can attest to this.) Erich Castorp has been eyeing Alma, whom Gropius now notices mostly because his table companion keeps staring at her at breakfast.

Does that connect? Yes, perhaps. And in an ordinary novel, it would mean something, suggesting a coherence to experience, an orderliness novelists try to suggest although God apparently does not bother. It isn't just a bowl of spaghetti before us but a single strand that patience and industry can untangle. The unified strand theory. It's like the unified field theory but with sauce. I don't worry about it much but its attraction I can dimly understand. Einstein's claim that God does not play at dice with the universe only makes sense if we can imagine a William Blake-ish God with a long white beard and an enormous pair of dice he flings down on the table. Table? What table? Ah, the universe. It was to make a surface on which to cast the dice that in the beginning He made the universe.

It may not be a satisfying explanation but it is an explanation. And by the same token, I have wondered why Mann never refers to Hans Castorp without using the first name. Other characters only get last names as if they were all English schoolboys together. But Hans Castorp remains unfailingly binomial. Could it be to signify his importance as the protagonist? (Call me Ishmael Peterkin?) To distinguish him from Erich, that neurasthenic cousin of his at Marienbad of whom we might otherwise think? Or because Mann has a son and a brother-in-law named Hans? It could be just an authorial tic. You can flip a coin. Or cast dice. (Or even one die, like Julius Caesar, who had mislaid the other somewhere in Gaul.)

You shake your head? You reject my invention? After all this foolishness you balk now, finding a final straw with which to beat a dead camel? Then let us try again. In Rio, where Manuel Bandiera lived for a time, his next--door neighbor was a German-Portuguese family. Sometimes, when Bandiera got up from the writing table in his study, stretched, and walked to the window he saw their daughter, a little girl of six or seven, playing some hopping game on the sidewalk. The girl's name is Júlia da Silva Bruhns and when she grows up she will marry Heinrich Mann, the merchant of Lübeck. (A lost play of Shakespeare?) Thomas Mann will be one of their sons.

I made that up. And I am not sure the time works. At any rate, it's a very far-fetched coincidence, but the farther-fetched these things are, the more significant they seem and the clearer their evidence of a providential hand screwing with the ordinary odds against such things. God is playing at dice with the universe, and they are loaded, as poor, dim Einstein never suspected. It would defy logic, and logic is the version of God that non-believers believe in. Physics, mathematics, cognitive science... those are boring beyond belief and are therefore beyond disbelief. (Does mathematics have a Kaddish? Are there blessings in physics?)

The spa in *8½* to which Guido Anselmi goes because his nerves are shot is never named, but it seems to be a fashionable one with lots of other rich nervous people around, comfortably uncomfortable. Guido's condition disimproves while he is there. He says puzzling things like "I really have nothing to say, but I want to say it all the same." More like Kafka than Fellini, no?

It would not be at all difficult for us to imagine a mustached, rather corpulent lawyer in a Panama hat, sitting out on the lawn in a deck chair where he takes the air and waits for his massage appointment. Unlike Kafka, he actually practices law. On the table beside him is a book by Thomas Mann that he brought along to help pass the time during his stay at the spa. He has not read much of it (he finds it boring, actually) but he carries it around with him. It invites people to start conversations. Even though he is a lawyer, he is shy about doing that with strangers. And is it *The Magic Mountain*? No, of course not. It's *Buddenbrooks*, but never mind. He thinks it is tedious and, if it doesn't pick up in another twenty pages, he will give it to the spa for their library and borrow or buy something else.

Another meaningless coincidence? Visiting the spa at the same time as Anselmi and the lawyer is Giuseppe Tomasi, Prince of Lampedusa. He has not yet begun to write *The Leopard* or even to think about doing so. He is floating along, living life, and enjoying himself, which is probably the best preparation for any venture into literature. (It is surely better than a creative writing course in the cornfields of Iowa.) Lampedusa never meets Anselmi, although he recognizes the lawyer—it is a very attractive Panama hat, after all, an authentic one made from the plaited leaves of the jipijapa palm. They have greeted each other with silent, reciprocal doffings of their hats. (Tomasi's is a splendid, pearl gray Borsalino.) Had they spoken, the lawyer might well have given his copy of *Buddenbrooks* to the future writer. And it might have influenced his style. (But for better or worse? That's impossible to know.)

Come on! The jipijapa palm? Oh, yes. Or, more appropriately, *si.* I am sorry to disappoint you, but that's real. It is also real that the hats do not come from Panama but rather Ecuador. A *superfino* hat can hold water and is flexible enough to be crushed down and passed through a wedding ring. Ah, the modest pleasures of facticity!

I have allowed myself to get carried away. We are not making guacamole but have slighted the *avvocato*, which is not only unfair to him but to us as well, for his has been an interesting and inventive career. He is the man who figured out a way around the morass of permits and approvals that are required to build anything in Italy. The process used to take years until—Amilcare, let us call him—found a provision in some obscure regulation that exempts those structures that are already existing. An existential real-estate lawyer? *Exactamento!* He was the one who asked himself, while sipping a corretto in a pleasant café in Milan, what does "existing" mean? This is before Sartre and those other exemplars of left-bank frivolity addressed the question. Sartre was never aware of real-world problems of realty. It was all *tarte* in the *ciel.* Amilcare, however, did research (unusual among Italian lawyers) and in one of those dusty elephant folios discovered that what it means is that a structure exists if it has a roof. One can see the primitive logic in that most builders work from the ground up and therefore put on the roof at the end. At the end and on the top. But what if they changed their strategy, started with the roof, and built downward from there?

Beh! A stupid idea. But original. And for an original idea, stupidity is seldom a fatal flaw. Suppose you had a construction firm that was not altogether on the up-and-up. In unmarked trucks they could sneak onto a piece of property under the cover of night and erect a roof. Just a roof. On poles. Up and up. It would then be a structure with a roof. It could also be described as a roof without a structure, but that seems not to have been contemplated let alone forbidden. Whatever it was, it would exist, enjoying all the advantages of existence—like exemption from the permits, licenses, and *documentazione* the government had devised to annoy its citizens. *Sorprendente! Stupefacente! Strabiliante! Sbalorditivo!* (And other Italian synonyms for "amazing.") Hegel said that the real is the rational and the rational is the real, but an Italian lawyer knew intuitively that this was nonsense. The irrational is the real and the unreal is the rational. Hadn't Georg Wilhelm Friedrich ever ventured forth from his study to look around? What lies at the heart of his work? (Or, more accurately: What lies, at the heart of his work!) The secret of Hegel is this: As Aristotle made explicit the abstract Universal that was implicit in Socrates, so Hegel made explicit the concrete Universal that was implicit in Kant.

Does that do anything for you? (Me, too, neither.) And it certainly isn't going to help you in the real estate business, which makes the more modest but also more profitable claim that realty is real. (And personalty? Is personal! Which is why those flight attendants ask us not to forget any of our "personal belongings," as if there were another kind that we might have brought aboard to store overhead among the shifting items.)

This dimwitted but profound observation is what made Amilcare a rich man. And even respected. None of his colleagues at the bar thought of this as chicanery but as a clever (and successful) manipulation of the rules of the game. What in the law is real, after all? Notional laws about theoretical structures? *La legge è la legge*, but who can take any of it seriously? Amilcare found several crews that for enough money could do impressive work in four or five hours. Avoiding the *polizia* was not difficult. How could they possibly guard every open piece of land on the peninsula? And the islands, don't forget. (In Sardo, the word for amazing would be *sõnaraamat*. I have no idea how this is pronounced, but it doesn't matter. Most Sardinians mumble anyway.)

Oh, before I forget. Guido Anselmi bears a striking resemblance to the late Marcello Vincenzo Domenico Mastroianni, which ought not to be surprising because he played Anselmi in the movie. But that was an accident, or the end result of a process that is aggressively random. Fellini's first idea was to get Laurence Olivier to do it, but that fell through. Lord Olivier wanted more money? Or his Italian wasn't good enough? Or he had other commitments that would keep him busy when Fellini wanted to shoot? Any or those or all, or God was just playing with his die without anything particular in mind, but casting is casting and that was enough to affect the movie. My choice would have been Gary Cooper, playing against type and saying hardly anything, in which event his accent would not have been an issue. Mastroianni was very good, of course. Old M. V. D. Mastroianni, which suggests that his parents named him after the Motor Vehicle Department. (They didn't but I did, and my poetic license is valid for another four years.)

OK, OK, OK, OK, OK, OK, OK, OK, OK, OK, OK, OK, OK, OK, OK, OK, OK, OK, OK, but where is this going? Where has it gone? Indeed, what is it? Believe me, if I knew, I'd tell you. If you know, please write or call. It may be best to start modestly (always a good plan) and call it a book. Yes, of course but what does that mean? Not a text, but a book, an old-fashioned physical book made of paper. I think of the one that Varlam Shalamov found in an abandoned Kolyma shack. (He wrote about the Gulags at least as well as Solzhenitsyn.) It was an edition of the poems of Yevgeney Baratynsky, whom I am not making up. Pushkin praised Baratynsky and Akhmatova and Brodsky rediscovered him and put him back on the map, admittedly in very tiny letters. He is a bit too sweet for my taste but he's very good. Shalamov and his two companions found the book and discussed what to do with it or, more specifically, how to share it fairly. One of the companions ripped out the introduction so that he could use the leaves as cigarette paper. The second ripped out the notes and the index so that he could cut them up and make them into playing cards. Shalamov got the main text, which he could keep as poems and read them, or perhaps memorize them and then use the pages as toilet paper.

"You see?" La Trine asks, "you see? That's one of the risks of literature."

"Among many," Harington concurs. "Why would anyone write if it weren't forced on him? That is the question."

"Not 'To be or not to be?'" Lord Olivier asks, with that slightly raised eyebrow of his and the enviable enunciation.

"It is, if you put a roof on it," Amilcare jokes. (His mood has improved considerably since he gave up on *Buddenbrooks*.)

"The toilet paper option doesn't work on a Kindle or an iPad, does it?" (That's me, I'm afraid.) They all look at me with stares of disapproval mixed with incomprehension. They do not know me and the iPad has not yet been invented.

So? So, back in Vermont, the Walloomsac is still running gaily down the mountainside toward Bennington. What is striking isn't the sunshine overhead, or the water, or the rocks, or all of them together, but the momentary glints that give us the feeling of... not discovery but recognition. They can evoke a *yes* from somewhere inside us, which is, like them, as dazzling as it is brief.

There is something hypnotic about water running over smooth stones. If we stare long enough, we can persuade ourselves that it or they have something to tell us. The sight and the sound together are calming, reassuring, and teasingly suggestive. What else matters?

I have no idea.

II

HOOSIC

The same water, same stones, but the name of the Walloomsac changes to the Hoosic, which is, in Algonquin, "The Beyond Place." It sounds too poetic to be reliable. Or maybe "the stony place," which seems like a guess, because the river is, indeed, stony and, for most of the year, there are more stones in its bed than there is water. Who knows Algonquin, anyway? Some Algonquins, maybe, but what makes us think that they are telling palefaces the truth. They may not scalp anymore, but they still can pull legs. The same wiseacre who explained that Walloomsac, its tributary, means "the swimming place" might have made up another piece of contemptuous nonsense. A guy comes in to buy moccasins and toy drums but what he wants is information. That is not what the trading posts are for, but the Indians are generous with misinformation. The truth—assuming there is such a thing—costs more. Heap wampum! Anyway, what difference does it make? What's the point of naming water? There it is, but different from moment to moment, and there are the stones that also move but more slowly. Call it whatever you want.

The Algonquin language? There are several and they are a subgroup of the indigenous Chippewa. The name applies to a large group of people of many tribes. In Massachusetts alone there are the Wampanoag, Massachusett, Nipmuck, Pennacook, Passamaquoddy, Quinnipiac, Mohegan, Pequot, Pocumtuc, Tunxis, and Narragansett. Did they all speak the same language? Or was there a trading language—like Swahili or Yiddish—and then the local, tribal languages? (I assume that their comedians would use the trading language in dialect jokes for flavor and because of its otherness. For nasty dialect jokes they would use Iroquoian.) So Walloomsac and Hoosic, which sound funny to us, were intended to sound that way.

To try not to smile, therefore, out of tact or political correctness, would be wrong and even ill mannered. "Hoosic." "Gezundheit."

James Fennimore Cooper wrote about the Algonquins. Was there an Algonquin shoemaker who used the last of the Mohegans? (Mohicans, Mohegans, and Monhegans are variant spellings of the same tribal name, but orthography was never the Native Americans' strong point.) The last of the tribe, in any case, was Uncas, the son of Chingachgook and he would have been the last because there were no full-blooded Mohegan women left for him to marry. But Uncas is killed by a Huron and dies before Chingachgook does, which actually makes the father the last Mohegan. If Cooper had been writing about Indians that lived in the west, he might have made a little joke, calling his book *Le Dernier Cree.* (I would have.) He wasn't fooling around with the title, though, setting a trap for students who haven't read the Leatherstocking Tales and therefore mess up on quizzes. He never imagined that there would be quizzes. I find it hard to imagine it, myself, even though I know it's true. And anyway, what kind of title would *The Penultimate Mohegan* have been? (I like that, too, but mine is a minority taste. As for kreplach and matza brei.)

Chingachgook means "big snake," and comes from the Lenape language. (Is that what the Mohegans spoke? And did the Lenape speak Mohegan? Or was this just more nonsense they told Mr. Cooper to see how far they could go without bursting into whoops of laughter, which would have ruined the joke and probably terrified the novel-ist. Chingachgook's name would surely have been difficult for Cooper to pronounce because of its initial voiceless velar fricative, something like the *ch* in Bach. The character is based on an Indian John (or, more clearly, an Indian named John), an itinerant basket seller, who, for all we know, might have been the last of the itinerant basket sellers. (Strictly speaking, he was an itinerant seller of baskets, because there are not and never have been itinerant baskets.) Would Cooper have noticed such a grammatical oddity? Very possibly, because he went to Yale. He didn't graduate, having committed some ridiculous offense against the propriety and good order of the university. One story has him leading a cow up the winding staircase of the bell tower of Battell Chapel, where it had to be butchered because you cannot make a cow back down a spiral staircase. This is unlikely, though, because Battell hadn't been built when Cooper was at the college. Another account has him putting a donkey in a professor's chair, which is difficult to visualize both for us and for the donkey. A third report involves an explosion in his dormitory. This one is less amusing but the least un-likely. There have been a number of proposals in faculty meetings for a James Fennimore Cooper prize (no money but a handsome plaque) for the student who gets expelled for the stupidest reason of the year, but it always gets voted down. Members of Cooper's family have been proposing a posthumous honorary bachelor's degree for him, but there is no precedent for such degrees, which seems to me to be a lame excuse. Cooper made out well enough even without the diploma. And as far as I know, none of those Indian tribes gave him a name that means "prankster who never graduated from Yale." Enough time has gone by since his undergraduate peccadillo so that he can be forgiv-en—and even honored. But would Yale be honoring Cooper or would it be the other way around? He remains a poor little lamb who has gone astray. Bah, bah, bah!

He has an odd reputation, not because of the Yale business but be-cause of the smart-assed essay of Mark Twain's that makes fun of his prose. "In any Cooper novel," Twain says, "it is a restful chapter...when somebody doesn't step on a dry twig and alarm all the reds and whites for two hundred yards around. Every time a Cooper person is in peril, and absolute silence is worth four dollars a minute, he is sure to step on a dry twig. There may be a hundred handier things to step on, but that wouldn't satisfy Cooper. Cooper requires him to turn out and find a dry twig; and if he can't do it, go and borrow one."

It would be hard to disagree, but Kay Seymour House, who has read all of Cooper's fiction (!!!) says it isn't. She has found no twigs at all. This is impressive because it isn't true. The last sentence of Chapter 3 is: "Ha! there goes something like the cracking of a dry stick, too—now I hear the bushes move—yes, yes, there is a trampling that I mistook for the falls—and—but here they come themselves; God keep them from the Iroquois!" The professor can play fast and loose with the text because she is certain that no one else will have read it. And her search engine was set for "twig" rather than "stick." She is not demonstrating scholarship but nerve. And freedom! Her liberation from the drudgery of accuracy.

If Cooper were alive, he would be indifferent to the controversy especially with Chingachgook's place in the culture so well established—and he's not even the hero. Hawkeye is. (Bela Lugosi played Chingachgook in a couple of films, and Lon Chaney, Jr. walked a mile in his moccasins. As did Jay Silverheels, who probably was glad to have better lines to deliver than "Get 'em up, Scout," which sounds lame after the Lone Ranger's ringing "Hi Yo, Silver.")

It is peculiarly American, to be an established writer even though nobody reads your books—not even professors who write about you. Cooper is "important" because he and Washington Irving are the first American novelists. But then who reads Washington Irving anymore, either? (You take my point? I have your nose!) These writers transcend their work and float above it with their names on the plinths of library entrances.

Books that succeed in spite of themselves? Without readers and, therefore, without words? It is an intriguing idea. (Who actually read Fuckhole's Pendulum?) A perfect work of art, the frightening blank page an author faces each morning is waiting for someone to put the cap back on the fountain pen, lean back in his ergonomic chair, and simply declare that it's finished. Flawless! (And who would argue with such virginal immaculaticity?) Literature is an intellectual experience, and this, surely, would be intellectual. Like that Rauschenberg white painting in San Francisco that the museum is instructed to have whitewashed every three years. Rauschenberg doesn't even do it himself. He just issued the instructions and specified that it shouldn't be the curatorial people but maintenance workers who perform the task. Art is whatever we say it is, and literature can be, too. Poetry readings would be a hell of a lot more fun. Flowery and inaccurate introduction and then the poet gets up, shambles to the lectern, looks out balefully at the not very numerous audience, and says not a word. Makes no sound whatsoever. Ideally, he doesn't even move. He is like one of those living statues in Harvard Square or the Boulevard Saint-Germain, but without the metallic makeup. The silence extends itself across the seconds from the brief John Cage interval (for which he demands royalties) to a further and grander instance of sensory deprivation. The audience, if there is one, waits for a while and then, I suppose, starts to giggle. Or to hurl insults. Or vegetables. Or ask questions. The questions are supposed to come at the end, aren't they, but when is the end and who decides? Maybe some of them get up and leave. All that is a part of the poetry! Why not? In any case, the poet should make sure he gets the check before the reading starts. If not, his lawyer is not bound to silence and can speak for him. (Speak softly and carry a big twig) The university is likely to pay up because it's not a lot of money and for one of their lawyers even to look at this foolishness will cost more than the miniscule honorarium. Still, it is fraudulent, isn't it? But isn't all fiction fraudulent? Or shouldn't the question be whether all life is fraudulent. Proust says somewhere, "*La vraie vie, la vie enfin découverte et éclaircie... c'est la literature.*" What we wake up to in the morning and get out of bed for is only raw material, a crude draft on foolscap that we mistake for the real thing.

Can poetry be fraudulent, too? Why not? (And what difference would it make?) Is April the cruelest month? If we are to stand up in court and discuss which kind of fraud goes under the rubric of art and which under the criminal code, we'll be a laughingstock. (Have you read Cooper's Laughingstocking Tales? No? That's all right. No one else has, either, not even Professor House.)

Ideally, the audience would sit there for a certain time, realize what was going on, and then...clap. But not all at the same time. It would be like the Amidah in Jewish services with people sitting down whenever they have completed the silent prayer, the faster ones first and then the slower. In this instance it would depend on when each person "gets it." A number of poems could be running simultaneously, different ones in different heads. But that happens, too, with old-fashioned poems with words in them. In any event the ideal is not something to strive after, although the poet may have that in mind. Or he may have had it in mind at the first readings he gave but he doesn't bother anymore. He doesn't want to risk disappointment. He has relaxed to the point where he can welcome whatever happens, as Kaye Serra recommends in her splendid book, *The Wisdom of Acceptance: The Acceptance of Wisdom.* She also wrote *Serendipity Will Save You* and *Mental Health in an Age of Insanity,* which I haven't read either

What could be the title of such a performance? "The Universal Solvent"? "The Extinction of Language"? "A True History of the Truth"? It is pleasant to imagine the anger of the department chairman at being swindled and ridiculed in this way. He would disapprove, which is his right, but he would also try to get the assistant professor whose job it is to arrange these visiting writers' appearances fired. Or at least not renewed. No tenure for you, young Dr. Smartheim! The students, of course, would protest. They seize any opportunity to protest about anything at all, and this infringement on the basic academic freedom of speech (or silence) would produce outcries (or silent vigils?) to bring attention to the administration's flagrant disregard of principles. And the university should also divest itself of any ownership of petroleum and coal companies, as well as those that do business with Israel, Russia, China, Myanmar, Swaziland, or Malta. (Malta? There is a comedian loose somewhere, a sophomoric sophomore for whom I have no small sympathy.) And they should restore hot breakfasts in the dining halls! And they should lower tuitions, increase the funding for undergraduate social programs, and change the school colors to mauve and avocado, in recognition of the LGBT community!

But I digress. (From what?) We were talking about James Fennimore Cooper, were we not? He had in Cooperstown actually met an Indian or two. Across the ocean, François Auguste René, Vicomte de Chateaubriand didn't bother with such vulgar empiricism but dreamed up his noble savages *ex nihilo*. Of his Natchez tales, *Atala* is the one we best remember (most of us not having read that either). It is the touching story of the love of Chactas for Atala, who happens to be his sister, which would not be an obstacle except that she has converted to Christianity and now has scruples about incest. Romantic hokum? Of course, but even hokum has to be invented by somebody. We may not like it but we must concede that it requires a curious combination of shrewdness and denseness. And like Cooper, Chateaubriand was outrageously successful.

At one point, Cooper goes to France. (He actually did that, although it shouldn't make any difference.) To educate his children, perhaps, or just to have a loaf of really good bread with good Normandie butter. A perfectly legitimate reason, I'd say. It is not inconceivable that he and Chateaubriand met. But there, I (we) have conceived it. All that remains is to fill in the details and enjoy the encounter and whatever it teaches us. Cooper would have wanted to meet Chateaubriand not only because the vicomte was a novelist but also because his chef was Montmireil, who devised that thick steak to which Chateaubriand's name is attached and by which it survives. Even those who have never read a word of *Atala* appreciate the steak with a nice Béarnaise or maybe a mustard sauce. It's like Peach Melba, which keeps Nellie Melba's name in the mouths of those who know nothing about opera. There are the composer's Tournedos Rossini, and Nesselrode pie, which is named after the Russian count. Poire Belle Hélène isn't named after a person, however, but Offenbach's opera. Bananas Foster is named after Richard Foster, a friend of Owen Brennan, the proprietor of the New Orleans restaurant. Suzette was a mistress of the Prince of Wales (later Edward VII) and they were dining at the Café de Paris at Monte Carlo where the desert was invented for her. The prince's wife, meanwhile, Alexandra of Denmark, gets credit for Gâteau Alexandra. a kind of chocolate meringue layered with chocolate mousse. Nobody is sure whether Beef Stroganoff was named after Alexander Grigorievich Stroganoff of Odessa or the diplomat, Count Pavel Stroganoff. Cherries Jubilee was not named for Irving and Thelma Feingold whose celebration of their fiftieth wedding anniversary was catered by Queens Caterers--but it could have been. These associations are arbitrary and whimsical, and some stick and some don't. Some become words in the language while others are mentioned only in large gastronomic dictionaries or disappear entirely. Fame is not earned, you see, it just happens. The Greeks thought they had it figured out—that you do something splendid, excelling on the battlefield or winning a chariot race at the games, but it then requires a poet to translate ephemeral success into "kleos," which is enduring renown. Go ahead, think of winners in the Olympic games who were not mentioned by Pindar or Bacchylides. (Whom am I kidding? Name some who were!)

But after all that meringue and mousse one still wonders about Chateaubriand's interest in meeting Cooper. The idea of an American novelist in those days was disjunctive and even absurd, like a three-star Michelin restaurant in Montana, or a Greenlandic poet. Whatever their expectations (which are mostly erroneous because we can't imagine the future, let alone predict it), the two authors would have found interesting things to talk about. They shared a hatred of the French revolution, for one thing. And the vicomte's idea of Indians, unblemished by reality, was purely philosophical, having to do with the question of man's natural character. His Natchez tribe were really Nihilonians, whose descendants we see everywhere.

Was Hobbes right? Are we brutes and beasts only partially redeemed by civilization and religion? Or are we innocent as newborn babes who are corrupted by our experience in society? These are fascinating questions, if you are fifteen or so. We may assume that this was the subject and wonder whether either of them could have enlightened the other or changed the other's mind by a jot or tittle? It is doubtful. We approach, however hesitantly, the question of the efficacy of words, spoken or written, in which we believe despite the evidence of our uncomprehending eyes staring at a text from the

Etruscan or one of those mystery languages. (Did the Lenape write anything? Or the Cree?)

At a basic level, it is convenient to have labels for things. A "chair" indicates something on which it is possible to sit. But not so fast. Was the word (or idea or form) prior to the thing as Plato argued, or did the thing come first, as Aristotle said? Novelists don't care because we are making it up. There don't need to be "real" chairs. It's better if there aren't. Once upon a time, and a very long time ago it was, a beautiful princess sat down in her gilded thing. Chair? Why not? The idea of a chair keeps changing anyway. An authentic Louis XIV chair has a tendency to morph into an object in a museum with a sign on its seat warning the patrons not to sit on it. Oh, excuse me, I thought it was a chair. It is dressed as a chair, is it not? It fooled me completely. The guard is not amused. Men dressed as policemen come and eject you from the museum. It is very lifelike. A trompe Louis (in the sense that it is no longer the Louis XIV chair the museum bought?). It is not even an exhibit by this time, but a happening. And you are not only the audience but a participant now, in which case you should get a refund on your admission ticket. Which turns out not to be an admission ticket but a "contribution" because of the sign announcing in smallish letters that admission is free but suggested contributions are...and then, in large letters and numbers, the prices for adults, seniors, students, and oddly the blind. So you are not entitled to a refund. It was a gift. And you don't want to be thought of as an Indian giver, do you? You are in a foul mood and, at least for the moment, you are convinced that Hobbes was correct.

Indian giver is a slur, I suppose, like Gypped or Jewed. But the Indians had no sense of property, so if one of them "gave" you something on Tuesday, he saw nothing wrong in taking it back on Friday if he needed it. Things just floated around like re-gifted fruitcakes at Christmas. Objects had lives of their own. (Don't think about this for too long, or highly trained medical professionals will suspect you of incipient autism.) Indian Summer is a season of warmth that is a gift but only temporary. As if other things weren't. At least in part, "Indian giver" is, therefore, a compliment, if we look at it intelligently—which, in our culture, is unlikely.

Where are we? Cooper and Chateaubriand were about to get together to talk about life and art. And recipes. (What recipes could Cooper contribute? Indian pudding maybe. Or succotash, which is msíckquatash in Narragansett and means boiled corn? Chateaubriand might have been amused by these primitive preparations. "You don't use real Indians in the pudding do you?" he asks. "Cooper manages a pained smile, having heard the line before. "And you, sir, do you use real shepherds in your shepherd's pie?")

They don't meet at some fashionable café in Paris. Chateaubriand is in hiding. He's a *vicomte*, remember, and the sans-culottes are still after him even in 1826, furious at him for being an aristo and still alive. They seek him here; they seek him there... They are easy to recognize, however, because, as the name suggests, they do not wear pants. But worrying as he does about these bare-assed bastards, René has to keep an eye peeled, which is a disgusting metaphor, isn't it? Or a recipe for a dish that never caught on. *L'oeil ravigote*, perhaps?

What catches on? Some of these names survive even though they have lost any connection with a person. For instance, who was Betty? I always assumed she was a black cook somewhere in the antebellum south, who made this terrific dessert thing they named after her, the Brown Betty. But that is a guess merely, and nobody knows. Or say that nobody else's guess is any more persuasive than my own. Evidence? A recipe card, perhaps? (She would probably not have been able to read and write, so it isn't historians we need here but anthropologists, who are very tentative about anything that does not involve tree rings. Foster's survival with that banana confection is pure chance, which is, in the end, all we can vouch for. Brennan had other friends, other customers, and he could have named the dish after any of them. Bananas Finkel, Bananas O'Doule, or himself. Or Chef Paul, who created it. But whether that was Paul Something or Something Paul I have no idea. There is a rue Paul, which should be a street in the quarter but isn't. *Domage.*

Ingestion is followed by digestion, but if the sequence is disturbed we get indigestion, that seems like an intensifier but is a contradiction.

Pick a small city in France you've never been to. Besançon, maybe, or Pau, which isn't pronounced pow but po. (This would make students at their Lycée Saint Cricq PAU boys, but never mind.) Now imagine a side street with a workingmen's café, and put the two of them at one of the small, round tables outside with a carafe of the local white wine between them. Cooper is delighted, thinking that this is the real France—real, in this case or even most of the time, meaning something different from what one imagined. Chateaubriand thinks this is not at all real but something a sappy, tourist might dream up, especially one who loves the *le peuple* and admires them for their sincerity. (He knows that they sincerely want to kill him and worries a lot about sincerity unless it is governed by intellect.) Anyway, there they are, in a reasonably safe place where they can sit and exchange views. They are like any two writers, praising each other's work but then adding a qualification of some kind (because each thinks he is better than the other).

"It has been said," says René, "that I write about the noble savages. This is a *canard*. (Not *aux framboises*, alas.) If I wrote about life in the time of the Valois, would they say I was interested in savage nobles? Does no one read anymore without turning everything into abstractions or metaphors? Or politics?"

James agrees with him at once and offers what he intends to be a comforting observation, that writers are not responsible for their readers' thoughts or emotions. Being misunderstood is not merely a risk but the inevitable consequence of the act of publishing.

They are not so much distancing themselves from their audience as they are declaring (without quite saying it) that there is a bond between them, both of them being popular writers who are not exactly comfortable with popularity.

There is further polite talk in which they discover unexpected similarities. Chateaubriand's chateau is not all that different from Cooper's grand house in Cooperstown. It seems unremarkable to both of them to carry the names of the towns they live in, or, actually, to live in towns that carry their names. Eventually, Cooper raises the question that has been bothering him—about incest. Why does Atala's refusal even to consider an incestuous relationship with Chactas mean that she is enlightened and civilized? The Egyptians were perfectly civilized and among the Ptolemies marriages between brother and sister were the usual practice.

"You know that," René says, "but many readers might not. Anyway, if I'd wanted to write about the Egyptians, I could have done so. Since Napoleon's campaign there, Egypt has been very much à la mode here. But you and I write romances, not fantasies, *n'est-ce pas*? And Egypt is fantasy. Indeed, as far as I am concerned, America is fantasy, too."

And this isn't? James is too polite to say that but he thinks it. After all, the major industry in Pau is smuggling. And second to that is basket making, because the smugglers need them so they can carry more. The Palois (which is the word for the townsmen) are willing to oblige. This would be a wonderful place for Indian John, Cooper thinks. He could settle down and perhaps open a shop, the hardest part of an itinerant basket seller's job being the itineranancy. The Berkshires, the Catskills, and the Green and White Mountains are, as one might expect, very up-and-down-ish. Like the Pyrenees. But there is not very much smuggling in the American mountains. Ours is along the seacoast.

"I usually read my books aloud to my children and nephews," Cooper says. "Do you do that?"

"Certainly not," Chateaubriand replies, his eyebrows raised at least an inch. "Why would I?"

"To see what amuses them and what bores them?"

"To trust their judgment more than my own? Certainly not."

He is beginning to get on Cooper's nerves. And Cooper on his.

Chateaubriand is impressed with Cooper but not in a good way. He is a writer, but he earns a living doing this. He makes literature into a trade. Who would have thought such a thing was possible? Writing is an acceptable, even an admirable hobby but Cooper does it for money. There are names for women who have sex for money (either prostitutes or countesses) but no equivalent insult for journeyman scribblers.

Some upstart comes out of the woods and presumes to take up a pen—a turkey quill, no doubt—and he thinks that the ink stains on his fingers entitle him to join the community of letters. What foolishness. The French are thought to have been friendly to the Americans, but that isn't exactly true. They hated the English. And the enemy of my enemy may or may not be my friend but he is very possibly useful, if you don't trust him too far. Cooper! A *tonnelier*! That's somebody who makes barrels. It's an honorable craft, but it's a craft. It would be an absurdity for Chateaubriand to stroll down the hill walk through the village talking to smiths, tailors, bakers, cooks, wainwrights, chandlers, and farmers, but those are the names one finds in America all the time. Menials passing themselves off as gentlemen. Is there something in the water?

Chateaubriand has always despised the revolutionaries' slogan about liberty, fraternity, and equality. For one thing, it's self-contradictory. The more liberty you have, the less equality there will be. And the fraternity is a purely notional ligature that is supposed to hold the other two together. Let them have *travail, famille, et patrie,* which is a noble way of saying that they are entitled to work themselves to death, achieving a grave in the patrie, as long as they replace themselves with another generation of worker to take their places. (Actually, that wasn't Chateaubriand's thought at all. I gave it to him. It was the slogan of the Vichy government and was imprinted on their *monnaie*. It is not very ambitious, but that is what René would have liked about it.)

Cooper, meanwhile, thinks the Frenchman's attitude is insufferably condescending. Aristocratic. This is what Americans ran away from. He may have a right to it because of his ancestry, but while Cooper didn't graduate, he is still enough of a Yalie to be unwilling to take shit from anybody. No wonder the sans-culottes are still on the nobleman's trail.

On the way back to Paris, Cooper's annoyance blossoms into real anger. The idea that Atala is superior to Chactas because the missionaries have got at her with their high-flown Christian (or European) ideas is offensive. Racist, too, probably. Back in American, we may fight the Indians when they act up, or even when they don't and are just living on land we want. But aside from a few crazies few of us try to convert them. What would come of that? Fraternity and equality? With the Indians? And the Blacks? Not without a lot more mess than Chateaubriand seems willing to imagine. It feels un-Catholic to Cooper who is not a Catholic. (He was an Episcopalian, I believe.) The sensible Roman idea, he has always thought, was to live a merry life and then, making a good confession at the end, get into heaven without difficulty. An insistence on virtue and good deeds is awkward. As if one could earn his way into paradise. Which is why missionaries generally fail.

The trip up to Paris is uncomfortable and very long and by the time he arrives, he has decided that Chateaubriand was guilty of bad manners, which, in the end, is the only law people believe in. Should he have let etiquette go and tried to engage the vicomte in a real conversation? What was there to lose? They were unlikely ever to meet again. (Actually, they never met in the first place—we are supposing all this, remember.) But it would not have done any good. You cannot change people's minds by talking to them. Words never matter—even if both parties in the conversation are writers. One uses words only to defend the positions to which one was born, Chateaubriand but Cooper, too. And this is a depressing thought. True, probably, but too upsetting ever to set down on paper. In which case, he has fundamental doubts about his calling. If it is just a way to make a living, one would do better in land speculation. Or fur trading with the (heathen) Indians. Both of these are a lot less work.

In Paris, he can relax, though, because he has come to visit Sam Morse. Both he and Morse were students of Benjamin Silliman's back in New Haven and they have a lot in common. In any event, Morse is a painter, and painters don't have ideas mostly. Or if they do, the ideas don't matter. Which is a relief. Writers think they can think, but for painters what matters is getting the fold of a drapery right or the angle of a chin or the set of a subject's lips.

Where shall we imagine them? A café somewhere? We did this in Pau. How about a brothel. No, not that kind! A brothel where they serve broth, good bread, and excellent butter. Beef broth, chicken, and sometimes fish. No? There are no such places? A pity, as they would say in that Florentine palace. Let it be in the parlor of Morse's hotel, then, in a large, showy room with an enormous chandelier overhead. (The building had formerly been owned by a marquis.) They are across the table from each other with a bottle between them. It has been a while since they have seen each other but they are able to pick up smoothly from the last time they were together. They talk, as friends do, about the political situation in France, which is always drastic but seldom serious. Charles X is on the throne. (Really? Was there a Charles X? Look it up if you doubt me.) Charles is trying to restore the power of the throne and get rid of all the squabbling factions that have made governing the nation impossible. He wants to set the clock back fifty years, even though he knows his chances of success are minuscule. Still, he has been told what life was like back then and how things worked. There are probably people around him, however, who are trying to reason with him and advise him that whatever he does should be done slowly. But he is the king and he doesn't like being contradicted. Or even reasoned with. If there is a divine right of kings, it follows that they are divinely right and not subject to backsass.

If you are an American, this kind of brouhaha is reassuring. This is what we left behind. And they, too, had a revolution that was supposed to improve life, although what they achieved was not quite paradisiacal. The main trouble with the French Revolution was that it was conducted by Frenchmen, who are dangerous when they take off their toques (and pants) and emerge from the kitchen. Or, no, I take that back partly. It was conducted by French intellectuals, philosophes, who do not allow vulgar empiricism to taint their elegant theories. Let the people rule? Sure, but the people, when they get excited as they often do, are a mob and mob rule is unattractive. They had the American model, but that was temporizing and complicated. Their taste (except in art and furniture) was for simplicity.

Still, wonderful bread. And fine cheeses--because the aristos insisted on these small comforts, having little else to worry about. This may be why they behaved so stupidly. Louis XVIII (Charles' elder brother) fled from Napoleon twice and was restored twice, the second time coming into Paris escorted by the Duke of Wellington and his army after the battle of the damp clearing in the forest (which is what Waterloo means). Having undergone these vicissitudes, Louis was less arrogant that most of the Bourbons who preceded him and he resigned most of his duties to the council. He granted all kinds of demands for reform and, although unhappy about it, recognized that one must bow to necessity.

His younger brother Charles d'Artois (who would succeed him as Charles X) was infuriated. "Kings bow? You bow? *Qu'est-ce c'est! Ma foi! Sacre bleu.*" (And other suchlike expostulations.) I recite all these details in order for us to understand Charles' *point de vue.* As Sam and Jim agree, Charlot is acting in this crazy way because he is crazy. He had to watch his brother achieve every day new depths of failure, both political and physical. (Louis was obese and afflicted both by gout and gangrene, which meant that he was often in a foul, not to say malodorous, mood.) And finally, he was dead so that Charles assumed the throne (and the throne assumed him). He resolved to undo much of his brother's cowardly mischief.

"That is why Scott has it easy," Cooper says. "He writes about excess and extravagance here in Europe, which Europeans know about and are willing to believe. I have to explain everything. Nobody here or even at home knows about Indians or cares."

"Why not invent them, then?" Morse asks. He has an annoying habit of tapping on the table with his forefinger, not in a regular way but with shorter and longer pauses. One might think he was inventing some sort of code.

Cooper smiles, nods his head and says, "But, Sam, I do. That's exactly what I do. After all, it's fiction, isn't it? Do you realize how long it would take to explain that the Mohicans' descent is matrilineal?"

Cooper knows what he is and isn't doing. He's an intelligent fellow. Because he is a novelist, let us assume that he is correct about Charles X, who, at this very moment, is in the palace (which one? who cares?) jumping up and down on a pogo stick and hurling scatological insults at the chamber of deputies none of whom is in attendance. Who are they to tell me what to do? Who are they to pick my ministers? They are shitfaces and have only the right to be dumped out of the window in a chamberpot to fall on the heads of their countrymen in the street below. Liberty is a nonsense. Fraternity is a joke. All that blood but they are by no means brothers. And equality was always an absurd idea on its face. Presumptuous! Worse than that, unrealistic. I should be the one to tell them what to do. I am the king, and they are shits.

Is this what he always thinks? Yes, but he is not usually so excited about it. Polignac, his minister, suggests that they might distract the people (as Napoleon had done) by conquering something. Give the people parades and a reason to be proud. So he conquers Algiers and restores the idea of empire and *la gloire.* Then there was the Franco-Trarzan War of 1825, a conflict with the forces of the new Amir of Trarza, Muhammad al Habib, who had attempted to establish control over the French-protected Waalo Kingdom. (One can't make this up, or rather one can but it takes a great deal of work and still doesn't sound convincing.) Was there a Waalo Kingdom? Or is it a line of furniture at Ikea? Are the reference books putting us on, some underpaid hack having taken the opportunity of slipping in imaginary kingdoms now and then if only to see whether the editors actually read this stuff? "The Waalo had a complicated political and social system, which has a continuing influence on Wolof culture in Senegal today, especially its highly formalized and rigid caste system. The kingdom was indirectly hereditary, ruled by three matrilineal families: the Logar, the Tedyek and the Joos, all from different ethnic backgrounds." Aha! Like the Mohicans. Yes, and what an amazing collection of papers there could be on their similarities and differences from young anthropologists (scholars who make apologies for anthropoi).

These military adventures of Charles were successful but too trivial to placate the mob or satisfy their demands. Now the shitty chamber of merdacious deputies wants to get rid of his minister, le Comte de Villèle. (They really want to get rid of Charles, but that will come later.)

Dangerous? Silly? Perhaps, but Charles learned a different lesson from their wanderings than did his brother. Louis had been nervous after two restorations about losing the throne a third time. Charles didn't give a damn. What could they do to him? Unseat him? He'd already been in exile often enough to have realized that it's not so bad. You go around the world with your retinue, attend parties, and take part in hunts. No politics to worry about. No rabble nipping at your heels like badly trained dogs that, for some insane reason, you are no longer allowed to whip. Why not? The rights of man? Those are merely to work and die. Or fight in the army and die. Everything else is by the king's grace and pleasure.

Let us leave his majesty there for a moment. He may be jumping up and down but probably not, I admit, on a pogo stick, which was invented only in 1920 by Hans Pohlig and Ernst Gottschall, from Germany. Get it? They flipped a coin, I think, and if it had come up tails, it would have been a Gopo stick. ("Who in hell needs this?" asks Hans. "Nobody, no one in the world," Ernst replies, "but that's the beauty of it. It is useless like sport or art." It is possible to jump without it, but unless you are very strong not quite so high.

I'm losing you. What's this about a pogo stick? But think how even if it wasn't true it was true. His rage was extravagant (over the top?) and the image --he is wearing his crown, of course--is striking. Without question, if I had written merely that he was "hopping mad," that would hardly have so vivid. You see? I did it for your sakes, and are you grateful? Even admiring? No, siree (or whatever the politically correct version would be that includes females). Not at all. The way some of you pounce at any opportunity to find fault is irksome enough to make me reach for my own pogo stick. And I am an old man, arthritic and un-athletic, and never managed more than five hops on that dopey toy even when I was young and fit. But that only intensifies the power of the trope, doesn't it?

The news that week is typically laughable, as the two Americans agree. Charles has enacted the Anti-Sacrilege Act, which criminalizes blasphemy and impiety. (Who would be in favor of such things? Me, for one.) The act was never expected to have any practical effect except to insult the revolution and the enlightenment. For the King to be wasting his time on such stuff demonstrates his impotence and irrelevance. But it is dangerous to say so, at least in French. The best exchange between the two Americans is Morse's observation that Charles X was probably the last of the Bourbons and that perhaps Cooper, with his interest in relicts, might like to stay for a while and write a novel about him. (Have there been any? None that I could find.)

Cooper smiles politely but he has to force it. The success of *The Last of the Mohicans* has not endeared the book to him. On the contrary, it has attained its independence and has established its own career, leaving him behind. It is a prodigal son who has left home and, while he spends a lot earns a great deal more. He has been prodigiously prosperous so that he has more than enough fatted calves of his own. What can a father do but produce that same forced smile and, at least in public, assert his pride in his son's achievements?

Neither Cooper nor Morse knows what we do--that in a couple of years, Charles will have to dismiss le Comte de Villèle and appoint Jules de Polignac, who will try to placate the left but in doing so will infuriate the right, which is to say Chateaubriand's faction. The government falls. It is Chateaubriand who is at least in part responsible for the July Revolution. And my point is? That history is going on all around them, Cooper especially, although he is unaware of it. The intrigues of Parisian politics are every bit as demanding as the Adirondack wilderness trails, but the woodcraft is different. (And the chairs.) The metaphor, or if it isn't a metaphor, at least the comparison, seems to make both muddles more comprehensible and more acceptable, but that is a dangerous illusion. *Les Illusions dangereuses* was not the book Choderlos wrote but it isn't a bad idea. And it could be just as subversive.

That's not what this book is about, though. I'm not sure, myself where it is going. If I were, there'd be little point in writing it. The general direction seems to be toward the last of the whatevers, which is always poignant, even if the tribe or species was deplorable and dangerous. No more smallpox germs? (Well, Russia has some and so do we, stored away in some lab, but there are no more free-range viruses (Variola major and Variola minor). Good, but the world seems diminished. A fortiori, the contemplation of the last of the Mohegans or Bourbons--or carrier pigeons, or dodos, or two-toed toads—can be an occasion for sadness. Why? Was dodo meat particularly delicious, or did it just taste like chicken? No, it's bigger than that and more frightening. What Cooper was talking about in his novelistic way was death, of an individual and of a tribe. The end of the world, no? Morse's droll remark turns out to be the key, which can often happen. Some smart, throwaway line, and we have a new view of things. There is a paradigm shift (although these days most paradigms are automatics). It was never the Mohicans we were troubled about but ourselves, because unless we are too arrogant to admit it, we know our turn will come, too. To come right out and say this may annoy some readers. One has rather to imply it clearly enough to evoke the emotion without being off-putting. Here again, the lie (all right, obliquity, but it's still a departure from verity) beats the truth any day of the week, which would be Lundi through Dimanche at the time we're talking about. The days had had different names in the revolutionary calendar when there were three ten-day weeks every month: Primidi, Duodi, Tridi, Quartidi, Quintidi, Sextidi, Septidi, Octidi, Nonidi, and Decadi. Easy to learn, but useless now (not that I have anything against uselessness). One must concede that it is perfectly rational. None of our ridiculousness about Sun-day, Moon-day, Tyrs'-day, and the rest of it. Who believes in those Norse gods these days? But then the next logical step takes us to Hegel's remark in his famous stand-up comedy routine that the real is the rational and the rational is the real, which is funny because it is so obviously wrong-headed, as those of us in the club who are still sober enough can understand at once.

Charles X was so busy trying to restore the royal prerogatives of the *ancien régime* that he didn't even have time to design a chair. *Menuisiers* and *ébénistes* were standing by, waiting for instructions, but *pas un mot*. Baroque? Rococo? Neo-classical? What would please him? Napoleon had had both consular and empire chairs, often with sphinxes, winged lions, and laurel wreaths on them, or lots of Egyptian frou-frou. Sometimes there were swans, creatures of Venus representing Josephine. Not far from the *Palais Royal*, Morse and Cooper are sitting on a very good empire sofa at an ormolu table. (Charles' style, given the peripatetic life he led, might have been the simple, folding campstool.)

Cooper was better than Twain would have us believe. And he actually knew something about Indians. Look, this is from his introduction to *The Last of the Mohicans*:

> [The Indian] draws his metaphors from the clouds, the seasons, the birds, the beasts, and the vegetable world. In this, perhaps, he does no more than any other energetic and imaginative race would do, being compelled to set bounds to fancy by experience; but the North American Indian clothes his ideas in a dress which is different from that of the African, and is oriental in itself. His language has the richness and sententious fullness of the Chinese. He will express a phrase in a word, and he will qualify the meaning of an entire sentence by a syllable; he will even convey different significations by the simplest inflections of the voice.

Not too shabby. It has a Ciceronian grace that is seductive, seduction being the first job of any novelist.

Morse's condition is different from Cooper's. He is a miniaturist and does portraits, very good ones. He's up there with Charles Wilson and Rembrandt Peale. Rembrandt was Charles' son. (Did you know that among Rembrandt's siblings were Raphaelle and Rubens?) But to get back to Morse, he thought of himself as a painter. The telegraph was a parergon as was the code that brought him fame, the popularity of which has already begun to dwindle. Who sends telegrams anymore? Who learns Morse code? Semaphore, yes, but this? There's Twitter now and old-fashioned email. Morse's name will have a low-level survival in history of art textbooks. And there's a building at Andover named after him. (OK, but then who were Bancroft or Bartlett or Day? I haven't the faintest notion.)

Among the Indians... But wait. We are not supposed to call them that anymore. It is politically incorrect. They are "Native Americans" now. (I am a native American, too, having been born here.) Or you can use their tribal names: Lenape or Wampanoag. But just as the Gypsies now choose to be Roma, the Indians want something else, too. The Stanford Indians are now the Crimson, for the Great Spirit's sake. The Cleveland Indians persist in their discourtesy, which they can do as long as there is place called Indianapolis, Indiana. But there is much ignorant outrage about the Washington Redskins. (They used to play in Boston where the baseball teams were the Red Sox and the Braves, and this was a clever way for a football time to appeal to the fans of both clubs.) I have been asked whether I'd approve of a team called the New York Yids, and the answer is emphatically yes! Yiddish cheers! And they could play their sport in skullcaps—except football, of course, but that wouldn't be right for the Yids.

We are, as Theodore Roethke might observe, in the far field. Closer to the subject (if there is one) is the question of empiricism. Cooper had met some Indians and Chateaubriand probably hadn't. In one sense, this was an advantage for the Frenchman. He could make up whatever he liked, having let go of the anchor ropes and floating high in the sky as the Montgolfier brothers would soon learn to do. The view is different from up there and certainly less subject to change. Empiricists consult reality and rely on it, confident that this will give them an advantage in their search for truth. You remember Dreiser's fetish about railroad timetables. Vera Similitude, his reference librarian, encouraged such accuracy. But what did she know? She had repressed even the truth about herself, which is that, like Marian Paroo (no kidding) in *The Music Man*, she is waiting to be swept off her feet by a dashing if disreputable Robert Preston.

The most advantageous strategy, I think, is to be a little empirical but not altogether beholden to the facts on the ground. The happy medium. (Is she happy because she only talks to cheerful ghosts?) Glance at the actualities and then forget them, letting your imagination soar above them. One of the briefs in Dreihaus, a Supreme Court case this term, used the term "truthiness," that Stephen Colbert had invented and that seems now to be coming into general use. The issue before the court was whether or not the state of Ohio could criminalize false political speech, and in an amicus brief Ilya Shapiro, a Cato Institute lawyer, made a distinction between truth and truthiness—which has no basis in fact but feels right. It is an expression of a gut feeling that may be true or merely truthy. This is a great stride forward in literary theory and the lawyer deserves praise and recognition for invoking Colbert's coinage and his insight that there is such a category. (I love the lawyer's name which you can pronounce just the way he does, but if you think in French it means "There is Shapiro.")

Truthy is what novels are. They feel real, even though we know they're not. They take liberties in order to be faithful to the truth. Whether he knew it or not, this was what Cooper did. He had known (slightly) Indian John, but Chingachgook bears little resemblance to him. "Want to buy a basket?" ("Want to buy a duck?" was Indian Joe Penner's line.) He was mostly a stereotype, or would have been if the stereotype machine had been invented. Conventional novels, after all, do not depend on accuracy of information but rather on plausibility.

Just enough stuff to elicit from readers their cheerful assent. They are the willing suspenders of disbelief. (Are there reluctant suspenders? Is that why most men wear belts?) Putting it another way, good liars know how to fold in a certain amount of truth to make their palaver persuasive. Cooper describes Lake Champlain and Lake George, and yes, there they are, small, empty, blue spaces on maps of New York State. So our trust in the author commences and it is up to him to keep it going. Having won our confidence, the novelist can leave timetables and maps behind and attend to what Henry James called the truth of coherence, a higher plane of artistic meaning (if, that is, novels can be said to have meanings).

Still, "Chingachgook" is hard to swallow. What kind of name is that? It is either authoritative or ludicrous. Do we believe that in the Indian languages it means "great snake" and conveys the sense of its bearer being able to understand and see through complication and deviousness. Or was this Cooper's private joke, a random conjoining of ill-assorted syllables? Gachchingook is no less unlikely. In a trivial way, I feel sorry for him. I could, if I liked, rescue him from the oblivion of the never-having-been-created, which is as dark as that of the no-longer-alive. Each of us is one in a million but who is so exquisite or punctilious as to give a moment's thought to his brothers and sisters, all dead now, the other sperms among whom he once swam? Every baby who is born into this life is the survivor of a holocaust. The last of the spermatozoa! Disturbing? Perhaps that is why so many of us are depressed and behave badly.

Gachchingook could have been featured in the novels as the not altogether reliable companion of Eagle-eye, whose "real" name would be Fatty Bumppo. It is, like hamburger meat, 93% nonsense and only 7% truthy. Is that enough? (More fat in the meat, 20% probably, makes a better tasting burger. And a livelier novel.)

Improbably, after listening to Morse's suggestion, Cooper writes a couple of novels set in Europe, *The Heidenmauer: or, The Benedictines, A Legend of the Rhine* set in the German Rhineland in the 16th century) and *The Headsman: The Abbaye des Vignerons* (set in Geneva and the Alps in the 18th century). Nobody but Professor House and perhaps a few of her students has read either of these books in the past hundred years and very few, except for specialists in American Literature, have heard of them. Even stranger, there is *The Monikins*, a satire on British and American politics, set in Antarctica in the 1830s. (This sounds as nutty as Anatole France's *Penguin Island,* which, as I need not remind you, is about a flock of penguins a nearsighted priest inadvertently baptizes, so they become a problem for God who worries they may now be entitled to souls.)

I once started to read the Anatole France novel. (You should, too.) But I couldn't finish it. Or I didn't want to. The set-up was so delicious that I preferred to imagine various endings myself and not be limited to the one he chose. Let us get just a little less frivolous, if only for a millisecond. Cooper, not a dolt, was shrewd enough to figure out that there was more money to be squeezed out of his Indian stories. Keep sending out the not-quite-repetitive manuscripts and they will produce the pleasingly repetitive checks he needs to eat and pay for his children's école. (That was another reason for his excursion to France: the schools were better.) So why didn't he? What was the point of striking out in a new direction? To go head-to-head with Scott? (Sir Walter made money with his novels and even with his poems, and nobody thought his commercial success was undignified.)

It would have been easy. But that was the trouble. It would have been unavoidably clear to Cooper who did not want to admit to himself that what he was doing was wrong, somehow. Not just because it made money but because that was the primary motive and it was therefore manipulative, catering to a taste and sensibility that were not his own. It would have been "inauthentic," as the Parisians would say a century-and-a-half later, sipping at their little cups of coffee in some sidewalk café. His effort to satisfy the tastes of the public is exactly what would have alienated him from that public.

So? So what's wrong with that? *Rien du tout!* But you have to be a grown-up to realize this, and novelists are mostly children with nonsensical ideas about how the world works. Novels are lies, and only a lunatic would insist on honest lies, whatever those would be. Memoirs are lies, too, and histories, and pretty much anything else authors put on paper. (Except maybe eye charts, where we squint and try to lie but usually fail.) Still we pretend to one another (writers, readers, scholars, students, and patients of ophtalmologists) that there is a lofty truthiness to the written word and that it is in some mysterious way good for you.

In short, Cooper didn't want to go slumming. So he wrote those books that no one has heard of. They've done him no harm however because nobody remembers them. Think of Eos and Tithonus, and how she asks Zeus for immortality for her lover but forgets to mention anything about eternal youth. Gods have a nasty sense of humor and Zeus makes Tithonus immortal but not ageless, so that he deteriorates and dwindles but never dies. Figure that a goddess asked for immortality for Cooper (or his reputation) but forgot to mention his novels so that librarians have to make painful decisions every few years

about de-acquisitioning his books (except for the Mohicans). It isn't
a pretty process. In San Francisco some years back, they built a new
library that had less shelf space than the one it replaced so they had to
get rid of a lot of their books. There was a law against selling them or
giving them away—so trucksfull (truckfulls?) were hauled away one
night and dumped in landfills. (Would our dear Miss Paroo have done
such a thing? Hard to say. The problem never arose in River City.)

Would Chactas and Chingachgook have got on well together?
Probably no better than Chateaubriand and Cooper. Different vibes
for different tribes, except that Chactas was originally a Huron. Chateaubriand made him one of the Natchez because they were even
more obscure. American Indians seem to have been every bit as xe-
nophobic as the nations of Europe were and are. Human nature con-
tinues to express itself, despite the grandiose intellectual systems we
propose for its betterment. We make peace treaties with one another,
but they never last. As soon as they prove to be inconvenient, we tear
them up, or just forget them. If the behavior described in the treaties
were within our powers, we wouldn't need to write it down, but that
is merely a way of saying that in an ideal world, life would be better.
Quelle surprise! Or is the lesson here even more depressing--that the
very act of writing anything down makes it immediately untrue.

Morse surprises Cooper with the information that Chateaubriand
had visited the United States and had written an account of his travels, mostly invented but with some nuggets of reality here and there.
He claimed to have met George Washington—which was almost certainly a fabrication. His book sold well, though, and the French believed what he said, especially about the beauty of Niagara Falls by
moonlight. (Beautiful? It's a great deal of water pouring over a cliff
and is very loud.) He visited Boston, New York, Philadelphia, and Baltimore, which would have been the likely places for him to go, but he
also claimed to have traveled in the "wilderness," which was a vague
denomination for everywhere else. The deserts of Louisiana! (Well,
there aren't any, but Manon Lescaut and Des Grieux die of thirst there
in Puccini's laff-a-minute opera.) So Louisiana. And the Indians? The
Hurons morph into the Natchez, which is a more southerly tribe and
the name of which is chewier in the mouth. He never met any of them
because he never went south of Tennessee, as if there was a sign on
one of its roads, proclaiming, "Here be dragons." And he probably had
no pressing need for any baskets. It was essential, however, for him to
claim first hand knowledge. The reading public (much smaller than
what we have nowadays, when the riff and raff read books, or at least
the captions under the photographs in magazines about celebrities)

would have been offended. They like their fiction to be true and think that otherwise it is a waste of time to drag their eyeballs across the lines of type. If for no other reason than politeness, then, he would have had to say he was conversant with some of the American aborigines.

[Conversant?

"How," says one Indian.

"How's yourself?" the other responds.

"Ugh." Except that Cooper spells it "Hugh," which one is tempted to pronounce as if it were a preppy first name.]

But back to Paris:

"I wonder why he never mentioned any of this to me," says Cooper.

"He probably didn't want to risk any questions he couldn't answer," says Morse. "It would be harder to deceive you, wouldn't it? You're a native American, after all."

[Cooper does not say, "Hugh!"]

"What a strange man!"

"Complicated," Morse agrees, but we must understand that the word is often employed as a polite synonym for "demented."

It is also possible that Chateaubriand neglected to mention that he had spent eight months in American journey in 1791, because I hadn't known about it myself. The conversation between the writers with such different social and political views didn't seem to require any "research" (which is a dignified way of saying that one glances at the internet). Only now, pages later, out of idle curiosity, did I take a cursory look and Lo and Behold, there it was. ("Lo! The poor Indian, whose untutored mind sees God in clouds, or hears him in the wind," Alexander Pope wrote. I have no idea who Behold was.)

What to do, then? Go back and rewrite? As a penance for my sins if nothing else? Nah! I told myself that I could fit it in later somewhere, and it has been floating over every paragraph since my belated discovery. Several times it appeared to be about to descend onto the page, but I waved it away, flapping my arms like that poor, desperate rabbi the Rothschilds hire to stand in their Lafite vineyard and act as a scarecrow in the area where the grapes grow that will be used for wine that will be kosher for Passover. No kidding. The worry is that some crow (or other avian) will fly overhead and drop a crumb that has leaven in it into that special preserve. (Do the Rothschilds really care? My guess is that they have the rabbi standing there so he can take the blame if any such event should happen. And, probably, the rabbi knows that, too, which is humiliating but also means that he can relax and wave his arms less energetically.)

What? I throw myself on the mercy of the court but, if I may, I point out that the Rothschilds' vineyard and its rabbi popped up legitimately, while Chateaubriand's biography did not naturally occur to me. Both are artifices, but the biographical stuff would appear to be labored. It is all but impossible to allude casually to the fact that he was born on 4 September 1768 in Saint-Malo, France, the youngest of 10 children, and grew up in his family's medieval castle, sleeping in a turret bedroom that he suspected of being haunted. True, but so what? (I do like the turret bedroom, though.)

On the other hand, as Kali says (she has as many arms and hands as the sculptor can manage gracefully and would be more effective than even the most vigorous rabbi in those Rothschild vineyards), my laziness may have helped us. It often happens that we learn important information after the fact. And then there is a sudden, retroactive understanding of a piece of behavior that was otherwise mysterious. And more often than not, we regret our disapproval, which we would never have felt, let alone expressed, if only we had known. So let Morse tell these things to Cooper. It would have been likely because Morse had been in France longer. He'd come to Paris to learn to paint. For a writer, this would make less sense, because, as I understand it, they speak a language there entirely different from English. (This seems have made little difference to Hemingway, Fitzgerald, Samuel Beckett, and *les frères Jacques*--James Joyce, James Jones, and James Baldwin. And a slew of others who went perhaps for the bread. Or the broth. Go figure.

When Chateaubriand was 24, he married Céleste Buisson de Lavigne, who he thought was rich. He was mistaken. They remained married, nevertheless, until her death in 1847, because it would have been dishonorable for him to divorce her only because he had guessed wrong about her finances. He was energetically and famously unfaithful to her, but there were (and are?) limits to honor. Notionally, Morse is explaining this to Cooper, but the conventional quotation marks are not going to fool anyone, are they? So why bother? The point, if there is one, is that Chateaubriand is not quite so unpleasant as we first thought, as even Cooper has to admit.

Quotation marks generally signify accuracy, that these are the exact words the speaker used on such-and-such an occasion. But they can also mean that what they surround is not true. On the boardwalk in Ocean City is a stand that offers orange juice its sign claims is "fresh squeezed." The proprietor thinks that this is an intensifier, but what it suggests is that the juice is not at all fresh squeezed even though he is making a claim that he admits is false. (Complicated. Or demented.)

Quotation marks in novels also indicate falsity, no matter what the author may have intended.

Not that falsity is altogether a bad thing. I am charmed by the invented meeting with Washington. Cheeky. And what was Washington going to do? Sue?

Chateaubriand didn't publish the book until he was back in France. And it wasn't at all defamatory. It praised the President and it wouldn't have been seemly to sue the Frenchman for excessive flattery, if only because it would have been difficult to prove damages.

Well, of course. Obviously. But flattery does have risks, doesn't it. A writer's reputation is just a bit too grand? There will come a critic to take him down a peg or two. With delighted savagery. Think of Mark Twain beating up on Cooper. Or of Dwight Macdonald going after James Gould Cozzens. And we who read it were abashed (why hadn't we noticed these defects ourselves?) but also relieved (we'll never have to read Cozzens anymore!). It is like watching wrecks at auto races, which demonstrate what we should have been able to figure out—that this is a dangerous sport we were right never to have taken up. A low profile is better. Better yet is complete obscurity.

Critics do this in the name of truth, justice, and the American way, but also to make a name for themselves, or to soothe their envy of the victim's celebrity or income, or to establish, yet again, that the public is generally wrong when they presume to form opinions about literature. (That last part, I fear, is correct.)

It is safe to say that Chateaubriand despised the public. They are not so bad in the abstract but when they are actualized they are often unattractive rabble crowding around a guillotine to cheer the murders of their betters. (From whom did those revolutionaries buy their baskets?) Who were they to have opinions about him? His insertions of flummery and misinformation were a clear indication of his contempt for those members of the public from whom he wanted to distance himself if only because they were dim enough to believe him. The Galatea myth is the wrong way round. Assume that Pygmalion has made his beautiful statue. Good for him! But why would he want to turn it into a real woman who will get fat, turn crabby, hound him about whose turn it is to do the dishes, and behave the way women do, so that the exaltation of first love turns into an exercise in diplomacy and endurance. So if he has made the mistake of turning her into a living woman, he picks up another piece of marble fresh from the quarry and kills her. For her sake. To keep her from deteriorating any further. Carrara boom-de-yay!

Chateaubriand fights on the side of the Prussians against Republican France. Between battles, he is scribbling in his notebook, writing the manuscript that will become one or maybe two of his novels. And wouldn't you know? A bullet strikes him in the chest but the manuscript protects him so that he is not killed but only slightly wounded. Do you believe him? I don't, not for a minute. But I like the claim because it makes his notebook the equivalent of a Bible, a boast of which he would not have been unaware. He makes his way to Ostend, then Jersey where he recuperates, and then to London. Bizarrely he gets a job teaching French in a school in Sussex. (*"Quand le soleil se lève, Maurice se lève aussi."*) I can't guess whether he was an effective teacher but his accent would have been excellent.

Would he have fretted about his condition? I can't guess. Or, actually, I can but I prefer to think that his noble birth and absurd upbringing might have instilled in him an indifference to his surroundings that we in the middle class find enviable or even disturbing. Think of those Russian counts and princes, got up in military grandeur and making their livings after their revolution as doormen at Parisian restaurants. Their good humor earned them tips, of course, but it may have been authentic. They smile at the vicissitudes of life. Anyway, there he is, almost resigned to his duties in the school, reading out *dictées*, correcting spellings and accents in the students' papers, and drilling them in irregular verbs, and this, he supposed, is what the revolution comes to, *hein*? He thinks back to life in the chateau and imagines how his tutor would be delighted that they have changed places. They never really liked each other. It is amazing what one is able to do: present, *je peux* (or *je puis); in the past definite, je pus;* imperfect and future, *je pouvais,* the subjunctive, *que je puisse*. No, it makes no sense. You just have to learn it. Memorize. Drill! (Oddly, *pouvoir* has no imperative. It would probably be something like *puisses*, but what would that mean?)

I don't know about you (there's an understatement!) but I find myself beginning to feel some sympathy for the poor sod. Nothing has changed. He is dead and cannot possibly care. And I am the same tetchy guy as the one who felt some antipathy toward him a few pages ago. But thinking either clarifies or confuses. It changes things. Just brooding about him, I find that his quirkiness speaks somehow to my own. (We don't like people for their accomplishments or their virtues anyway but for some oddness about that them that is immediately congenial.) Perhaps, the imaginary interview with George Washington could become a genre. Historians are disqualified because they know too much and their knowledge is likely to get in their way. But a brief meeting with the rather stern personage on the face of dollar bills?

Dare I disturb him?

-Mr. President?

-Yes? What can I do for you?

(I should have prepared for this, at least figuring out in advance what would be a good opening question. But it is too late now.)

-If I may ask, sir, do you remember ever meeting the Vicomte Chateaubriand?

-I never laid eyes on him. Or he on me. I should have remembered.

-What about James Fenimore Cooper? Did you ever meet him?

The former president shows some surprise. He thinks for only a moment and then replies:

-I don't believe so, but I have read some of his writing. His descriptions of the actions of the French and Indian War were quite accurate. And vivid. Wars are not easy to write about. There are men who have fought in them and men who haven't, and it is very difficult to speak honestly to both groups. He does that well, I think.

-And the rest of the book?

-I do not generally read novels so I cannot possibly comment.

He rises from his desk. It is the signal for me to depart. I thank him and am about to extend my hand when I remember (How? No idea. But I do.) that he doesn't like shaking hands. He prefers bowing. So I bow. He bows. I am dismissed. I put the dollar bill back in my pocket.

It is, of course, a great honor to have met and spoken with the father of our country, even if the interview was brief and notional. My understanding is that he is a busy man, although dead, and agrees to see very few people. I cannot explain why he showed me such special favor. I am hardly important as a historian or prominent as a pundit. So it must have made an exception for me because of the subject: he wanted to get it on the record that he had never met Chateaubriand, that irksome and presumptuous Frenchman who, even if he does not endorse fraternity and equality, does take liberties. The president did not deem him important enough to speak about *sua sponte*, but in answer to someone else's question he could allow himself to declare that they had never met. Still, I am delighted to have been the bearer of his message to the worlds of literature and history. It was also extremely interesting to visit Mount Vernon, where I have never been but where I locate him, partly, I confess, to see the great house and have it in my mind as the appropriate and in some ways revealing background for him.

The only Mount Vernon I know is the one in Westchester County where the New Haven and the Putnam lines converge on their way to

Grand Central Terminal. I have ridden through it in a train or an automobile hundreds of times, but have never stopped. So far as I know, there isn't much to see there, anyway. I don't know Yonkers, either. I don't even know what a Yonker is.

We both know that this interview with President Washington was a fiction, and yet, as with some fictions, I find myself believing in it at least a little. Lies we keep repeating take on the feel of truth. And for Chateaubriand, a novelist after all, that process might have been likelier than in some other, harder-headed, harder-nosed persons. The line between what we tell ourselves and what we remember blurs. It is impossible to distinguish the fact from the wish, and in our confusion we opt for the more attractive of the possibilities. Would it not have been interesting to meet Washington and to exchange even a few words with him? I can attest to this and therefore I find it difficult to blame the vicomte for his report of his encounter.

Why stop with Washington? Could I not interview any of the presidents? Could I not have a useful and enlightening conversation with Buchanan, say, or Fillmore, about whom most of us know very little. Fillmore was an unpopular president, but there is one remark of his that I found curious enough to commit to memory: "In my view, secession on the part of the Southern states would be illegal; but if they should secede, I do not understand that there is anything we in the North can legally do about it."

One has to admire the breezy honesty of the man. Lincoln's solution was almost certainly correct but involved a hideous number of casualties and deaths. An unthinkable number. And perhaps for that reason, Fillmore could not think of it. In this way, the limitations of our imaginations define the limits of reality's possibilities. It is almost true that "poets are the unacknowledged legislators of the world," as Percy Shelley declared. (I'd refine that perhaps to claim only that they are the world's unacknowledged secretaries of health, education, and welfare, or perhaps of the department of the interior, even while admitting that most of them have little experience with bureaucracies and only the vaguest notions of efficiency.)

--Excuse me, Mr. President, but what did that odd comment of yours mean?

Fillmore looks up from his toddy and shakes his head.

--It means what it says. It says what it means. There was no rational way out of our predicament. My one goal was to keep the country from a bitter civil war and I am the butt of ridicule for that. If I am remembered at all, it is only because of my unusual first name, which people in your time think is amusing. Is it?

--There are people who think so, yes.

--I am not a duck. And I was in the serious business of trying to prevent a war. Slavery would eventually have gone away, as it did in England and the rest of the civilized world. But we didn't have to kill each other. The Civil War was nothing to be proud of. It was a tragedy. Better an uneasy peace than a tragic war, no? What I was desperately trying to do was find some compromise that would at least postpone the bloodletting. On the union side alone the number of killed and wounded was 650,000. Add in the Confederate casualties and the collateral damage among civilians and you have more than a million. I may have failed but I certainly tried—hard enough to antagonize both sides.

--Thank you, Mr. President.

Disgruntled, disgusted, he waves me away. Outside, it is a cold, gray Buffalo afternoon. It feels like snow.

Spooky to be able to do this. But that's the fun of fiction. In historical novels, it often happens that some King or Queen or General comes in at the end to sort out the complications of the plot which have been occupying our attention enough to lull us into accepting that this is what Don Carlo, or Queen Elizabeth, or Napoleon might very well have said. (I can't think of a novel in which Charles X plays such a role, but it would almost be worth attempting such a project if I could keep the pogo stick for him. I could indicate each jump with some kind of pictograph: ⊠. And I'd keep it short. Short books are harder to publish but there is much less typing.

--Your majesty?

⊠⊠⊠⊠⊠⊠

He is too occupied to reply or even to acknowledge my presence.

Stupid? Perhaps, but it acquires a spurious respectability if one calls it "counterfactual history," of which many academics may disapprove while others continue to invent their what-ifs, because they are fun. The South wins the war. Or they don't win but hold out until the northerners are exhausted or get bored and give up. The South becomes, essentially, a South American country, from the Virginia line downward. We know what happens to such countries. They have joke governments. The Union has manufacturing and shipping and more people. So they are the dominant power. The south staggers along in its grandiose antebellum way, but then there comes (from the north) the cotton gin (Samuel F. B. Morse painted a portrait of Eli Whitney, actually.) and other such farm machinery that is better and cheaper than Negroes and mules. One by one, the confederate states come to realize that their hard-won victory was essentially meaningless and eventually they secede from the confederacy and rejoin the Union, even though they have to free their slaves to be welcomed back.

--All of them?

Who? Fillmore again? We were done with him, I'd thought. He came up accidentally, a distraction from a distraction, but is unwilling to go away. He has a cause, which is generally tiresome. He offers the refinement that those southern states were not all the same:

--South Carolina was governed by madmen. It always has been and is even today. They seceded from the Union but they were the last to join the confederacy because they were reluctant to share their sovereignty, even with a group of like-minded, cigar-smoking, julep-drinking men. I can easily imagine a return of most of the other states, but South Carolina might hold out, an independent nation, if rather a backward one. A Caribbean country on dry land. Cotton, sugar, rum, and pretentiousness. That would be enough to get by with. Where is it written that North America should be only two or three countries? The European model is the more natural, because it depends on old enmities, religious differences, and the general tendency among large groups to break into smaller ones.

Would that be a bad thing, I ask, an independent South Carolina?

--Bad for some. Good for others. They might continue slavery there just out of stubbornness. And to attract tourists, who would be an important source of income for them.

I cannot disagree. His parting remark is that in politics, one cannot let reason get in the way, because there is a fundamental unreasonableness to the world that eludes and confounds sensible men.

I had thought of him as a mere figure of fun. Instead he turns out to be an alternative, and perhaps even a better one, to Lincoln. Had events turned out as he had hoped, we would have Millard Fillmore on our pennies and five dollar-bills. There would be a handsome Fillmore Monument in Washington, DC. Fillmore would be on Mt. Rushmore. There would be a Fillmore, Rhode Island and a Fillmore Nebraska. There are also Fillmores that were actually named after him in California, Illinois, Indiana, Michigan, Minnesota, Missouri , Nebraska, New York, Oklahoma, Utah, and Wisconsin. Weirdly enough, there is one in Saskatchewan. (I'd have thought there would be a chain of gasoline stations with his name, but apparently not. There is, however, a Fillmore character in Disney's *Cars*.) I am saddened, meanwhile, to find that Cooperstown was not named after James Fenimore but his father, William, a judge and a politician hardly worth remembering unless you are the historian of Otsego County. Or a member of the Cooper family.

If William Cooper should present himself, I am not at home.

There are no defenses against these associational pop-ups be-cause any defense requires the use of the their own weapon. It would be like going on a hunger strike when the city is besieged. Nothing has changed and the opposing army is still outside the walls, jeering probably, but we have redefined our terms to be less flattering to them and more to ourselves. Clever but useless. Which could be my motto. *Inutile* sounds more refined, no? More philosophical, almost. Poulenc (or someone with the same name) used to substitute "Honolulu" for "Hallelujah" in church music, thus draining it of its theological mean-ing and bringing it down (or up) to the realm of art. The "Honolulu Chorus"! It would be a good motto, too, but who would understand it? (No one, but that is not a fatal defect.)

We pause in our travels. We have to take our bearings. With no idea where we are, we want to husband our energies. We have no map, no compass. The sky is cloudy and we don't know what time it is, so we can't figure out our direction from the position of the sun. What would Fatty Bumppo recommend? That we walk downhill and keep on going down, until eventually we find a little stream or a brook, and then walk in the direction of the water's flow, which will also be downhill. We still have no idea where we are or where we're going but we can be fairly certain that we are not going around in circles which is what happens to greenhorns. Or tenderfeet. *Our Greenhorns have Tender Feet* sounds like the title of a movie or a novel (but not this one!). Will we find water? Will it turn out to be the Hoosic? No, I don't think so. That would be too predictable.

Too predictable for what? Hard to say. It would feel too neat, too pat. The butler did it. Everybody did it. The narrator did it! It was an absolutely random bullet from the apartment across the street, or bet-ter yet from another mystery entirely. (Has anyone done that?) These are all desperate ways to make an ending of a mystery satisfying. Mys-teries depend largely on their endings. But every such gesture fails, because life isn't like that and novels are (or pretend to be) simulacra of life. How to make them random, with a tantalizing tendency that nonetheless refuses stubbornly to satisfy itself (or us) and leads to frustration rather than fruition?

Katabasis, the march down country, which Xenophon ought to have written about. The lift, the elevator, the ascenseur, the ascen-sore...they all imply that the device goes only upward. If that were true, think of all the office workers and apartment dwellers, who would be stuck up there on the 78th floor (or the 13th, even though many buildings pretend not to have one).

They go down, too, at least half the time. "Down, into the base court," as Shakespeare said, giving the line to a king rather than a doorman. Richard the Second, or, if it comes late in the play, Richard, the Fecund, because in the quarto for some reason in the running head the S changes to the old fashioned long s that looks like an f, which is what invites the joke. One can also refer to him as Dick da Deuce.

Richard was the Last of the Plantaganets, so he's a member of our relicts club. In the Shakespeare version, Henry assumes the throne and hints that he wishes Richard were out of the way so that Piers Exton leads a gang of cutthroats to Pontrefact Castle where they kill Richard. It makes a nice ending but it was fiction. There was, however, a factual faction that wanted to seize Henry at a tournament, murder him, and restore Richard to the throne. This aborted attempt was the Epiphany Rising, of which I confess I had never heard. (The name sounds like some rock musical of the sixties, but never mind.) That plot against Henry is what prompted the him to order that Richard be starved to death in his cell at Pontrefact. It makes a kind of sense, I suppose. Starvation is a slow and dreadful way to die; beyond that, there might have been some implication that this unusual punishment was a reminder to the prisoner that after he had abdicated, he should have had better control over his appetites. I don't ordinarily think of Henry IV as a witty king, but this kind of droll gesture might have amused him, whether he thought it up himself or took it from the court fool.

But is this what the book is about? The curious coincidences in the lives of these men who were the last of something? I wouldn't have thought so. And if it is, I have no notion of what sense it would make. The last Mohican? The last Plantaganet? The last Bourbon? We could as easily get excited about the last carrier pigeon. The last wooly mammoth. Or the last bar car on the Metro North commuter trains, which they took out of service just last week. Their time was over and they were a bit slow on the pick up. And anyway, what do they have in common? That they occurred to me, that their names arose in the random activity (or whatever it is) of my mind. None of them had any idea that they'd be appearing here, and I shouldn't be at all surprised if they are all hopping (pogo-stick!) mad. Or would be if they were alive. Or, in the case of Chingatchgook, real and alive.

What is interesting is that the conjunction, even if meaningless, seemed for the moment promising. I am reading this just as you are (albeit more slowly) and when I saw that they had something in common, I thought, aha, that must mean something. All the police procedurals have someone like Holmes telling someone like Lestrade that there are no coincidences. There are, but what he's saying, not to the

Lestrade but to us, is that this is an important plot point and we are to register it. We may be fooled. It could be a red herring. Or a blue porgy, which would be an even bigger distraction. By the time we have discovered the murderer, we'll have forgotten the instruction, or will have forgiven it because the detective hadn't intended to mislead, even though that was in part the reason for his creation.

I am not telling you anything that you don't know. (That would be dangerous for a novelist.) Picture this: you are a kid in seventh or eighth grade. And your assignment is to write a "book report," which is an odd locution. Grownups never do this. We may write reviews or essays, but not reports. The only practitioners of the genre are schoolchildren. But what can they say? What does the teacher want to know? Mainly that you've read the book. She doesn't care whether you liked it or not. That's not your job. Who are you to have an opinion about *Silas Marner*? Does anyone ask in geometry classes whether you liked the new theorem? That would be ridiculous. (I thought angle-side-angle was the most attractive.) So you rehearse the plot, which doesn't inform the teacher of anything. Presumably she has read the book. (Probably many times.) But if you get the characters and the action right or are reasonably close, you will have demonstrated that you read either the book or the Cliffs Notes. Or maybe just looked it up on Google, which will give you several accurate synopses. Your experience of the book as a piece of literature is not what she is interested in, which is a very bad lesson for an English class. (What to do? Keep your head down and make sure that your subjects and verbs agree in number.)

Is that what this is, a book report? Is the past never past? We can get sucked back to a deep-seated memory but when we're there we can't do anything differently or better. That is the real charm of counterfactual history, asking "What if?" or "If only?" and coming out with an altogether different and maybe better present. Suppose it is just that and my inexperience tells me (correctly) that I have no idea what I'm doing. There is an honesty to that, and an admission of ignorance is Socrates' idea of wisdom. What English classes teach us is how to pretend we are not at sea whenever we open a book. In other words, they tell us how to deceive, how to perform, how to present ourselves as knowledgeable. I am an old man and I have no idea how to talk about a book, or write one, or even read one. What is a book, anyway, but an extended exercise in wonder that seems worth our strenuous effort. It beggars the imagination, which is an odd phrase. Do beggars have limited imaginations? Probably, because they are thinking only of food and dry clothing.

What, here, seems to be asked? Those lasts are appealing, not because we are all sentimental preservationists but because each of us knows that he is the last of himself. His children are related, but they are not him. And it is the wise and generous parent who can love a child because of his differences. The child is not a Xerox copy. He is a new creature, which means the parent, facing extinction, is the last of a breed of one. When he is gone, there will be nothing of him left but his offspring who are only loosely connected. Reading Cooper, then, each of us is Chingachgook (or Uncas and then Chingachgook). We may wish it were otherwise, but if wishes were beggars' horses, my grandmother's trolley could fly.

--That is not what I meant, Cooper says.

How do you know? You might have meant it and been unable to recognize the unendurable thing you were saying.

--What are you, some kind of mystic? What you suggest is absurd.

It is, but I cannot explain to him that it is also true. Psychiatry has not yet been invented. Much of the human mind is unexplored, central Africa before Dr. Livingston trekked through it. Or without the metaphor, before Dr. Freud. If we knew what we meant when sitting at our desks, it would not be worth dipping the quill or unscrewing the fountain pen. Or typing the password to get to the home screen. There would be no question to wrangle with, Jean. (Jeans may not always be wranglers but Wranglers are usually jeans.) Perfect knowledge, if there were such a thing, would not need novels. Poems, maybe, but not these quizzical excursions in prose.

I'd put it even more strongly and suggest that when a novelist thinks he knows what he is doing he is like a liar concocting a story the lapses and inconsistencies of which are the only clues to what he is talking about. His intention is irrelevant and distracting. My strategy for solving this problem is not to have an intention and to let one oddity suggest the next. This is my version of Cardinal Newman's *Apologia Pro Vita Sua* (his famous apology for his herring). Yes, of course that kind of schoolboy humor is distracting, but we must ask ourselves what it is distracting from. In any event, it interrupts the flow of the conversation, but there is no subject one wants to take too seriously. Just beyond the light of the intellectual campfire, wolves lurk and, however engrossed we may become in the topic before us, we must remain alert to their threats behind us. Sometimes they howl; more often they creep up on us silently and one of us may go a little way into the trees to pee but never return. We must keep our wits about us but not on too close a leash. Serious people often make that mistake. They disapprove of us but it is only the frivolous who have any chance of surviving. Let us toast each other with another drink, the last of the mojitos.

The best feature of Charles X's reign, aside from his exertions on the pogo stick, was his style. He had principles and didn't care what anybody said about caution and circumspection. He was a king. When he abdicated and fled, as he was forced to do in 1830, he was suc-ceeded by Louis-Phillippe whose ideas were much like his own but was willing to prevaricate, obfuscate, and make meaningless gestures. He removed the royal lilies from the doors of his carriages, as if that would do any good. He pretended to be a middle class person hop-ing to keep the support of at least of shopkeepers and rentiérs. In a more sensible country, it might have worked. But the French are not sensible. They rose up again in 1848 (give them a millimeter and they want the whole damned hectare). Charles had departed with some dignity. Louis Phillippe runs out of the back door of the Tuilleries with his wife, Maria Theresa of Savoy, and they hide in a gardener's cottage in Honfleur. They have nothing but the clothes on their backs. They manage, however, to get in touch with the British consul at Le Havre, who smuggles them out of the country as "Mr. and Mrs. Smith." (How long did it take the consul to come up with such a name? It was better, but only slightly than "N. Cognito".)

So in the end he's just another rejected French king; his pretend-ing to be a member of the Elks, the Rotarians, the Kiwanis, or whatever their French equivalents might have been, did him no good. On the reign it raineth every day. To demean yourself for a reason is a dismal thing, but to do so and not achieve your purpose is pathetic. Ridicu-loony. Pardonnez roi!

There is no evidence but I like to think that Charles understood all that. Nothing he did would affect one way or another the history of his country and, indeed, that of all Europe. 1820, 1830, 1848 as we all learned in school. Waves of revolution in which malcontents and visionaries combined to destabilize the existing order in the hope of something better. At best, this is a desperate bargain in which you are buying a pig in a poke. I always thought that the poke was supposed to conceal the scrawniness of the pig, but it's worse than that. More often than not there was a puppy in it or a pussycat, neither of which is edible except in times of famine--in which case they would eat the poke, too.

Poke? Polk? Pocahontas? Popocatepetl? We could skitter off in any of those beckoning directions but we will pretend to be an outpa-tient, which is the best most of us can manage most of the time. We will Persevere. Which is how word got out to Concord that the British were coming.

The social, political, and economic changes in France in the *dix-neuvième* may have made Charles' retrograde ambitions irrelevant. But for an historian (you can do it that way but you shouldn't aspirate the h) there would have to have been an explanation. And for Richard II? No such luck! His political environment was not evolving. There were no changes he had to deal with and nothing for Anne the historian to explain except the return of Bolingbroke from exile to reclaim what he thought was rightfully his in the interminable, doggy-dog struggle for power. Each against all. It may not be intellectually interesting but can still be fun to watch (from a great distance) or read about. Richard was sentimental, which is a dangerous proclivity in a monarch. Worse than that, he was poetic. Shakespeare gives him a lot of wonderful stuff to say—his lines are much more elegant than Henry's. But Shakespeare seems not to have had much confidence in poetic rulers. They are distracted, and the main thing in the king game is to keep your eye on the orb.

Speaking of Bill, his formulation about how "The fault, dear Brutus, is not in our stars, but in ourselves" is horse frockies. It is neither in our stars nor in ourselves. There isn't even any fault, or blame, or cause and effect. Why study history then? Because it is comforting. No matter how bad things may seem, there is evidence that they have been just as bad before. Or worse. And we're still here, aren't we? The Russians had it right in the time of the tsars. There is nothing to do but sit in the doorway of your humble cottage and wait. Eventually the tsar will die and there will be another one, maybe slightly less terrible. We can hope for Ivan the Merely Pretty Bad. Or Nikolai the Annoying. But at least the individual Russian does not feel implicated or responsible for the outrageousness of what is going on around him. He leaves it all to the higher powers, the counts, the princes, the tsars, and God, all of whom are off their medications. He will shout "Long live the tsar!" if he has to, but he knows, as the tsar does, too, that the wish sooner or later will be disappointed. The tsar is a man and will die. None of that expensive regalia can blind him or us to that grim truth, which is the only ray of hope in the peasant's heart. If he smiles, he does so because he rejoices in the absurdity of what he and the others are shouting. "Slava! Slava!" Actually that means glory, but what glory will there be in the tomb? What is also comforting is the unanimity of the crowd, calling out what each member of it knows is absurd.

There is no history. There are only sequential but not necessarily connected events.

--That's ridiculous, Anne tells me.

Yes, it is, isn't it? I agree entirely.

--The historian's job is to make sense of what has happened.

But what if it doesn't make any sense. You are then imposing on randomness an appearance of order that is necessarily a falsity.

--Are you saying that there is no meaning in life?

I don't go that far. I don't have to. You're an historian. You tell me then, in a few words or even a few more, what is the meaning of life? If you can whisper that into my ear, I'll follow you anywhere.

She has no answer. She furrows her forehead and then vanishes, leaving behind her only the odd but by no means unpleasant scent of old, leather-bound books. (And maybe patchouli.) Have I been rude? That wasn't my intention. But it does seem to me that if there is no meaning in life it must follow that there is no meaning in history either. It's just now, now, now, and then not. The rest ought to be silence but Horatio is wrong. The rest is fiction, which is where we are.

No, no, you say. If the rest is fiction, it isn't this kind of fiction but something sensible with the recognizable qualities of a novel. Plot and characters, at least, and maybe an interesting setting. But where is that written? I ask not where is that novel written but that rule? Expectations are snares and delusions. (If a snare is a delusion, it is not a snare, but never mind.) We pride ourselves on our ability to think ahead, but this can also be a defect. Animals have no expectations, which is probably why they don't understand jokes, almost all of which are demonstrations of our inability to rely on our powers of thinking ahead. An animal, indulging itself that way, would not live long.

I don't believe I've ever read that anywhere. And I am certain that I've never had such a thought cross my mind. It arose from the prose, which is the best gift fiction can offer us: obiter dicta that occur to the author along the way and are too good to discard. As a reader (I am also a reader, after all), I think, yes, that's true. Or, even better, that's interesting.

Sue Asponte takes the floor. (Remember her, from a few pages back?) She is about to say something but, as happens to us all some time or other, she forgets what it is and resumes her seat. I admire her for her refusal to fake it.

People put a lot of value on the truth of character. But what is that? A vague tendency. St. Augustine fretted that "no one is so well known, even to himself, that he can be sure as to his conduct on the morrow." Or never mind the morrow; he had no idea what he was about to do five minutes from now, and he was a smart fellow. And a saint. I have no idea what I am going to do either, nor—it logically follows—do any of my characters. There are tendencies and habits. And here, there are associations, more or less free, but there are also pop-ups, things that appear to me without warning or excuse. Novelists ignore this because if they took it seriously they would all be creating unshapely and awkward books like this one. In the name of truth, which is blazoned on fiction's flag. (And Harvard's, but they do it in Latin and break up VE RI TAS into syllables, as though it were a difficult word).

I said earlier what I believed at the time to be the case—that Henry IV ordered that Richard be starved to death. But it seems there is no evidence for this. It is possible, therefore, that Richard starved himself to death. Why would he do that? Why not? He was depressed and it would have been an extravagant and melodramatic thing to do. Better yet, there would be people who would suspect that Henry IV had some hand in it. True or not, the rumor would be troublesome to the king and would give some credence to the notion that he was not the legitimate ruler but a usurper and murderer. There would be revolts (and, indeed, there were, several, during the course of his reign). Too complicated? Too far-fetched? We must remember that Richard had plenty of time to brood about this in his quarters at Pontrefact and he was, in any case, a broody guy. He had been wronged. He was the victim. But this way he could penalize the victor and make Henry's life and reign as difficult as possible. With luck, he would be overthrown, too. And then his successors, one after another, would kill each other, again and again, in a delightfully extended series of gory punishments that each of them would have deserved. What could be lovelier?

Talk about drama, this is every bit as interesting as the play Shakespeare dreamed up, even though there is less action on the stage--unless we can dramatize Richard's venomous visions. We could steal from Beckett (not Tom but Sam) and put Richard onstage up to his neck in a pile of what appears to be shit, but unlike the protagonist of *The Playground*, he would have a very large, very elaborate crown on his head. The action going on around him? It would be what he imagines and even wills into being. The noblemen, the clergy, and the rebels (Owen Glendower, Harry Percy, and others) would think they are acting on their own but we'd know that they were following Richard's vengeful script.

Can that happen? Well, stupider plays have gotten themselves produced. But what I am asking is whether a character in life can realize a plan of someone else's contrivance. I don't see why not. In any case, each would be supposing himself to have free will, and both would be wrong, which is witty enough to be diverting. We could even underscore the artificiality of the dramaturgy by having Richard occasionally replay some scene that he particularly enjoys. In any event, the important thing isn't whether these things can happen but whether we can shake the confidence of the members of the audience (or the readers) that the world is what they think it is and their actions are their own—as they must be if they are to have meaning.

What could capture our attention more than the sight of a man starving himself to death, whatever his reasons. The will to commit suicide is impressive in itself, but for most methods a person has to work himself up to an action that will take only a moment. People who have jumped off the Golden Gate Bridge and hit the water right (or wrong) so that they have survived report having had second thoughts on the way down. Understandable. Oddly, in their support group meetings (there is one, at Moffitt Hospital, I think) many of them say they have a new life and that are devoting themselves to good works and charitable causes. If the leap is not a life-ending event, it is life-changing. But in his cell in Pontrefact, Richard had to keep his resolution from hour to hour, from day to day, taking nothing but sips of water while waiting for the torment to end. It is the suffering of a martyr, except in a wicked cause, and for such people there is no process of canonization of the kind St. Cyprian of Carthage described in his treatise, *De laude martyrii*. Unless Mephisto has saints, too.

The logic was clear. He was going to die anyway, sooner or later. The only questions were how and when, and the answers were within his control. Why not go in such a way as to inconvenience the Lancastrian upstart? It was a good idea, but not nourishing. He had to reaffirm it, even as his warders put before him bread, wine, honey, and whatever other tempting comestibles they thought might weaken his resolve. No, and no. And again no, a thousand times an hour. It is nuts, of course (were there nuts, too?) but entirely consistent with Shakespeare's view of Richard's character and that of historians as well.

Henry IV understood what his pesky predecessor was up to and realized that even if he was dead, Richard was still a problem. Henry had the body displayed at St. Paul's Cathedral to show the people that Richard was truly defunct. Dead as an halibut. Let them see with their own eyes! They came in droves (and left it high dudgeon?) not convinced. A fiction arose that this was the corpse of someone else, who looked like the former king, while the real Richard was hiding out somewhere in the country, waiting for his moment to come back with soldiers and the massed populace to take back the crown.

Henry had ordered that the corpse be quietly interred at the Dominican Priory at King's Langley, Hertfordshire, but that wasn't persuasive to anyone. So he had the body moved to Westminster Abbey and put in the tomb Richard had had designed for himself.

How can anyone govern under such conditions? Even an absolute monarch must give way before willful and invincible ignorance. Richard was still alive? Or maybe he was dead but had come back, a revenant, a ghost but more substantial. Like King Arthur. Or maybe even with King Arthur. Once a story like this gets going, it keeps on spreading, acquiring new and ever more marvelous twists and turns. There is not much difference between wanting it to be true and believing in it. The good old days? Those were Richard's. An undisputed claim to the throne? That was Richard's too. Seizing power is easier than holding on to it. It is riding the tiger. Or the greased pig.

So. Did Richard starve himself or did Henry have him starved. Nobody knows. (So we all get to vote.) But the convention of this curious excursus allows me to revive him. They found Richard III buried under a parking lot in Leicester, presumably in a handicapped spot, but he didn't have a lot to say. We can chat with Richard II, however and ask him what happened.

He glares at me.

I rephrase. May I ask about your death, your majesty?

--No. I prefer it this way. I get sympathy one way and the other way I get sympathy as well as credit for being clever. Why should I give up either of these advantages?

For the sake of truth, sir?

He laughs. The laughter of dead men is unsettling.

--The only truth that matters is that I am dead. You can believe whatever you like. It makes no difference to me.

But the play has it wrong. Doesn't that bother you?

--No, it's a good play. I've seen it often.

How is that?

--How is that? How is this? Don't be tedious, young man.

I let him go. I am pleased to be called "young man," which he has a right to do. He is more than 600 years old, after all.

I admit at once that this is an absurd colloquy, but it is also the case that while I was writing it there was a part of me that was persuaded, at least enough to make a few corrections as I went along. Corrections? How could a nonsense be incorrect? The wraith, no matter how insubstantial, has a character. Is a character. And as I have begun to realize, despite the bishop of Hippo, character is all that matters. Actions are complicated and are surely as subject to interpretation as literature. Character presents itself but we don't think about it. We simply react to it. The simplicity is paramount. By instinct, dogs like some people but not others. The smell maybe? The posture or carriage? No dog has ever confided in any of us to explain itself. But we have the same reactions, more physical than mental, that we try to deny because we don't want to seem arbitrary or prejudiced. The denial is incomplete, however, because we are aware that we are doing it. The rules of good manners or political correctness or of the Fair Employment Practices Act are not to be questioned, so we blame ourselves and assume that we are the ones who must be defective, snobs and bigots.

To reverse the argument would be to make it more palatable and even perhaps persuasive. If there is "love at first sight," then there can be its opposite.

"First sight" is an exaggeration, however: what the phrase means is at first encounter. Or very early on. Dr. Elliot Cohen describes the phenomenon, defining it for us (as if it needed definition). He cites Bertrand Russell's theory of knowledge by acquaintance and goes on to explain that, "Such acquaintance can be cognitive (what she says to you, and what emotions and attitudes she expresses); auditory (her tone of voice); kinesthetic (the way she moves her body); olfactory (her scent); tactile (how she feels such as in an embrace); and even gustatory (as in the taste of the first kiss). This does not mean that all such kinds of acquaintance are requisite to "love at first sight"; however, this knowledge cannot meaningfully be restricted to the visual perception alone.

In simpler words, what he is saying is that the traditions of western literature are not entirely wrong. Girls look forward to the prospect of being swept off their feet by some Prince Charming who has come to the castle to awaken them. Men fear it, knowing how it can disrupt the orderliness of their lives, promising ecstasy but often bringing disgrace and ruin. But it happens, and everyone knows what Dr. Cohen is saying with perhaps less charm and sadness than the subject deserves. He does serve a purpose however, in that he confirms what Dante and Petrarch told us centuries ago. My own view is that people who didn't believe those poets are not worth convincing. If you gots to ask, you never gets to know.

Even so, it occurs to me that we could summon either of those poets to our conclave if I had the nerve. But I don't. Kings, presidents, novelists are pieces of cake, or of cheese, or of cheesecake. But Petrarch is too alive for me to impose on, or to impose him on you. There are limits, after all, to my presumptuousness. I back off. (I. Bakov, deputy assistant acting minister of cultural affairs, who warns me that there are lines that should not be crossed or if they are will be crossed out, and that the OGPU has a file on me. The OGPU sounds menacing even though, today, it has something to do with pogo sticks.)

Another, lesser poet, perhaps? *Forse* Pietro Cardinal Bembo.

Who?

Exactamento! Many of you will never have heard of him. Not long ago, I offered a translation of some of his elegant poetry to a couple of university presses but they declined even to read it on the ground (reasonable but cuckoo) that no one had heard of him. I could have argued that this was precisely the reason to publish his work, but you can't talk to an acquisitions editor. Or a dial tone. (How can there be dial tones if there are no dials anymore?)

Anyway, Bembo. One of Lucrezia Borgia's lovers. The author of at least one poem that made it onto the Index Librorum Prohibitorum. And then he was elevated to cardinal, which was quite a hat trick and got him a big red biretta. And his name is attached to an attractive typeface:

Bembo

Bembo Italic

Bembo Semibold

Bembo Semibold Italic

Bembo Bold

Bembo Bold Italic

Bembo Extra Bold

Bembo Extra Bold Italic

Nice, isn't it? Plain and clear with the most modest serifs. Bembo had nothing to do with the design, though, which is recent, a 20th-century revival of an old-style serif face cut by Francesco Griffo around

1495. It was made under the direction of Stanley Morison for the Monotype Corporation in 1929. It has a double-story a in lower case and the capital Q's tail is centered under the figure. The uppercase J has a slight hook, and there are two versions of the uppercase R, one with a straight tail and one with a curved tail. Right? Right.

Bembo was a celebrity, one of the leading lights of Venice in which there was no shortage of glitter. I'm not making any of this up. It would have taken a lot of work to do that. It is all real but silly enough for readers to doubt, particularly when its source is altogether unreliable. But the truth of a statement is not affected by the harlequin suit I sometimes wear at my desk. (Theodore Roethke used to write in the nude, or at least that's what he said. Maybe he was kidding. Or coming on to—or frightening off-- attractive graduate students.)

But never mind Roethke. Bembo is the one I'd feel comfortable talking with (and to and for). He is a magisterial fellow and looks very severe. The eyes, which sometimes twinkle, are piercing, the nose is long and sharp, and the white beard is longer than mine in Titian's great portrait. His head is turned a quarter to the right to suggest that he knows we are there, waiting upon him, and sooner or later he will turn to look at us. His right arm is flexed and his hand is in a position to suggest that he is explaining something. This allows Titian to show off a little with his rendition of the white lace of the *rochet* above Bembo's wrist as it protrudes from the crimson *mozzetta*. Still, having read some of Bembo's work, I know that Titian was accurate but not telling the whole story, for the cardinal had a certain frivolousness about him, and I share his belief that frivolity is the only sensible and civilized way to confront the difficulties of life that do not arise even from malevolence (which would be reasonable) but are only random. Most of the time.

--The worst sin is to lose faith, my son.

You're kidding, your eminence. (I say this in such a way to blur the grammar so that the verb can be transitive and the sentence can be heard as "You're kidding your eminence." I am not being disrespectful but merely playing to his fondness for wordplay.)

--I'm quite serious, sometimes, although few people have noticed it. The question you should have asked is faith in what? You sit down at your desk and read yesterday's work. It is disappointing. Always. But is it good enough to continue? Good enough not to throw away? There is no way of knowing and that is where faith comes into it. You rely on faith—in yourself, in the work so far, in your efforts of the previous days or months. We write with words but it turns out in the end to be an exercise of the spirit. I may not be much of a cardinal, although I do love the regalia, but I know something about writing.

That's true, your eminence. I agree.

He purses his lips.

-- "Eminence" was a form of address that Urban VIII introduced some years after my death. I prefer the earlier style of address, which was "Illustrissimo." It resonated better. But never mind. In your book, you have written a number of times that you don't know where you are going.

I have, yes.

--If what you are writing is supposed to be a representation of life, an enactment of it, then it would follow that you wouldn't know where it is going or what comes next. Or when it will end. That's how life is, after all.

I am delighted to be so well understood but not surprised. You are said to have been a brilliant man. But....

He makes a dismissive gesture and interrupts.

--Your audience, as you imagine it, is brilliant. But we agree that life is impossible to predict and doesn't have a plot.

I don't want to interrupt him so I just nod in assent.

--It can have a direction, but you don't understand what that is. Would you like me to tell you?

I am not sure. Wouldn't that ruin it?

--Trust me. It won't hurt anything.

Then I am eager to hear.

--It is about me, he says and flashes a sudden, wicked grin.

I am surprised to see how yellow his teeth are. I ask him if he is serious.

--Quite serious. It is about writing. About words and even letters. I am a poet, a man of the church without any particular belief, and perhaps most important, I am a font. "In the beginning was the word," never made any sense to me. Obviously, in the beginning were the letters, without which there could not have been words. Thus, the font of wisdom. You and I know this, although it is impolite, and impolitic, to say so.

I am not comfortable with this. The conversation is too theoretical. I should anchor it, give it a setting at least, in a grand Venetian chamber that has not been properly maintained. In fact we are in Ca Bembo, the splendid palace on the Grand Canal near the Rialto Bridge. (It still stands there, as much as anything in that collapsing city stands, and they have refurbished it some and rent out apartments to tourists, but they are very pricey.) There is gold leaf on the frames of the wall panels but it has fallen off here and there and needs restoration. The velvet curtains on the windows are also threadbare in places and in need of attention. Bembo seems indifferent to his surroundings, but I am not so serene. He has the advantage, of course, of being dead. But that is a condition to which it few of us aspire.

I tell him that it makes no sense, this late in a book, for the major character to announce himself. It seems arbitrary.

--Verisimilitude, my son. You live from day to day and year to year, and then, quite late in your life—your story—you meet someone who turns out to be a close and important friend. His appearance and your meeting are arbitrary, but are you going to object because it hasn't been properly prepared for? You have spoken about wanting not to be dishonest. In life, this often happens and, therefore, in a book, it could and should. Why do important characters have to be introduced early on? Are your best friends people you knew in high school? Or even college? You grow, you change. One might speculate that if you had met this important person a decade or two earlier, you might not have appreciated each other. You weren't ready. But how to convey that observation in declarative sentences?

I take it that your unexpected appearance means that I'm ready, or at least that you think so, Illustrissimo.

--I do. We have so much in common.

We do?

--Both of us, considering our talents and achievements, are re- markably obscure. Or, to put it more bluntly, nobody has heard of ei- ther of us. I used to be famous but not any more. More people know of me as one of Lucrezia Borgia's lovers than for my writing.

Lovers? *The Catholic Encyclopedia* says that you and she had a Platonic friendship.

--Consider the source. Do you believe in the Immaculate Concep- tion, the Dormition and Bodily Assumption of Mary into heaven, Je- sus' return from the tomb, or any of that? You make up stuff and it's fiction. You make up a lot of stuff and, if it's wild enough, it's a religion. Besides, who said that Plato was celibate? I wrote a book about Pla- tonic love and dedicated it to Lucrezia, but everyone understood it as a joke. What difference does it make, though? What the body does, the body soon forgets. What the heart and the spirit do they can re- member forever.

I have no idea what to say. I change the subject and ask, Why did you choose to appear to me?

--Why not? You are an admirer of Petrarch, as am I. That com- mended you to me. And I knew that you needed me. For a reprobate to do a good deed once in a while is agreeable, if only to keep people off balance. As do some of the details in your book. *Mozzetta* and *rochet*, for instance. They are the right words but you had to look them up. So even while they are true, they are also a kind of falsehood. To keep readers off balance as they are most of the time in life.

You like my book then?

--I'm not in a position to judge, am I? And whatever I say, who would believe me?

I would.

No, you wouldn't. You are writing my words after all. And therefore you cannot trust me or believe anything you have me say, can you?

Again that sudden smile. Or more accurately, it appears suddenly and then fades gradually.

Given the life you had led, were you surprised to be made a cardinal?

--Not at all. No one deserves a red hat. We are all unworthy, some more than others.

He raises his index finger either as a caution or in emphasis.

--It is a figure, I think, of heavenly grace, which can elevate anyone, even the least likely. I was amused, perhaps. Pleased, surely. But not surprised.

You seem to have become more devout since your elevation.

--Exactly. Seem. But the idea of grace is a philosophical one and it is interesting to follow its implications. Even a pagan like you could do that. But do sit down.

He indicates a chair with a very high back, designed not so much for sitting as to display on its backrest an elaborate needlework of a hunting scene with a great deal of foliage in a delicious range of greens.

So what happens now? (It is not unprecedented for a writer to ask of his characters what the next paragraph should be.)

--That is up to you. As it would be in life. There are constraints, of course. Whatever you do or write should be in character, but by your age you should know yourself well enough to grope your way forward.

It is vertiginous.

--Yes, indeed. Blessed Mary, ever vertiginous. But remember that it doesn't matter. In literature and in life. Grace, or luck, or whatever you want to call it plays a greater part in our careers than we dare admit. Look at me, for example, a cardinal. All you have to do is write, "And then," and you can go wherever you like.

He holds out his hand, palm down. I realize that it is an invitation for me to kiss his ring. Can I do that? Is it like shaking hands or bowing? Or is it a profession of a faith I don't have? I hesitate for an instant but then I kiss the ring.

And then? And then?

My expectation is that he will now fade away as the others have done. But this time I am the one who is fading. And I realize that I don't want to do this, that I am eager to stay there with him, that the present scene is more vivid and important than anything outside the room.I walk to the window and look out at the dirty water of the picturesque canal. It isn't the Hoosic, but in the right kind of boat I could theoretically get from here to there. If the idea of doing such a thing should ever cross my mind.

But it hasn't.

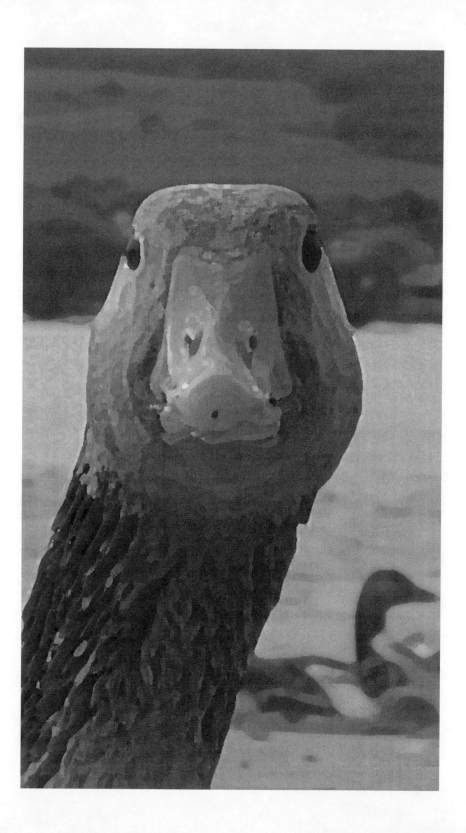

III

TOMHANACK

Not even a river, call it rather a small stream or, as its name suggests, a creek. In the summer it shrinks to a mere rivulet, but that does not make it unimportant. This, after all was where the Tomhanack Meteor decided it was a suitable place to fall to earth, distinguishing it forever from other, more impressive waterways. It therefore offers each of us a hope, however wan, that we, too, may be picked out in the random tohu and bohu (Martinů, again?) and be elevated to a significance that falls upon us like a meteor. Think of Jenkins, as you probably haven't done since school. His ear is famous. Thomas Carlyle used it to name a war with Spain. It isn't quite fame, but the name endures and those who are curious can explore easily enough to discover that during the war in 1731, off the coast of Florida, the Spanish patrol boat *La Isabela*, commanded by Julio León Fandiño boarded the British brig *Rebecca*. In a gesture of mannerist vainglory, Fandiño cut off the left ear of the *Rebecca*'s captain, Robert Jenkins, whom he accused of smuggling, and said to him in a loud voice, "Go, and tell your King that I will do the same, if he dares to do the same."

Who would believe such extravagance? This is not only a rhetorical question of mine but a practical one that Jenkins considered. The scar should have been enough, but for skeptics back in London there needed to be something more than the lack of an ear. The presence of the ear would be more persuasive, not necessarily the proof of anything but a dramatic exhibit to hold up at the right moment in a speech. So Jenkins had the ship's cook pickle it and put it in a jar.

"Aye, aye, sir," the cook replied. Or perhaps, "Ai, ai!" because it was disgusting. They sound much alike.

In a sane world, there would be a note from the producer's office saying, "Rewrite. This is too stupid. Audiences will laugh." But we're in the real world here, which does not bother with sanity but spins along doing whatever crosses its vast non-mind. Omniscient? Omnescient rather, which my dopey spellcheck underlines for me because it doesn't know the word. Of course, it doesn't: I just made it up. But it's a terrific word, coming from *omnes* (all) and *nescio* (I don't know). Very Socratic. [Nescio was also the pseudonym of the Dutch writer Jan Hendrik Frederik Grönloh, who was born on June 22, 1882 in Amsterdam and died ... Who cares when? In the sixties sometime.] The variation on the word came to me, falling from a cloudy sky, not a meteor maybe but a delicious innovation. And as the meteor lent a certain éclat to the New York creek, so my modest but useful addition to our vocabulary may make me not quite famous but known, as well perhaps as that Grönloh fellow.

Which is a low bar. (One of those seamen's dives in Amsterdam? No, I mean not difficult—unless, of course, you are dancing the limbo in which the meaning is reversed, just as "below par" changes its meaning in golf to become high praise.) Nescio wrote three novels, none of which was successful during his lifetime when it might have been convenient, but they survived him to receive some respectful attention later. But how famous is that? You ask anybody to name his favorite Dutch novelist and he's likely to answer, "I don't know," which would be absolutely correct. (Harry Mulisch would also be correct.) Or ask what was Grönloh's pen name? Bingo! Right again! ("I don't know" was also the third baseman in the famous Abbott and Costello routine.)

Who knows what he had in mind? Not me. Not him, either, if the soubriquet meant anything. I remember Socrates' lovely line, *en oida oti ouden oida*, which means, "The one thing I know is that I know nothing." It is not likely. He (Grönloh, not Socrates) went to an HBS school, a *Hogere Burgerschool* in which Latin and Greek were not offered. These were not schools that were supposed to prepare their students for university study but only to provide them with sufficient mental equipment to go into a job in industry or trade. He did obviously learn a few Latin words, his pen name among them. And he could have picked up Greek on his own, too, a smattering anyway, but that seems improbable. Still, with Nescio, one can never be sure. I am not sneering, believe me. (When I sneer, you'll know.) On the contrary, I admire him all the more for going to what was, essentially, a commercial high school and then discovering himself as a novelist.

The reason for the pen name? Apparently he didn't want his employees at the Holland-Bombay Trading Company to know about his writing lest they think of him as frivolous. He joined the company in 1904 and worked his way up to become its director in 1926. It was a position of considerable responsibility and therefore he had to maintain at least a façade of stolid dignity. (How did Wallace Stevens keep the information that he was a poet from other lawyers he dealt with in the insurance business? How did Dr. Williams keep his colleagues and patients from knowing about his poetry?)

One minute, you've never heard of Nescio and the next you don't know, which with him is knowing. Fame, it seems, can be negative like dark matter, which is said to fill the universe. Obviously it fills most people's minds. We try to improvise with whatever is at hand, but it is like learning Chinese from the little slips in fortune cookies, one word at a time, one meal at a time. (Intensive Chinese is when you take a look at your dinner companion's slip so you can learn that word, too.) In an internet survey carried out by the newspaper *NRC Handelsblad* in the beginning of 2007, that invited readers to name the ten best Dutch novels Nescio's trilogy (*De uitvreter, Titaantjes, Dichtertje*) came in at number eight. Worse than negative fame then (or one of its most pernicious forms) is the posthumous kind.

NRC? Those are the initials of the old *Nieuwe Rotterdamsche Courant* that merged with the *Handelblad* and survives in this minimalist gesture. At least so far. Back in 1970 when the two papers became united in holy parsimony, management must have thought the vestigial initials might help keep the loyalty of *Courant* readers, at least for a while. Sooner or later, someone will decide enough is enough and the initials will go away. Think of Pierce, Fenner, and Smith whose names came after Merrill Lynch on the letterhead (and over the doors where they had been cut in stone). Now that I think of it, before Smith, there had been a Beane following Fenner. What happened to him? Probably he and Smith were faultless (at least as much as Pierce and Fenner) but traders on the street referred to the firm as the thundering herd, so they thinned it. Brutal? (Not really.)

But back to Jenkins. Who could doubt his own eyes or Jenkins' ear that he held up in its by now somewhat cloudy bottle? There are always skeptics, not because they are disagreeable people or contrarians but more probably because they have been duped before and are trying not to let it happen again. Fool me a hundred times, shame on you; fool me a thousand times, shame on me. There was also the political question of whether it was good or bad at that moment to have a war with Spain. The anti-war people found it useful to express doubt. Researchers have discovered, however, that the incident happened as described when sometime in the late 1880's John Knox Laughton, KCB, the founder of the Navy Records Society, uncovered contemporary letters from Jamaica in September and October 1731 which substantiated Jenkins' account. Writing from onboard HMS *Lion* at Port Royal, Jamaica on 12 October 1731 [O.S.] to the Admiralty in London, Rear-Admiral Charles Stewart confided, "I was a little surprised to hear of the usage Captain Jenkins met with off the Havana," and he mentions the business of the ear. Beside that, in the Admiralty records files with the 1731 correspondence from Jamaica was a List of British Merchant ships taken or plundered by the Spaniards compiled in 1737, listing 52 ships, among them, *Rebecca*, Robert Jenkins, Jamaica to London, boarded and plundered near the Havana, 9 April 1731.

Convinced? I'd be. (I am.) But those morons in the head office won't care a Bagalhouce fig about whether it's true or not. (That is a moonshine fig, a small white, very sweet fig from the Azores: I put the adjective into the tattered locution to make it more specific and therefore more credible, even though I have never eaten or even seen such a fruit. I mention this because it demonstrates how the writer's craft itself invites falsehoods in the name of persuasiveness.) But the thing is that it doesn't make any difference whether the story is true or not. It was reported and widely believed, which made it a *cassus belli* and put Jenkins, in a limited way, on the record.

There are other notable preserved body parts. Cromwell's head, for instance. After his corpse was dug up, tried, and found guilty of treason it was condemned to death (redundant, but the rules of grammar have never been enacted into law) and hanged. It was then beheaded and the head, tarred, was stuck up on a post and blown down in a storm. A guard stole it and sold it. It appeared for a while in a museum of curiosities, and was finally interred on the grounds of Sidney Sussex College at Cambridge—in a secret place to keep it safe from seekers of souvenirs, or, if we may indulge ourselves by undoing a metaphor, headhunters.

There are also Einstein's brain, Galileo's finger, Napoleon's penis, Rasputin's penis (larger than Napoleon's), and Buddha's tooth, which is in a reliquary in Sri Lanka where it is visible by appointment. In each of these instances, the body part partook of the fame of the whole person. With Jenkins, to the contrary, the ear is famous and he is merely ancillary.

Fame is a double-edged razor blade, except that you can't shave with it. Some men and women put their fame to use, turning it into money or happiness. Others just enjoy it as they would a rare bauble in their vitrines. What it seems to offer is a kind of immortality. The looming prospect of death--which is always present while we always try to ignore it—may be held at bay, at least for a while, by a celebrity that may not be eternal but will last a little longer than we will. It is possible to conquer the world like Alexander, who died young but whose name survives in history books. Or it can be a single glint of light. Enneus, the Latin poet whose *Annales* is gone except for a few fragments, lives on in a footnote. He said he had dreamt that Homer's ghost had visited him and was now his guide in the composition of the poem. Well, okay. It is a pretty story. Such tributes are not unusual. His claim was more elaborate, however, because it mentioned that in the dream he learned how the spirit had survived all those hundreds of years in the form of a peacock. A long line of peacocks? An extraordinarily long-lived peacock? It doesn't matter. The cheerful weirdness of the idea spreads its gaudy tail and our memory of Enneus' encounter with Homer turns out to be more enduring than his own epic. Papyrus lasts only so long before it is lost or burned so that it disappears into the air. But air is better and is now where the old poet resides, that rarefied air scholars and literary people take into their alveoli with every breath.

My visitation from Nescio was less showy. He was a mere shadow that flitted past the windows of my mind as I was occupied with frivolous wordplay. Omniscient, remember? And there he was, not as a peacock but a rather dapper fellow in a tan fedora and what used to be called a lounge suit (it is indistinguishable from what is now a business suit, except that the latter are generally of darker fabric). I affected earlier not to know when he died because I thought it would be better to leave him floating in indeterminacy. But he died in Hilversum on July 25, 1961. He was fifty-odd years older than me, but we did overlap and were notionally contemporaries. No need, therefore, for any peacock or emu or condor. (Or, more likely, a goose.) Just a trim businessman--that was his main occupation--in well-tailored clothing.

His father was a blacksmith and shopkeeper. (Well? So? Gladstone's father was a greengrocer. Does it matter?) Maybe, because Nescio had to invent himself. His full name was Jan Hendrik Frederik Grönloh, which was also his father's name. So his "real" name was Fritz. Or that was the name he used. Except in his writing, which published under the *nom de plume* so as not to risk the derision of his friends. Jan Hendrik Frederik becomes Fritz who becomes Nescio. It's like the infinite regression of your image in the mirrors of a barbershop on opposite walls.

And why do I want to talk with him? And what do I want to learn from him? For one thing, he's here, having unexpectedly presented himself. For another, he's a Dutch writer, and they have different views of celebrity. If you write in a minority language like Dutch, your chances of being translated and read in English, French, German, or Italian are slender. Corollarily there is little probability of your making any money. How many Dutch speakers are there, after all? For Fritz, then, it was not something he thought about. And now that he is becoming established, albeit in a small way, is he pleased? Angry? Still indifferent?

His "establishment" quite suitably undercuts itself --his three novellas have been reissued as *Amsterdam Stories* in the New York Review Classic series. He's up there with Sigizmund Krzhizhanovsky's *Autobiography of a Corpse* and Jeremias Gotthelf's *The Black Spider.* Not the big leagues, maybe, but double-A, and there must be people who follow the Richmond Flying Squirrels or the Akron Rubber Ducks.

"I'm not sure I follow you," Grönloh says.

I'm sorry, I tell him. It was a self-indulgence. I was doing a number about secondary or tertiary renown. And some of the minor league team names are funny.

"That's intentional," Skyler Stromsmoe explains, appearing surprisingly to reprimand me. "Minor league ball doesn't offer the excellence of the majors but it has a relaxed, light-hearted attitude the fans like."

And who in the hell is Skyler Sromsmoe, you ask. He turns out to be the shortstop for the Flying Squirrels.

Grönloh is even more deeply puzzled. He is afraid that he may have shown up in the wrong book. I tell him not to worry about it and ask him what his life was like, writing well but without any expectation of much of a readership and even so using a pen name.

"I never worried about it. I thought of it as a hobby, like making model ships. You apologized a few moments ago for your self-indulgence, but I always thought that all writing is self-indulgent."

Stromsmoe asks if either of us want a Flying Squirrels baseball cap. Is he still here?

I thank him but decline. I feel sad about his appearance. He can't possibly know it but this is the high water mark of his career. He is thirty years old and is only batting .220, which even in this league isn't promising; unless he shows some improvement soon, he is unlikely to move up to the Fresno Grizzlies, let alone the SF Giants, and it will be a short career, which he'll almost certainly remember with regret for the rest of his life back in Bow Island, Alberta. He really comes from there. (One could take the sentence before the last and, with little trouble, turn it into an intelligent, ironic, but fundamentally sad novella, or even a novel that pretends to be sad but is actually very funny and self-mocking--but never mind. It has been done, anyway.) I thank Stromsmoe for dropping by and wish him well. He understands that, correctly, as the signal for him to leave.

Grönloh expresses some surprise at the news that his work has been reissued.

Should I tell him that it's a mixed blessing? The New York Review Press does some worthwhile books, bringing back deserving authors to whom insufficient attention has been paid. But they are a vainglorious lot and they publish some things just to condescend to their readers and embarrass them by pointing out the lacunae in their knowledge of books. You've never heard of him? What a clod you must be! If you had the wider familiarity with literature that we in the *New York Review* (or its press) have, you would have read these people before they went out of print. If you aspire to any degree of sophistication, even an unconvincing show of erudition to youngsters at parties, you must read these books, every damned one of them. If you want to disguise your inferiority, that is. And to be sure you don't miss any, we have a book club you can join and get all our books as they appear. (Does that come with a T-shirt so you can let fellow passengers on busses know how goddamned smart you are? Or can you buy the shirt or the book bag and not bother to acquire any of the books, which would achieve the same result?) [That's sneering, although I am sure I didn't have to say so.]

"You must understand," Grönloh says, "that in the Netherlands, we assume obscurity. It used to be that Dutch intellectuals wrote in Latin, as Erasmus did, for instance, because that was the way to communicate with those who spoke French or German or English or Portuguese. But for me to write in Latin would be pointless. Who studies Latin anymore? I'd have to learn it myself. If literature were like painting and we Dutch writers had a room to ourselves in museums as our painters do, no one would ever pass through it unless on the way to the *toiletten*. I am not complaining, mind you. There are certain advantages to our curious condition. It takes a lot of pressure off us.

"Come to think of it, Erasmus could as easily have written in English or French, because he knew both those languages and spent much time in those countries. He even taught at Cambridge for a while. But in his view, Latin had the best chance of lasting. So maybe the old bastard wasn't so smart, after all."

Why do you call him that?

"Because it's true, literally. His father was a priest. And if you have a double father, you have none, right?" A big grin lets me know he is joking and perhaps also apologizing for the joke.

I see what you mean, I tell him. I don't know a great deal about Erasmus, but I do remember one sentence of his: "There are some people who live in a dream world, and there are some who face reality; and then there are those who turn one into the other." It sounds very modern. Or do you keep up?

"I have little sense of time, actually. I do read some of the new Dutch novels, partly as literary works but also to get a sense of what's going on there. I'm not very assiduous about it, I'm afraid."

Whom do you like?

"You've mentioned Mulisch. I like his work. And Cees Nooteboom is very good, too, in a lofty, metafictional way."

I like him, too. Let me ask you about your books.

"I never talk about my books. I didn't while I was alive and to do it now would be ridiculous. Read them, if you feel so disposed. If you like them, let me know (and if not, not). I used to hide in them, but there's no need to do that anymore, is there? I can appear or disappear as the whim takes me."

His whim takes him. *Gegroet!* (I had to look it up, but it means Goodbye, as you doubtless guessed.) But in fiction, there are no goodbyes. I can bring him back as easily as I conjured him up in the first place. He may return or not, as his whim (which is mine) prompts. I had been about to ask him to say more about the curious condition of his secret life as an author. Was it only from the staff of the Holland-Bombay Trading Company that he wanted to conceal his other, not altogether respectable existence? Or did his anonymity (pseudonymity?) have a wider purpose? It is unlikely that many of his Holland-Bombay employees were habitual readers of novels (unless he deliberately recruited men of taste and refinement who were interested in the arts—which would be very strange).

Nescio! There is another closet novelist who worked in business and wrote fiction under another name. Ettore Schmitz! Name rings a bell? No? (That is in a way a mark of his success.) He wrote as Italo Svevo (Italian Swabian) and became a writer entirely by accident as is fairly well known now. He had decided to study English in the Berlitz School in Trieste so he could understand and answer letters in English that came into the Viennese Union Bank, where he was a correspondence clerk. A perfectly ordinary undertaking with an entirely businesslike motive. It was relevant to his literary career only because his Berlitz teacher happened to be Giacomo Joyce of whom you have surely heard. Beyond that, some literary critics claim that Schmitz/Svevo was the model for Leopold Bloom. Signora Svevo, Livia, was not the source of Molly but in some ways a prompting for Anna Livia Plurabelle in *Finnegan's Wake*. She is there both a character and also the River Liffey (in Irish, the river is called *Abhainn na Life*) and any three consecutive words that start with the letters A, L, and P refer both to the river and to Livia.) What this amounts to is literary fame without the tedium of unscrewing the cap of a fountain pen.

Svevo's novels, all self-published, were dismal failures. Even if they had had his real name and his address on the title page and his picture on the dust jacket, nobody would have taken any notice of him—except for his Berlitz teacher's kindness. Joyce read *Senilità*, told Schmitz it was very good, and suggested *As a Man Grows Older* for a title in any English version. He also read *The Confessions of Zeno*, a weird book about a man who is trying to give up smoking, and Joyce liked it well enough to send it up to some friends in Paris where it was translated and published by Valery Larbaud and Benjamin Crémieux. Almost immediately the French hailed it as a masterwork.

As Zachariah says somewhere, "a prophet without honor in his own country should maybe think about going to another country." (Or it could have been Isidore of Seville.)

Too grand? Probably so. Undeserved obscurity is the Italian habit. Think of Prince Lampedusa, sitting down rather late in life to write a novel about his experiences and his views of life. He submits it to some publishing house in Milan. And with a fine Italian hand they rewrap it and send it back. Drat! And then he dies. It is only posthumously that someone else in Milan, in a different house, gets a look at it and decides to publish it. (How many novels come in every year from defunct, legitimate princes, after all? And the novel is wonderful. (But that has never counted with publishers, even –or especially—the pretentious one.) Lampedusa, however, is not quite on point. The ordinary life of a prince is sitting in cafés and ...and doing whatever else they do. Svevo and Nescio had careers, and their writing was presumably an escape from the mundane constraints of real life. "Write about what you know," is what desperate instructors in MFA programs tell their students. But one could make exactly the opposite case: write about what you dream, what you crave and imagine. That works, too.

Nescio's *The Layabout* (or it could have been rendered as "The Moocher" or "The Schnorrer") is about a fellow who does nothing much except sponge off people. Not only shamelessly but gleefully, as a matter of principle. And he sees, really sees, in such a way as to impress his friend Blavink, the painter. He spends hours looking at the water, takes a break at noon for lunch, and then returns to his post, appreciating the subtle changes in the water's color and texture as the winds and the clouds influence it. He is not quite one of those Russian holy fools, but he has that kind of disturbing simplicity. He isn't quite a Buddhist beggar with a wooden bowl, either, but he is in a way related. He doesn't paint, doesn't write, doesn't do anything—that kind of activity would only get in his way and distract him from his calling as an aesthete of nature and of urban life as well. He is particularly good at seeing and describing canals, which means that Nescio, in order to prepare for the creation of one of his leading characters, had to teach himself to observe in that way, both with a child's innocence and an adult's sophistication.

So we have Nescio, or Grönloh really, walking the streets of Amsterdam, looking and trying to see what he would see if his eyes were sharper, his mind more receptive, his soul more open, in order to get some vague idea of what Jappi (pronounced Yappi), the eponymous moocher, will be like when he appears in the story. At that stage, names and fame are the least of his concerns. More probably it was the chance to take a brief break from the existence of a director of the Holland-Bombay Trading Company, which any of us can imagine even if we have never been to Holland or Bombay. (Or Mumbai! But the gin is still Bombay, because the men in the liquor business know the value in actual dollars and euros of a trademark with which nobody fucks. Does the American Kennel Club recognize the Zimbabwe Ridgeback as a breed? Are there Sri Lankan sapphires? Do you know a lot of rug dealers who sell Iranian carpets these days? Are there signs along the roads advertising Myanmar Shave? To hell with them: they are all natives speaking in opaque languages, and have no authority whatever within the civilized world.)

Then there is a very curious case of equivocal fame. I can't ever remember whether Chester Gillette was the real guy or Clyde Griffiths. One of them is the protagonist of *An American Tragedy*. The other is the guy who killed his pregnant girlfriend so he'd be free to marry the boss's daughter up in Cortland, NY—where they are proud of it because it is the only thing that ever happened up there. I looked it up. Gillette was the real guy and Grace Brown was the girl. Dreiser, sedulous fellow that he was and eager to be true to the truth, used the same initials, which is what makes it tough to remember which is which (a competitive volume to *Who's Who* that never quite made it). What's striking about this initial business is that Gillette used it himself when he checked into the hotel near Big Moose Lake in Herkimer County. (For reasons I can't imagine, Dreiser changed the name to Big Bittern Lake. So as not to sully the reputation of an innocent lake? Its notoriety is something the locals celebrated on the centennial of the murder, setting out wreaths to commemorate poor Grace.) Of course, Gillette had to dream up a name with his real initials, to match those on his luggage. (Clarence Gundlefinger? Carrington Gormsby, III? Probably a simpler Charles Green but almost certainly not Clyde Griffiths.) He'd gone there with Ms Brown planning to kill her, which he did the next day in a rowboat out on the lake, just as in the book and the movie (*A Place in the Sun* with Shelley Winters as the girl). He beat her unconscious with a tennis racket, which was neither in the book nor the film, but Gillette was working ad lib without a script or a director to tell him what to do. Or you can look at it the other way and criticize Dreiser and George Stevens for not using that awkward and amateurish detail in their versions. (Who would make up such a thing? But that is exactly why it was valuable.)

Actually, in the movie, he doesn't even kill her. It's equivocal. She stands up in the boat, it tips over, and all Montgomery Clift does is not try to save her, which is quite a different thing from actively bludgeoning her. The point was to preserve some possible sympathy for Griffiths so the audience wouldn't feel too happy when he is convicted and then electrocuted, so that he, too, is a victim. It's a tragedy, after all, even though the moviemakers, for whatever reason, decided that Kaiser Wilhelm's famous phrase was better as a title. (So that was what World War I was about?) A place in the sun is okay on the beach but at a bullfight avoid the *sol* and get a *sombre* seat, where you'll be more comfortable.

Dreiser is one of those peculiar writers of whom you can read any paragraph from any of the novels and see how bad it is, then read a whole chapter and find that it isn't quite so wretched, and then finish the book and realize that it is rather good. A triumph of the architecture of prose, and I wouldn't have thought such a thing was possible. Nescio's sentences are much better, even in translation. As are Svevo's. For that matter, I doubt that Skyler Stromsmoe's would be any worse, and that's assuming he had some hack helper, a sports writer like Dick Schaap, for *Stopped Short: A Life in Double A*. We can't blame Stromsmoe for the spelling of his first name. That was his parents' doing. And who were they? Beaver trappers? Hardscrabble farmers? Forgers of totem poles to sell to tourists?

[Stromsmoe muscles his way back in to reappear and insists that his first name is easier to spell than Schuyler. He also reminds me that one of the reasons I picked him out of the Flying Squirrels' line-up was that the name, spelled that way, caught my eye. "Yes, that's true," I tell him, although I never actually told him that or anything else. There's also a player somewhere whose name is Skylar, which sounds like some kind of coating they put on roofs. Or, as Sir Philip Sidney would have it, rooves (which spellcheck doesn't like).]

Nescio was a pen name, but there is a narrator in *The Freeloader*, a fellow named Koekebakker, which, in English, would be Cookie-baker. He is the one observing Jappi, the observer. But Koekebakker is a stand-in for Nescio, which in turn is a mask for Grönloh. It's a nest of diminishing Russian dolls that are not individually interesting but only become so in their nesting state. The innermost doll is exactly the same as the outermost, except for its size and the intelligent child realizes that the doll isn't so much the toy as the regressing sameness that poses the question: What else were you expecting? No one can play with these things for long without feeling chastened and, one may say, reduced. It is, thus, a sad toy, which is a thing only Russians would have invented. I think of little Gogol or Dostoevsky sprawled on the floor and opening these dolls and somehow I am inclined to suppose that they are sadder and sadder with each repetition.

Here Koekebakker is the one telling the story and from him, the fiction of a fiction of a fiction, there is a radiation of truth. Too clever by half? Or by a third? Or is it perhaps a Dutch treat, which isn't a treat at all because you have to pay your share. (Most references to Dutch anythings are put-downs: Dutch courage, uncle, twins, wife, and so on. The experts say that this is because England and the Netherlands were trade rivals a two or three centuries ago, but so what? I don't know a lot of anti-Hanseatic insults, although it might be pleasant one afternoon to dream one up. And then use it as if I assumed that readers would understand what I meant. [Hansdorpher, maybe?] The members of the Hanseatic League were, like the Dutch, trading rivals of England, and Queen Elizabeth got rid of them in 1597—or she tried to. But they are pesky critters and difficult to ferret out. Lufthansa still flies openly and shamelessly to Heathrow and it is the Hansa of Luft.)

Another significant feature of Nescio's novel is its series of protests, funny but also wounding, about the stupidity of office work, at which Jappi tries his hand from time to time in order to placate his father. His inabilities are not only impressive but even admirable. He puts letters in the wrong envelopes so that they reach unintended recipients. He knows it makes a difference but can't bring himself to care. He is incapable of the soul-deadening contortions it would require for him to become a minimally useful employee. These are of course Grönloh's own observations from his years at the Holland-Bombay Trading Company, or call them admissions. He knows that if there are any readers who ever had jobs, they will feel the same way, resenting the tedium and silliness that clerks experience hour by hour, minute by minute, and even tick by tick. No wonder that *trahison*, if there is any, is likely to come from the *clercs*. (The phrase comes from the title of a book by Julien Benda.)

"You have to just sit quietly and stay like that," Nescio has Blavink the painter say. "You have to just sit quietly and stay like that and long with all your might, without knowing what for." It is a spiritual exercise, altogether different from the Buddhist abnegation of desires. Blavink's recommendation turns us outward and responds to the richness of existence.

"Very good," Nescio says. "If I had to pick a single sentence that said what I mean, that might well be it. But any single sentence is incomplete."

Svevo, who is Triestine and therefore funnier than the Dutchman, says, "You need the whole novel. All those schoolchildren who have to write essays about books they've read would do better just to copy out the entire book in longhand. Several times, if necessary. One learns more each time through, if the book is any good."

"That would be cruel," Nescio says, "but it would work."

That longing you mention, did that arise from your office work? The question flashed into my mind because both of them served time as clerks.

"It may have done," Nescio says. "I don't remember."

Svevo suggests that it doesn't matter how it happened. "That would have been as good a way as any. Those long columns of figures that you add up and then add up again to check the result, even if you are using a machine, can put you into a trance. You feel that you are losing yourself. And a part of you exerts itself with that longing that doesn't even have a particular object. It is the soul's way of trying not to drown."

Nescio says nothing but he nods up and down. [The gesture signifies agreement or assent, unless the person is Greek, in which case it is negative, in order to deceive the Turks.]

"What we needed was a way to escape," Svevo says. "The pen names are us but not us. There are many people, I am sure, who have pen names but are not writers."

To this Nescio says, "I don't know," but he may mean it or he might be making a joke. Or both, of course.

I can't ask. I have to make do with what he tells me, which is the way we get on in most of life.

Stromsmoe is back. I have no idea why. I'd thought we were finished with him, a minor league minor character in for a single inning. But apparently not.

"What you guys need is to get out in the fresh air sometimes and get a little exercise," he says. "Just throw a ball back and forth. It'd do you a world of good, change your entire outlook."

It doesn't seem to have done you much good, I tell him. This is unkind but true.

"It kept me from brooding. Still does. That I'm not quite good enough is my problem, not the game's."

"That's sporting of you," Nescio says.

"Well, it's a sport, isn't it?" Stromsmoe answers. No trace of a smile. Deadpan, perfectly.

Does know he was being witty? Or was this just an accident, the way some plays on the field can be accidental when the ball happens to take a fortunate hop from the turf to land in the pocket of a fielder's glove and he looks, for the moment, like Cal Ripken. The odd thing is that it doesn't matter. As far as the individual play is concerned, he did what he was supposed to do and gets credit for it. For all the statistics they keep in baseball, there is, on the field, only the present. Does he field the ball? Does he throw it to first in time to get the runner out? There's no philosophy, just the action. And only then come the numbers.

Averages don't count with novelists. Think of Forty Mad-dogs

Ford. All those boring books, but then *The Good Soldier, The Fifth Queen* and *Parade's End*! The other books are forgotten, erased as if they had been written on a Magic Slate. (A lot of books should have been written on Magic Slates.) This is perhaps the only way in which literature is less cruel than baseball. But seriously (but not too seriously), have you ever heard of *Return to Yesterday, When the Wicked Man, The Rash Act, It Was the Nightingale*, or *Henry Knows How*? (These are obscure enough that I wouldn't blame you for suspect me of having made them up. Well, the last one I did actually, to trouble the wrong kind of reader or, more accurately, the kind of reader who cares about the wrong kinds of things.)

Ford and Conrad wrote a couple of novels together, but I suspect that Ford wrote them and Conrad just let his name go on the title pages to boost sales (and get a share of the royalties, of course). It was certainly nothing like "by Joseph Conrad as told to Dick Schaap."

In any case, what their joint efforts featured on the title pages (*The Inheritors* and *The Nature of a Crime* was not one but two assumed names. No mention of Józef Teodor Konrad Korzeniowski or Ford Hermann Hueffer. They were both trying to sound British, which is a curious ambition. Had I been Conrad's editor, I'd have told him at least to keep the acute over the o and use the z and the f in Józef. It gives a touch of elegance—like Italian suits or Parisian hats. But it's no use crying over milk spilt under the bridge.

Stromsmoe asks, "What's the matter with collaborations? It's like having a pinch hitter. It happens. The object of the game is to win, after all."

"Is it?" Nescio asks quietly.

"It depends on what you define as 'winning,'" Svevo suggests.

I send them all away. I don't quite believe in them anymore and I suspect that even the most patient reader has begun to have doubts. Restive. Restless. They seem like opposites but they mean the same thing--an anxious inability to sit still and rest. As T. S. Eliot said, "Teach us to sit down." (Which isn't all that easy, it turns out. Michael Caine once explained how crucial it was not to be either too slow or too fast, so that the camera can follow your movement and you don't look nervously jerky or feeble.)

So who is left, here? No one? How can we continue with the game?

Stromsmoe says, "We're gone but we're not gone. We're like players on the bench. In baseball, you can't put a man into the game who has already played, but here you have no such rule. That's what makes me uneasy about this thing of yours—that there aren't any rules. What makes baseball real isn't just the players and the umpires, which change from day to day, but the rulebook, which is always there, not only during the game but also before and after. It's something to rely on. It's real, the way life isn't."

This is suspiciously intellectual for a shortstop, never mind a double-A. I don't say anything but my face shows my doubts.

"Don't tell me you're surprised," Stromsmoe says to me. "You put a guy in and you're never really sure what he's going to do until he's done it, you know? That's what makes the game interesting. It's predictable but only so far and not always. As gamblers find out, sooner or later. You think I'm dumb because I'm a jock, but that doesn't always follow. A novelist should know that."

I sit corrected. I suspect that Stromsmoe is enjoying this, getting back at me for picking him out of a lineup and making fun of his name and his limitations as a player. He is a tall, lanky guy whose hair is starting to recede, which makes him, technically, a highbrow. Why did I not notice this before? Another thing I hadn't noticed was that his ambition and obscurity are not much different from Nescio's or Svevo's. Or my own. He is a reasonably good athlete and was ranked second nationally in NCAA Division II in stolen bases (52 of 55) when he played for Southern Arkansas University.

This is a joke university, not because it is worse than most of the schools in the division but because of the name. It was supposed to be University of Southern Arkansas, but some state legislator down there, one of those good-old-boys, a moonshiner who lived mostly on roadkill, realized that the initials would be USA, which he thought would be sacrilegious. (So if you see someone with a T-shirt that says USA, he's either a patriot or an alumnus of the University of San Antonio.)

But just look at those guys in minor league ball. They are pretty good; they have to be even to get to that level. Stromsmoe is almost certainly a better ballplayer than I am a writer. He hastens and chastens my will to make known.

May I call you by your first name?

He gives me a scornful look, as if to question my honesty, or maybe my sanity. It's my book, after all, and I can call him anything I like, as we both know. But I want his permission, nonetheless. (Is there a cloister somewhere of Nuns the Less who pray to St. James the Less, the younger brother of Matthew and the least well known of Jesus's apostles? No, but I wish there were.)

We both understand that I can delete the preceding page or so. I am in control here, or at least that is what I have been supposing. Even this is not quite exhaustively true, however. I should feel less than honest if I were to undo those lines, and Skyler knows it. This has always been his backup strategy. If he can't get a hit, he'll take a walk or bunt his way onto the book's base path. After enough time in the game, one learns a little shrewdness. (Really? Then where is mine? Or isn't shrewdness precisely what I have been running away from—shrewdness, facility, professional competence? If it is going to be worth anything—worth doing, I mean—writing should be risky; otherwise it can never expect to discover anything new.)

From out of the gloom, Nescio's voice is faint but clearly audible as he says, "If I may make a comment? The difficulty is not with writing but with ambition, the desire for achievement by which one can distinguish himself from the herd. There can be two outcomes, both of them sad. Either he fails and feels worthless, or else he succeeds and feels lonely. Neither of these is what he expected when he was young. That ignorance is perhaps the greatest advantage the young have over us older people."

Ignorance, is it, or innocence? It is a serious question I am asking. The words mean different things. Ignorance is not knowing; innocence is not harming. Not nocent. *Primum non nocere*, and all that Latin stuff doctors use without knowing any Latin.

"Yes," Nescio says. "They are different, indeed. But the practical results are often indistinguishable."

We are, the three of us, in one of Nescio's vivid settings, standing together on a hill overlooking the harbor, with the sun just about to set and making a shimmering golden stripe across the water as it does at the close of every day. That gold swath looks to a childlike part of ourselves like an inviting path, but of course children see all kinds of marvels in ordinary things. The real marvel is that as adults we can still sometimes respond as we did decades ago and interpret the streak of gold—or by now reddish-gold—as a roadway that leads from our confusion to a settled truth, or at least its temporary semblance.

I like Nescio's writing because it is at once utterly sad and also restrained. He never allows himself to stray into sentimentality—as Hemingway does, I'm afraid, in the novels if not in the short stories. Skyler has never read Nescio, which is not surprising. Neither he nor Hemingway is in his league. (And the only Faulkner he is likely to have heard of would be Craig, who played for a while for the Hagerstown Suns and is now coaching at some high school. William? Where did he play?)

But the ballplayer would not find the Dutchman congenial. Sad? Sure, but who isn't? Life is almost always disappointing. It may not be true but I remember reading that all the Nobel laureates in literature—every single one of them—have been clinically depressed. And they are a group that has been by and large successful. Well, mostly. Who were Eyvind Johnson, Erik Axel Karlfeldt, or Frans Eemil Sillanpää? (Usually, when they can't think of a worthy recipient they award it to some needy Scandinavian although sometimes, as in 1935, they don't even give one at all.)

I remember Tom Hanks saying in some movie, "There's no crying in baseball," which is true. Skyler would extend the prohibition, or, because he thinks baseball is the world, would extend it and forbid crying *tout court.* Playing in the minor leagues may not be glamorous but it does build character. I commend to you a clip on YouTube of Skyler giving a talk to some of the locals in Etzikom about what a thrill it was to play on Canada's national team in the competition for the World Baseball Cup so that he was playing for his country... All athletes say such predictable, ah-shucks stuff about how their victory was a result of team effort and every man played his best. But Stromsmoe seems actually to believe the words that he has been trained to mouth. This is another edgy instance of fiction turning into the truth. I daydream about some player answering a reporter's stupid question and telling the world what he really thinks—that they won because they got more runs than their opponents, who made a lot of errors and were generally stumblebums out there, that it was a long sweaty game, and what the fuck is there to say about it except get off my case and let me go take a shower? It'll never happen. The owners wouldn't stand for it and the candid young man would never again be allowed inside a ballpark even to sell hotdogs. (Etzikom? It's an Alberta hamlet, *vaut le detour* because of its windmill museum. It's about twelve miles east of Foremost, if that is of any help to you. And, I'm temped to say, fifteen miles west of Hintermost, but one can't have everything. I like to think of it as a quaint place with a corner restaurant: Sam 'n' Ella's—Fine Food.)

Stromsmoe isn't likely to approach such refreshing candor. (He'd spell it candour, of course.) He has drunk the Kool-Aid, as they say. (Correctly, it should be the Flavor-Aid, which is what Jim Jones put into the poison down in Jonestown, but that doesn't sound right even if it's true. So? So? It seems we have all drunk the Kool-Aid.) Skyler really believes the blather he is spouting about his pride in playing for his country. "O Canada, /Our home and native land! /True patriot love in all thy sons command. /With glowing hearts we see thee rise, /The True North strong and free!" But after the first two words, the Canuck fans lapse into English and French simultaneously, which is fair but unintelligible. Neither the Anglos nor the Franks will yield

precedence to the others and this is their demented solution, gib-
berish rather than clarity. Nobody can ever make out the words: "*Ô
Canada! But af! /Terre de nos aïeux, /Ton front est ceint de fleurons glo-
rieux! /Car ton bras sait porter l'épée, / Il sait porter la croix!*" (These
words do not mean that you carry an épée in your bra, which is smarter than just wearing a crucifix, although it would be lovely if they did.)
Anyway, Skyler's heart beats just a little faster at the sound and the
jumbled words and he really was proud to be playing for his home and
native land, God help him.

"Why are you picking on him? Why give him such a hard time?"
Nescio asks me in a whisper.

Why? What kind of question is that. *Hier ist nicht varoom.* That
was true in the concentration camps but it has always been true on
this side of the barbed wire, too. It is as he said. I noticed the strange
spelling of his name. That was enough. It was luck, good or bad, mine
or his. How many minor league players make it into novels? When
he's back in Alberta driving a snowplow (a ten-months-a-year job), he
can tell his buddies about it as they down a couple of cold Molson's.
If he ever finds out, that is. (I am fairly sure that this isn't the kind of
book he'd be likely to read. Or his friends, or their friends. Or any
Canadians, for that matter. Of course, I could translate the book into
French and then do a simultaneous recording of it in both languages.
It wouldn't be a novel any more (is it now?) but a "happening," a venture into a new and even sillier art form than heretofore. I could also
buy a dog and call him "Tofore" so I could shout, "Here, Tofore!" which
has a nice Henny Youngman brevity. ("Take my wife. Please.")

Youngman used to carry a violin, not to play it so much as wear it.
As Jack Benny did, too. It was a way of acknowledging the death of a
loftier dream than doing standup. Or I imagine that it could have been
an impish reference to the paintings of Mark Chagall who has violin-
ists floating through the air, each of them hoping one day to come to
earth and get a gig somewhere as standup comedian. "Good evening,
ladies and germs. I just flew in from Vitebsk and boy are my arms
tired!"

Nescio says nothing, but inasmuch as he is a character here, I
know with some certainty that he is wondering whether I have been
taking my medications. His *Weltbild* is of necessity Dutch, and his
work is a demonstration that Dutch stolidity is no defense against despair. Mine, perhaps, demonstrates that mania and logorrhea don't
work well either. Or that given enough time, those monkeys will stop
trying to reproduce Dickens and just do ... monkeybusiness. (An honest expression of their views about life an art that none of us will rec-

ognize, let alone admire.) Or, to give it its more pretentious name, *"le baarbouinisme."*

I tell him that if I were worried about people's feelings, I'd be obliged to consider my own, which would be a disagreeable undertaking. We do what we do and we get what we get, which is rarely what we deserve. Your pen name was at least in part to afford you the freedom to assert sad and unpleasant truths, no?

"It was, indeed. And I was anxious not to seem unserious. Un-Dutch."

I understand.

"But as I look back on it now, it seems perhaps unnecessary and even vain. As an author, I was altogether obscure. There were members of my own family who had no idea I was a writer, even though I had mentioned it to several of them. Or they knew I had a hobby and would sit in the study sometimes and write things, but they never expressed any interest in reading any of them. Had they done so, they might have asked me questions about what they had read. Stupid questions or more probably just irrelevant ones. And I would have had to conceal the disappointment I could not have kept from feeling. One takes such pains, such risks, and exerts such effort, and the true fiction is that anybody cares or even partially understands. The reader is fictional."

I agree with him (which is hardly surprising) but I see a corollary that had not previously occurred to me. The worst writers, the ones with the least imaginative capacities, have real audiences. Because they need them. Jackie Susann, Danielle Steele, Harold Robbins, Stephen King and their like are all empiricists who are authors only because the public says they are. On the higher level where some of us try to operate, there can never be such confirmation. We are snow leopards high up in the mountains subsisting on food that is mostly imaginary.

And Stromsmoe's fans are imaginary, too. He has to ignore the rubes in the Flying Squirrels Diamond and imagine himself in AT&T Park on Willie Mays Plaza where a much larger audience is waiting for him to hit a ball far enough out of the park to land in the water of the bay where the souvenir hunters wait in their boats.

This makes it hard for him to keep his eye on the ball in either of the games in which he is appearing simultaneously, which may be why his average is only .210.

I look around, apprehensive lest Stromsmoe make another of his appearances. Nescio will turn his head slightly to the left and raise his eyes, letting me know that he was right and that I should not have continued to tease the poor Canadian. I should not have picked (on) him in the first place. It was unworthy of me. Or more tellingly, it was too easy. He is on third base and looks uncomfortable in his baseball get-up, the hat of which is particularly unsuited to his 1920's Triestine notions of style. He knows nothing about the game and has never heard of Abbott and Costello, but *Ecco come va.* He is also uncomfortable making his posthumous appearance here in our book (I include you, too, imaginary readers).

I discovered this weekend in an exhibit of protest art at the Boston Museum of Fine Arts an empty, open coffin. The explanatory placard had a schedule of the days and hours during which Lazaro Saavedra, the artist, would appear and lie in the coffin, as if dead. A prehumous appearance. I supposed it probably happens. With the curator's permission, however, the artist could provide a stand-in, couldn't he? An impersonator. Who in Boston would recognize Saavedra or be able to spot an impersonator. Even the artist himself is an impostor, because he isn't dead but is pretending to be. And seeing him—or someone—lying there, we are invited to feel sympathy, not only for him but for all the sufferers of Cuba, which he comes from. Or was it some Central American country? It doesn't matter. Indeed, we needn't limit our pity to the Caribbean and Central America. *Mors ubique est,* no? Why not therefore mourn them all? Or at least think of them, although, when we do, we think of them alive because they don't have much to say to us in their actual state of defunctitude. We pretend, but they do, too. In the event, Saavedra had visa problems and never showed up, so the public had to imagine a body in the coffin—particularly during those hours when there was supposed to be one and wasn't. Those times would have been more particularly poignant, but that would only be apparent to history of art majors and other such exquisites. My own suspicion is that there was never such a person. A dealer in New York or Boston arranged for the work to be exhibited at the MFA, thought up the artist's joke name, and had a coffin shipped to the museum. Lazaro has to have been invented for the occasion, too. (Which would make it a nonce, which is an invented word like wug, blicket, dax, toma, pimwit, zav, speff, tulver, gazzer, fendle, and tupa.) [Make a sestina out of any six of them, why don't you?]

Back home, I took a liberty and imagined Nescio lying there in the coffin. And then Svevo. And then, of course, myself, which was less depressing than I might have expected.

It was something of a relief when I visited the museum's men's room (relief is the point of such visits) and found no placard announcing when Sr. Saavedra would appear to sit in one of the stalls and make his position clear to the world that Cuba, Central America, and perhaps the entire world is incrementally excremental. But I did think briefly of the possibility, which means that he or the prankster dealer in New York had won.

But why Saavedra? Because it is Cervantes' last name that nobody uses or even remembers? Because it is Daniel Ortega's last name? There is also an Indy car driver from Bogota named Sebastian Saavedra, but he is an unlikely reference and if we ever think of him again, even for a nanosecond, he and Stromsmoe will find each other, get on famously, and maybe open up a sports bar in Etzikom offering sandwiches that have mysterious names: the Speff, the Tulver, and the ever-popular triple-decker Fendle (with the duck pate).

It would appear that I have written myself into a cul de sac, which is not a grand cru St. Émilion, but ought to be. That is an *Appellation d'origine contrôlée,* but if you remove the acute accent from over the E you get the name of a restaurant in Fort Worth and are on the Trinity River rather than the Dordogne. Just from that little mark there. Vertiginous. And a bit fruity with a delicate suggestion of huckleberries. (So you see? (Culs de sac are where attorneys general generally live.)

"You seem to be spinning your wheels just a bit," Svevo suggests. And of course he is right. I know what I'm doing, however—which is trying to stop time. Our day-to-day lives are like garbage chutes in old-fashioned apartment buildings in which malodorous stuff comes hurtling down at random moments to some repository far below. The only way to escape these iterative downpours is to leave the building. Or stay put and contrive to freeze time, which is what happens with writing. I can posit a subject and then, not immediately but after lunch, or even perhaps tomorrow morning supply the predicate for which it has been held in suspension. Not impatiently, because patience and impatience assume the movement of and the knowledge of passing time, but in a serenity I can almost imagine. More astonishing than these pauses in composition are those occasions when I can set the manuscript's clock back, return to an earlier page from yesterday or last week, and remove one of those distracting adverbs about which, as you have noticed, I am often too lenient so that they have maintained themselves since the first or second draft.

I venture to imagine that there must have been something like this refuge from life and time that drew Nescio and Svevo to the *secrétaire.* If they were as shrewd as I believe them to have been, they would have let it be known that there was to be as little noise as possible, as few distractions from the work at hand, which demanded an entirely focused concentration. (It doesn't: think of all those Hilde Johnson types batting out copy on their noisy typewriters in a city room in Chicago in which the Ritz Brothers could have performed without attracting much notice.) The trance, if it happens, can withstand all kinds of racket. If it doesn't happen, the writer can always blame anything or anybody else. Sibelius used to prohibit any humming or whistling within a thousand meters of his house because he didn't want alien melody lines intruding on his ever so delicate sensibilities. Was this a joke? Did he fall for it himself after a while? It is difficult to imagine any real noise anywhere in Finland except the occasional screech of the cranes flying overhead. The entire country is one of those snow globes that you can shake to produce the whiteout of a storm. There's a herd of reindeer. And a tiny house, in which a Sibelius one might see through the wrong end of a telescope is playing a minuscule piano, a Kleinway, perhaps.

No? No.

But why not? Is it not the wish of any intelligent person to free himself of the vicissitudes of time and change? We order our lives, devote ourselves to projects that may extend beyond the span we have been allotted, and act as though we were ignorant of the most fundamental characteristic of the mortal condition, which is mortality. And then, from the sky, a bolt of lightning that Lucretius says could not possibly come from Zeus because there would be no reason for him to destroy his own temples—except forgetfulness or bad aim, neither of which comports well with godliness.

Our struggle against contingency and serendipity is a rebellion that is destined to fail, as we well know. But we fight nonetheless with our weapons of sophistication and buffoonery because those are all we have. One can't kill time but one can contrive to pass it. Like a kidney stone.

"Right!"

Who is speaking? Can we never be rid of him? It's Stromsmoe, who has been sitting on the bench with a learned patience. "There isn't any time in baseball either. Games go on, theoretically forever. Now that there are lights, they don't even have to call them for darkness and they go on and on. Eight games have gone to twenty-two innings and have lasted for seven hours or more. But as long as the score is tied at the end of an inning, they go on to another one."

And that is your idea of timelessness?

"It sure as hell feels like it, which is as good as."

I suppose so. Tennis, too, I'd imagine.

"Not anymore. They have those sudden-death playoffs."

It is a nice metaphor.

Stromsmoe doesn't comment on metaphors. It would be surprising—but also out of character—if he did. It isn't that I dislike surprises. This manuscript is full of them. I never expected, for example, to encounter a tiny Jean Sibelius inside a snow globe, playing a tinkly arrangement of *Valse Triste* on his itsy-bitsy piano. But in an altogether irrelevant display of fastidiousness and responsibility let me suggest that such a talent on Stromsmoe's part would be too far out of character to go unexplained. And I'm disinclined to do that. I am stopped short by the short stop (if he could chuck wood).

The opposing manager, of the Akron Rubber Ducks say, waits for Stromsmoe to come to the plate. Then he switches pitchers, bringing in a southpaw. And Stromsmoe is yanked without having had a single swing of the bat and is done for the day because he can't come back. (Oh, how I wish.)

It can happen, just as it can happen that he gets the count to three and two and then keeps hitting foul balls. For the rest of the afternoon. They don't keep records of the number of foul balls in a single at bat, but Phillies outfielder Richie Ashburn hit fourteen once. One of them hit a woman in the stands and broke her nose. Then, as she was being carried out on a stretcher, another hit her, although not in the nose. What are the odds?

And with books, I expect that Flaubert holds the record for the most revisions of a single sentence, although nobody keeps track of that category either. He'd wake up in the morning, read some of *Bovary*, take out a comma, and then have lunch. In the afternoon session, he'd put the comma back. A good day's work? A nonsense? Remember that he was a writer of fiction and could have made this up to impress his gullible friends, which is what I prefer to believe. It might well have been a simple exaggeration of his actual habits but enough to have departed altogether from the uninteresting realm of the real. (If he was going over it that many times, you'd think he'd have noticed that whenever Emma is feeling horny, the way he announces it is to have a wind ruffling a wheat field. Once, or even twice, okay. But it is frequent enough so as to blemish an otherwise pretty good book.)

We were, if I remember correctly, talking about vicissitudes. Dopey events that happen and nudge our lives a little or crush them altogether. They are not the results of anything and certainly they are neither punishments nor rewards. They are not part of any plot but are just incidents that follow one another on the string of time. They are the beads we strung together in kindergarten (shouldn't a German noun be capitalized?) without paying any attention to the colors. Whatever came to hand was fine. A sappy writer of children's books (or a writer of sappy children's books) might bestow intelligence on the beads in the box and let them suppose that the kindergarten kid was . . . God! (I have no idea how the book comes out: perhaps the little beads wise up and realize that their God has a lot of limitations. Or maybe the kid performs some kind of miracle, finding a red bead that has rolled under the radiator, say, and reuniting it with the green bead that was its best friend and has been grieving. All the beads in the box are converted and now offer prayers to little Stanley to bless them and keep them; may Stanley make his face shine upon them and be gracious unto them; may Stanley lift up his countenance to them and give them peace.

In the cartoon version of the book, there will be an accompaniment of some drecky pious music. It isn't that children have inherently bad taste. "They've got to be taught," as Oscar Hammerstein wrote in his saccharine ditty about how racial prejudice is a bad thing. (Really!) And miraculously anyone who ever saw *South Pacific* was immediately cured of bigotry just because of that song.)

What is delightful about language is its wiggle room. I find a tiny chink and through it I can invite you into an alternate universe. Or at least another dimension. There are thirteen I believe, but I don't believe it, as with so much in life. *Credo quia absurdum!* is a quip of Tertullian's and, while you may know the phrase, there are many fewer (or fewer many) who can claim to be on a first-name basis with Quintus Septimius Florens Tertullianus, that old Carthaginian cut-up. He was onto something, though. If a thing is self evident, then there's not much standing in the way of your believing it. You'll never get to heaven with that kind of caution—or even believe in heaven, for that matter.

Quintus was a Montanist, which has nothing to do with mountaineering. The church rejected Montanism and called it a heresy, so he would have done better to keep quiet. It had nothing to do with Yves Montand either, I'm all but certain. But silence is often preferable to speech; relying on it one can get away with a whole hell of a lot. Think of all those monks who maintain silence for months at a time or even years. Nobody knows what they are thinking, right? They could be Montanists, or Gnostics, or Arianists--any of those heterodox types. But they do not give themselves away, as most of us do most of the time. Wisdom is all very well, but discretion is simpler and just as effective. Maintain a solemn countenance and keep your mouth shut. Your associates may find you spooky but they will respect you and even fear you.

The other option is to spout nonsense as copiously as you can.

Here and there you can inject small but absurd truths to which few will object because they never know whether you're kidding and will give you the benefit of the doubt. Doubt is nothing like belief, may be its opposite even, but they both get you to the same place. DeFuniak Springs, or Shawinigan Falls. They sound ridiculous but for that reason they have stayed in my head for years. They may be perfectly pleasant places in which to live, work, play, and retire. When I was a kid, it was Shawinigan Falls. Now it's Shawinigan Cataracts and they have a team in the Quebec Major Junior Hockey League. The *Cataractes*, actually, so as not to annoy the fussy Francophones. (*Allo? Allo? Ne quittez pas!*) Ideally, every player should have cataracts, which would make their games more interesting to watch. (Against the Perkins School for the Blind, maybe.)

And DeFuniak Springs? It's just a lovely name. Frederick R. De Funiak was a president of the Pensacola and Atlantic railroad, and one of his workers thought it would be a good idea to name the lake and then the town after him. It was a joke name, after all, but the man who wore it was unlikely to object. The men building the line—in that unbearable heat and humidity and with those swarms of mosquitoes the size of sparrows--hated the place and took great satisfaction in inflicting such a name on such a place. The enthusiasts of the Chautauqua movement picked it out as a winter headquarters and they, or their successors, omitted the space after the particule but the kept the F in the majuscule--which only made the name sillier. That is so nonsensical that you would bet on it, if you could find some sport willing to take odds against the existence of such a city. Jean-Paul Sartre? Or Belmondo? Or Marat? (Or Jones, for that matter.) They're all dead now, though, and have come to believe in *néant*.

Is that absurdum enough for you to give credence to it? Or conversely, is it too absurd for you to doubt? Relax. *Dolce far niente*. Let us imagine that it is an eclectic restaurant in Toronto's energetic Financial District. Let us further assert that it's a bit pricey, charging $22.00 for a cob salad, and seven dollars more if you want chicken in it. (To be fair, we're talking here about Canadian dollars, the looneys and twoneys that still add up.) Let us go there, you and me, into a beauteous evening, calm and free. Don't say anything! Keep a solemn countenance. People will fear you, respect you, and perhaps one day, come to love you. You betcha. And the one of the Jean-Pauls may appear to pick up your check.

The Chautauqua movement is interesting primarily because it has three *u*'s in it. It is also a curious phenomenon in American (pardon the expression) culture. Education? Self-improvement? Who could be against those? First of all the movement was for Sunday School teachers, but they raised their sights and imagined themselves providing the equivalent of a college education to the poor who couldn't afford those pricey tuitions. (In 1898, a year at Harvard cost $150.00, and, no, I haven't misplaced the decimal point.) So what we're really looking at here is uplift. Ambition (which is almost always overweening). Perfectionism. Or to get down to the nitty and gritty, these protestant do-gooders were hoping to curb the appetite of their flocks for drinking, gambling, dancing, whoring, and theater-going (honest!) and get them to stay home and read books, although presumably not collections of plays.

It is easy to make fun of this. But it's our country right or wrong. And as Quentin Compson says, I think in *The Sound and the Fury*, "I don't hate the South. I don't. I don't hate it. Really, really, I don't." [Repeat *ad lib* until the words have lost all meaning.] It's hard to disown, is what he's saying. But did he try, really, really hard? *L'urlo e il furore* would be the Italian version, of the novel, of course, but also of the opera, which is pleasing to imagine, with a mad scene right at the start as goofy Benjy describes a golf game. Or does the worst ringside analysis in the history of sportscasting: "One would hit and then the other one would hit." Or is all this wrong? Or is it *Absalom, Absalom* in which Quentin comes back from Harvard to do assert his negative claim? Don't worry about it; try not to think of it. Then try not to think of Belgium. All those rashis in ashrams in India have with greatest difficulty trained themselves not to think of Belgium for days at a time. It is a spiritual exercise and one can make steady progress toward that tranquility to which we all aspire.

First, you don't think of Belgium and then, with your breath carefully controlled, you manage to extinguish all thoughts of any of the Benelux countries. And then, and then? The entire continent of Europe disappears into the primordial tohu and bohu (from which it arose--without the music of Richard Strauss, I am afraid. With our luck it will turn out to have been something embarassing from somebody like Emil Waldteufel or John Phillip Souza. Or both, alternating so that first one would play and then the other would play, the first few bars of each piece serving to rid the ear of the horrific dying quivers of the one that went before. An earworm, that would be, which is a calque for *Ohrwurm*, and we have an epidemic infestation of them. (Here is the one advantage that the tone-deaf have over the rest of us.)

An elitist, you say? A snob? Let me put it this way. When the Boston PBS stations is having its fundraisers and wants to attract the largest audiences with their most popular and appealing programs,

what do they put on? Reruns of Laurence Welk and that woman with
the bubble machine (Alice Lon, actually, "the champagne lady," whom,
if memory serves, Welk fired for showing too much leg). Nobody ever
lost money by underestimating the advice of P. T. Barnum. A snob
would have the right to sneer, which he would almost certainly exercise. But he might be redeemed, at least in part, by the pangs of pity
in his heart for the sordidness of the demonstration. Who can bear
to think of the Polka Hall of Fame in Euclid, Ohio, in which Welk is, of
course, one of the honorees?

Lawrence Welk,
Paul Wendinger,
 Henry "Will" Wilczynski,
"Whoopee John" Wilfahrt,
Gene Wisniewski,
Bernie Wyte Witkowski
Joe Wojkiewicz
Sylvester "Shep" Wolan
Frank Yankovic
Chester "Chet" Zablocki

What is even more bothersome, as "Whoopee John" Wilfahrt is
eager to point out, is Welk's lapse from authenticity to a kind of slick-
ness of which no one else on the list could approve. They were or are
grown men and understood about money and the necessity of making a living. They knew about responsibily—one must look after the
whole band after all and think of what is best for all of them together.
But a "champagne lady"? Whoopee John shakes his had and says, "Jesus Fucking Christ, you think we had champagne ladies back in the
Bohemian forests? I was a kid of ten when my mother bought me my
first accordion for a buck and a half. I practiced in the grain bin until
the noises I was making began to sound a little like music. But what I
was getting out of that squeeze box in the grain bin was a lot less annoying than what Welk produced for most of his life. He gave the rest
of us a bad name."

In fairy tales, the woods are dark, dangerous, frightening places,
but in their depths, there are pleasant peasants, squeezing out their
cheerful polkas as if the beasts, the robbers, the witches, and the ogres
were not hovering all around them. We can easily enough translate
those cute fairytale figures into the politics (read, bloodthirsty mad-
ness) of Eastern Europe. But with an almost heroic denial, they belted
out their cheerful tunes as if the world were a wedding. (Extra credit
if you recognize that last phrase as an echo of the title of a Delmore
Schwartz book of short stories.) Small wonder that these Polka Hall-

of-Famers don't feel comfortable about Welk's having joined them. His music doesn't have that authenticity which could be described as a thin-ice sparkle of gaiety over a deep lake of death and danger.

Am I right? Whoopee John doesn't answer but only nods vaguely, either in agreement or perhaps because he is sleepy and maybe a little drunk. They brought their accordions, concertinas, bandoneons, and organetti with them when they came to America from Slovenia, Slovakia, Slavonia, Albania, Moldavia, Freedonia, Sardinia, Sicilia and all those picturesque, grim places. Streets paved with gold were not what they were looking for. Streets that were not, from time to time, buried in mud or set ablaze would be quite satisfactory. They had few illusions and knew they would be pouring molten steel, mining for coal, paving roads, or at best herding cows somewhere out in the empty countryside around Shawinigan Falls, because they understood that life is hard wherever you are. Schnapps and music offer at least some temporary relief.

Whoopee John raises his head and then his eyebrows. He looks to be asking a question. What could he want to know? I think he thinks I ought to have offered him a beer by now. (He is my character and he can only think what I think he thinks.)

A beer?

"Sure," he says, but what he means is that it's about time.

I ask the tavern-keeper for a Bohemia Obscura, which is a fine dark beer brewed in Mexico, originally by Bohemian immigrants. National Bohemian is better known and is an okay lager but it is unremarkable, a product now of the Pabst Company in Los Angeles rather than the original Natty Boh guys in Baltimore. It doesn't have a whole lot of flavor so it is best served icy-cold to wash down mouthfuls of crab. (The National Brewing Company are the guys who invented the six-pack, which could just as easily been four or eight, but isn't because they set the standard back in the forties. Four would have been for pantywaists and eight would have been for pigs, who, if they were devout, could by two of the six-packs if they wanted to.)

I am certain that Whoopee Joe doesn't know any of this and doesn't much care. Beer is for drinking; talking about it is ridiculous. He picks up his schooner and takes a sip. (He is also uninterested in the oddment that an Australian schooner is smaller than a pint while, a Canadian one is larger. In Britain, meanwhile, a schooner is a large sherry glass, because sherry was delivered from Jerez in schooners. A smaller sherry glass is a clipper.) Old Joe has a beer-foam mustache which he doesn't bother to wipe away. A friend can give you a swallow of beer from his glass while you are up there performing, but he is not going to wipe away the foam on your upper lip, and you can't take one hand off the accordion to do that yourself. So you leave it and even get used to it there. It becomes a sign that you are not some goddamn amateur. Or a sell-out like Lawrence Welk. (My stupid spellcheck keeps correcting his name to whelk, to which I have no strong objection. A whelk is a kind of sea-snail, actually and, if you put its shell to your ear you can hear, albeit very faintly, "A one an' a two!" But only beneath a full moon and between the breakings of the waves on the beach that generally drown out its ridiculous and barely audible call.)

Life doesn't have chapters or even breaks and novels shouldn't either. But as a kindness to the few who have managed to get this far, I suggest that this is a good place to pause, freshen your drink, take a nap, pee, or whatever. I seem to be off on a new tangent. What sense does that make? Geometry makes no distinctions about the age of tangents, or not as far as I am able to remember.

I lived in New York for a while in a cheap apartment on the Upper West Side, before it was gentrified, and one of my most vivid memories was of the electric clock on our kitchen wall. I came into the kitchen one night, turned the light on, and saw three or four cockroaches scurrying toward the clock. Odd. So I took the clock down from the wall and found that it was entirely covered by a swarm of them that had been drawn to it, I suppose, by the heat of the mechanism. Horrified, I unplugged the clock and, holding it by the cord, carried it out to the incinerator chute in the hall to chuck it down into the hell where it belonged. Why do I mention this? It is the vivid demonstration of photophobia that seems to be a convenient trope for much of our experience in life. (Tropes will swarm, too, but not often in clocks.) A flash of light, and truths scatter, fleeing from our attention. "*Mehr Licht! Gib mir mehr Licht!*" Goethe quipped, but it is not always such a good idea. When you turn on the light you have no idea what you are going to see: as likely as not, it will be disgusting.

In Hamlet, after the players perform, Claudius says, "Give me some light, away!" to which Polonius adds, "Lights! Lights! Lights!" but this time the audience knows what the king would see if he were enlightened. And with Oedipus what comes to light in Thebes is blinding and, to make sure we understand that, the tragedian has the poor, ruined man destroy his eyes. "And God saw the light, that it was good: and God divided the light from the darkness." It doesn't say that the darkness wasn't good, but without it the light doesn't mean much. It was the separation, I think, that deserved that divine expression of approbation.

I have been resisting for some time the admission that this entire work, all three volumes of it, may be an exercise in obfuscation. Nowhere have I mentioned that my sister died a couple of months ago. And that I was not particularly upset. I hadn't spoken to her in more than twenty years and now that silence will stretch out to eternity. I am again an only child, as I have wanted to be since I was four. Our parents may be dead, but I have them to myself again. I should feel some twinge of guilt about this but I don't. I have been avoiding any mention of the subject. And shall continue to do so. But I am willing to allow that it may be the concrete wall at the back of the stage that the sets conceal. The wall is uninteresting and irrelevant, except perhaps for its subtle acoustic effect, and few members of the audience will ignore the actors and the play in order to imagine what the wall may be like. So to hell with it, right?

I shouldn't have said anything. Forget it. If the text resonates slightly differently, you can blame me for my unwarranted and unwanted confession. If I were you, I'd think of the author now as even more insensitive and chuckleheaded than before. Or, more to the point, I suggest that you enjoy the awkwardness of it, as you do in the summer at the beach when you see some poor vacationer mincing along on the hot sand. It looks as though he is dancing but he is in pain, each step searing the soles of his feet. What a dope! He could have bought a pair of cheap flip-flops and avoided this suffering but he didn't, and his progression toward the water is, let us admit it, comical, almost Chaplinesque.

So, *sur le pont d'Avignon*...

And where is Stromsmoe, now that I could use him? He has been offended by my exploitation of his funny name and his unimpressive career. There are worse careers in baseball. There were men who tried out for the Richmond Flying Squirrels, walk-ons I think they are called, and who failed. Ran to catch a fly ball, turned, were temporarily blinded by the sun (*mehr Licht!*), and missed it. An easy chance and they muffed it. And got sent home, their dream ruined but their lives, more probably than not, spared the further disappointments that Stromsmoe's flesh is heir to. He is the oldest player in the infield, old enough to know the score, translating his average and his age into a fairly reliable projection of his future, and yet he is unfazed. How does he slog along on his hard road? Does he pray to Stanley, the kindergarten kid the colored beads worship? No, but he has his rituals. For instance, when he gets a hit, he keeps on wearing that pair of socks until he gets another one. For luck? Or to punish himself as the socks begin to reek, first of old cheese and then of dead bodies? I have no idea, because I can't decide which is worse. There are ways, after all, in which the game allows for the passage of time. And its shadow, which is history. Or, to put it with less grandiosity, statistics. You come to the plate late in the season and you get a hit, but it doesn't do you much good because of the weight of all those earlier strikeouts. You get two hits in a game, which is very good, and it only nudges you up a couple of percentage points (calculated in the thousandths). And every damned morning, you're a day older, slower, weaker, and with eyes that are less and less keen.

If I were to grab him with one of those illegal choke holds, he'd break it and probably kill me. Or he might just answer the question and the truth would be that, no, these things don't bother him much. Not yet, anyway. They bother me though. I just walked to the farmer's market that happens every Monday in a parking lot about five blocks from my apartment. I had to stop and rest twice on the way. And I couldn't quite manage to stay steady, so I looked to be drunk or perhaps the victim of some dread neurotic ailment (not implausibly tertiary syphilis). I got there, bought a couple of bottles of one guy's terrific eggplant-and-tomato spaghetti sauce, got a baguette from the High Rise booth, asked a couple of produce guys for breakfast radishes. Neither had any, but one, who had heard of them, said that the myth was that the French eat them for breakfast. (Myths also say that they eat snails and frogs' legs, but that doesn't make them any less true.) I had to take a cab back home. Old? Frail? Fading? I should say so. And why shouldn't Stromsmoe worry about these things, too? He is a lot younger than I am, but he lives in his body as I mostly don't have to. Sorry, Skyler.

Sorry, reader. Another lapse, I fear. But at least I had a stick figure (never mind his .220 average) upon whom to project my troubles. My guess is that this is what appealed to Dick Schaap, who may have been a jock-sniffer but wasn't altogether stupid. He could see in the brief careers of these guys a vivid representation of the life we aspire to. The stardom, the fame. But then they lose it and wind up in the men's room of the Fontainebleau handing out towels and restocking the ice in the urinals. They age and turn into Palookas and stumblebums, which appeals to the nastiness in all of us. It's the penalty they pay. It was all metaphor, although he would have tried to dismiss the word. (I never met a metaphor for which I was sorry.) Schaap was smart enough not to be too smart.

Although it pains me to have to agree with him about anything, I can see the vividness of the drama demonstrating itself again and again. Alex Rodriguez, with all those steroids, hit like a sonofabitch but the injections may well have caused hypogonadism, which the doctors call among themselves "the teeny-weeny-peeny disease." Think of it: Madonna could blow him and floss at the same time. (Wouldn't that be a gas on YouTube?) Was the improvement in his batting skills worth it? He was pretty good without the drugs, but he wanted more, he wanted to be a superstar and world famous. Well, he's famous.

More often than not, these athletes, who know nothing about finance (some can hardly add and subtract even with a calculator), lose all their money to bad investments by crooked managers, who are anyway skimming, or they just piss it away and wind up owing more back taxes than they have left. (This will not be Stromsmoe's problem). Some of them get by signing things, which is an abrupt comedown (come-uppance?), but it's a cash business and the IRS has a hard time keeping track of it. (Do the Richmond Flying Squirrels even have baseball cards? Well, baseballs then. I doubt that Skyler gets asked all that often and, when he is, I'd think he'd be too flattered to charge.

Booksellers have signings, too, with authors reading a little and then inscribing books. The object isn't just to promote the writer who is making an appearance but to generate foot traffic, which is good even if they don't buy his book. The bookstore has ordered maybe thirty copies, which they can send back. The author signs nine on a good evening. And from the store's pile, he signs maybe ten more, not because he has any expectations of buyers wanting a copy with a "Signed by the Author" sticker on the front. No, authors are smart enough to know that a signed book is "defaced" and the store can no longer return it for credit. (You see, Skyler, there are indignities you have never imagined. Into each life a little shit must fall, which is how the line may have first occurred to Longfellow.) Nescio would not have appeared for book signings, because they didn't exist back then. It used to be the author's job to write, the publisher's job to publish, and the booksellers job to sell. That worked well enough until everybody got greedy. But the idea of Nescio at a table with a line of prospective readers holding his book in their hands is amusing. Would he have worn a ski mask or a paper bag over his head? Did he sign with a big question mark—and maybe the date? Wouldn't that have been too easy to forge?

The desire of the customer is to contrive a kind of intimacy with the author, unmediated by any text, which is the only thing interesting about him. The author, for his part, doesn't want to share himself out in tiny pieces. His books may be available to the public but his life is his own. This is one motive for pseudonymity. And it doesn't mean that the author is so pleased with himself, but more likely the reverse is true. He wants to keep his failings to himself. As Nescio says, in a short, memorable paragraph, "Now my spirit can abandon my damned self and rise strait up into the sky like blue smoke on a windless summer night, while a distant cow sorrowfully moos."

The aspiration is both unusual and recognizably true. What is most impressive, however, is how he invests himself so intensely into imagining the moment and conjuring up its details that he can hear the mooing of a distant cow. A nervy thing to put in there, it gives weight to the loftiness and persuades us. We can imagine the cow and her sound, and retroactively, the rest of the sentence.

But inscriptions. Some seventeenth century poet—Waller, maybe or Wither?—signed almost all of his books. Hardly anyone bought them, so he gave them away to friends and acquaintances. The curious result is that in the rare book trade, an unsigned Waller is worth more than an inscribed one, because of its rarity.

What are signatures, anyway? A personal imprint of some kind? Isn't the text enough of a personal imprint. You read a book and, if you love it, it stays with you. That's what you keep. The inscribed book carries no more of the writer's being than the scrawled name on the title page. (Or flyleaf, but I prefer the title page.) "Do you write with a fountain pen or do you type?" (As if the impliment were what had enabled the book and if only you had a fountain pen like that you, too, could be an author.) What difference does it make? Why in hell do you want to know? Shut up, why don't you?

I learned only recently that my dead sister hadn't spoken to her daughter either (my niece) for twenty years. One could say that my sister brought out the Cistercian impulse in members of the family: the Order of the Cistercians of the Strict Observance, no less. It was reassuring to hear about this disconnection. It allowed me to suppose that I might not have been the crazy one.

Is that true? Or did I make it up just now, like the moo of Nescio's cow, for its anchoring capacity? I don't think it matters to any of you, but if I were a reader I'd assume it was not altogether invented—although I might well be wrong.

It occurs to me that even better than pseudonymity or anonymity is silence. Novelists work with whatever they have to make a simulacrum of lived experience, and their own experience is conveniently at hand. Still, using these details means sharing them, which isn't altogether comfortable. Nescio has a story, "Little Poet," which is awkward in English because we have few diminutive suffixes. The *ie* at the end of doggie or cookie or dearie or daddy is one of these, and its effect is to make the noun more intimate. But there is nothing to be done to poet that isn't insulting (like poetaster). Anyway, the little poet is making a poem in his head. Or he is seeing his life as a narrative poem. He does not have to pick up a pencil because his art is entirely mental. That would be convenient. Nescio realized, and envied, its possibilities. There it is. No retyping, proofreading, submissions, rejections, reviews... None of that tediousness. I am not far from there, at the border of absurdity where most of the reading public does not venture to approach and those who do are bored or outraged. But it is quiet here, and sometimes I can hear the whisper of water over the stones of the Tomhanack. (Can you? Can you canoe? It was an ad for an inexpensive fragrance for men who wanted to smell like L. L. Bean customers. They still make it, a refined, spicy, lavender-amber concoction with a masculine blend of brisk citrus and accents of lemon and oak moss. It is recommended for daytime wear. I wonder what kind of women it is designed to attract: those hearty, horsey, outdoor types, who played field hockey in college.)

The little poet liked to contemplate such curiosities. The attractiveness of the idea of sports is much greater than that of the sports themselves. If no one but polo players bought Ralph Lauren's products, their sales would be minuscule. But the number of men who dream of themselves up on a horse with a mallet and one of those swell hats... Enormous. Lauren's Big Pony fragrance collection offers personalized bottles, yes with your name on them, in the Red, the Blue, the Black, and the Double Black which comes in a deep noir bottle and opens with mango and cocoanut and then reveals intensive spicy notes of Indonesian nutmeg, pepper and fried coffee with a touch of spice (cardamom and fir). You can have a beer belly, toothpick arms a wispy fringe of hair, and a beaten down look that most men who are paying attention develop in their fifties, but you can slap on a little of this elixir after shaving and you are a classy dude on a pony with a row of those blonde horsey girls looking at you with admiration and daring you to take a shot at the goal they are defending. (The fried coffee alone, which I suppose you could put in your shoes, will probably not do this for you.)

Ralph Lauren sued the U. S. Polo Association for using "his" logo of the guy on the horse with the mallet. The association pointed out that they had real horses and mallets and had been playing the game for decades. I love the idea of a fiction suing a reality for infringing on its logo. That would have delighted the little poet who of course bears a certain resemblance to Nescio and to me and other like-minded readers. The Polo Association, ably represented by Pimwit, Tulver, and Dax, won the case and celebrated by licensing their design to Sears, which puts them on tee shirts and sweaters in a size slightly larger than what Lauren uses. (Sometimes, as Nescio and Svevo can attest, businessmen do have a sense of humor.)

Those who cannot distinguish between the real and the imaginary are called psychotics. Or saints. The voices Jeanne d'Arc heard were not coming from St. Margaret, St. Catherine, the Archangel Michael, or anywhere outside her head but she believed them anyway. Charles VII (*le Bien-Servi*) didn't much care where they were from and was pleased to be crowned in Reims. And who would argue with him? He was the king, after all.

--Rabbi, my son thinks he is a chicken.

--Bring him to me. I may be able to cure him.

--But, Rabbi, we need the eggs.

There it is at its basic level. Reality has its claims, but so does the delusional, and one would have to be crazy to reject the benefits of fictions. Serious men considered Jeanne's case and differed about it. The English burned her at the stake, having convicted her of heresy, which had nothing whatever to do with her voices and her military triumphs but was limited to her offense of cross-dressing. (That, at any rate, was their story.) Twenty years later Pope Callixtus III held a retrial and posthumously vindicated her, which didn't do her any good but made a nice ending to the Church's version of her story. The narrative, as they have always understood, is far more important than the life. (If you believe this, good; if not, you are going to hell—or else to Santiago de Campostella. *Buen camino!*) Callixtus III, a Borgia, is otherwise best remembered for his Bull *Inter Caetera*, which reaffirmed the right of the Portuguese to enslave infidel Africans. When it comes to bizarrerie, those popes are infallible. You have to hand it to them, or they'll just take it.

I can't floss anymore without thinking of Madonna (you may now have the same trouble, and I apologize for that), but this morning, to keep her out of my head I was wondering about tonsorial, which comes from the Latin tondēre, which means to cut or clip. Is a haircut, therefore, a tonsorectomy? Or tonsorotomy? Either one sounds very serious. And both make spellcheck gag, but I generally take that as a compliment. Is it the case, though, that much thinking is merely intended to distract us from the unpleasantness that lurks below, ready to take any opportunity to appear in all its horribilitude? The fancy name for a haircut (which, having thought of it, I shall probably use now) was a way of getting rid of Madonna and A-Rod, whose job it was, and they performed it well, to keep me from thinking about my dead sister. I don't know why she and her daughter were estranged. It wasn't any of my business and isn't now. But because I don't know the details, I wonder about them from time to time, feeling sympathetic to my poor niece. It is bad enough to lose a sister whom one has already lost. For a daughter to have such a complicated experience with her mother, whatever the reason, must have been even more painful. The wound would have been deeper and the scar tissue more of an impediment than anything I can claim or admit to.

Is it not better to be contemplating the invention of "tonsorotomy"? There is a barbershop in Natick that calls itself Fanara's Tonsorial Parlor, which makes fun of itself, I do believe. "Barbershop" is already uppity enough, inasmuch as it signifies a place that trims beards, even though most people go to one to have their tonsures trimmed. Or "styled," which is losing its meaning, too. In W, an upscale hotel in Miami Beach, the maids put a sign on the door of the room they are cleaning that announces they are "stylizing the room." Great! Can you do something in Mission, maybe with a Navaho rug? No, they just vacuum, scrub the bathroom, make the bed, and replace the towels. Mostly they are not Anglophones and are not offended by the absurdity of the signs they are given. But even so, should one tip them more for this nonsense or less? Or about the same?

"These fragments I have stored against my ruin," Eliot says, but he doesn't explain how to use them. They are like the wolf urine gardeners splash around their corn and tomato patches to keep the deer away. And possums, too, I imagine. (Like TSE.) I can go for a long time without thinking of him. At the end of a month, I earn a token, the way dry drunks do at AA. (You can't just not read Eliot; you have to be in recovery. Not with a bang but a whomper.) And where do you buy wolf urine?

There was also an antipope named Callixtus III, whose real name was Giovanni, Abbot of Struma. He had a reign (or anti-reign, or parapluie) of about ten years. He was primarily a bargaining chip Frederick Barbarossa used to pressure Pope Alexander III about something or other, and he had only limited geographical support. He lived in Viterbo, which is close to Rome. I'd have expected that popes and antipopes would have kept their distance, like the little Westies and Scotties with magnets that repel each other. But apparently not.

Our expectations are as inaccurate as our memories. We float through a thick soup, occasionally catch sight of a slice of carrot or a lima bean, and draw conclusions about what kind of potage this might be. And are almost always wrong. But it doesn't make any difference. The soup is unaffected by our misprisions. The guy with the spoon knows, but he's not saying. In fact, he might be Stanley, the God of

Colored Beads who is holding the spoon the wrong way, as if it were a shovel, and is not paying attention to his food anyway. Naughty God! (How's that for a tee shirt?)

Amazon, I discover, sells wolf urine. Deerbusters is the brand, and you can get 32 ounces for $30. (Reduced from $35! Who can resist a sale on such stuff? Stock up!) They claim it is wolf's urine but it may just be Amazon clerks' urine, because the idea is to repel deer, and are these animals such connoisseurs as to be able to tell the difference? Amazon, being what it is, may not even pay its employees for their urine but only impose a very strict drug testing program—or what appears to be one—while in fact, they take the urine samples and pour them into a bucket for resale at just under a dollar an ounce. The beauty part, of course, is that the program works for the prevention of drug abuse almost as well as if they sent the stuff off to a lab for testing, because what sane worker would suppose that the test was a charade. Indeed, any drug abusers among the workers are probably buying clean urine, which they give to management, which resells it as having come from wolves. And no one's the wiser. I trust the fellow who dreamed up this system got a bonus. Anyway, has it ever been scientifically demonstrated that wolf urine repels deer and rabbits? Is it just an old wives' tale? Does it repel old wives? (Hot sauce also works and Deerbusters sells that too, by the half gallon. The deer hate it. It costs more than the wolf pee, but it is can also be used in jambalaya and gumbo.)

We appear to have wandered somewhat from our subject—or we would if we had a subject. But think for a moment. We were talking (all right, I was talking) about the borderland between the truth of fact and the truth of fiction. And the ingenious fellow at Amazon seems not only to have understood this but even to profit from it. If gardeners believe in it, it works (works at least in terms of sales). If the urine looks and smells like urine, and indeed is urine, the customer is not going to know whether it is from a wolf, a coyote, a lemur, or an elephant (which comes in very large quantities). Or Jeff Bezos. Will they all repel the deer? Who knows? Maybe there won't be any deer coming this way this year, and the property owners will attribute their absence to this wonderful, renewable, environmentally friendly substance they have splashed around the Mexican marigolds that surround their tomato patches to repel rabbits and, I think, mice and voles. But in that case is it the urine or the marigolds? Either way, they feel good, aglow with virtue just as they do when the get into a Prius with the slowish greyhound rescued from the euthanist's needle.

Do I make fun of my Cambridge neighbors? I confess to it. I can't help it, because they are so ridiculously self-satisfied. But I also see in each of them Nescio's little poet who makes up an epic as he goes along. He is both author and protagonist, and therefore every breath he takes is fictional. His mythology may not be appealing but it is indubitably a mythology, and it prevents him from seeing the paving stones, or bricks, of the sidewalk before him. What substitutes for those things is grander and more suitable to a Cantabrigian, Unitarian-Universalist, right-thinking, generous person who wouldn't care if deer devoured his tomato plants (which he doesn't have; and there are no deer in Cambridge).

So it *is* relevant. When there is no actual subject—as there never is in life—everything is relevant. Or, put it the other way and say, with greater assurance, that nothing is irrelevant. The world is fucked up? Yes, of course, but if His eye is on the sparrow, He is going to miss a lot in Southern Sudan. Or maybe He is paying attention to football games between rival Catholic high schools, with both teams praying in the locker room for victory. He may be omniscient but evidently He can't focus his attention. Bupropion sometimes helps, but what is the recommended dosage for a god?

Evidently? Is there evidence? The entire fun of theology is that there is never any evidence. It is pure intellection, a positing of logical systems that do not, in the end, depend upon logic but faith. I do not criticize theologians. On the contrary, I admire them for their nervy exertions that are entirely mysterious to me. And mysteries are not always bad things. "Behold, I tell you a mystery; we will not all sleep, but we shall be changed, in a moment, in the twinkling of an eye, at the last trumpet..." Do we believe that or do we believe in the beauty of the language, or of the music in Handel's setting, and give ourselves over to that? Or, to pose the question in its most difficult way, is there a difference? There remains a glimmer of hope in the possibility that the trumpet shall sound, and the dead shall be raised incorruptible, and we shall be changed. You bet your life! (Say the magic word and a duck will descend from above with a fifty-dollar bill in its beak.)

This is not at all where I expected to go. But as you have already realized, I have no outline. This is an exploration, and the nature of exploring is to venture into territory that is unknown and somewhat frightening. For me, the possibilities are rich because there is a lot I don't know. Has my sister been raised? Has she been changed and become incorruptible? Or at least a nice person? That is difficult for me to imagine. Incorruptible and uncorrupted? I remember her when she was about five and we liked each other. Loved, I suppose, if that describes the relationship between siblings. We were supposed to love members of our immediate family. That was not only expected but assumed. And we had no reason to doubt it. The rift came later. Rifts, really, for it wasn't any one thing that caused the estrangement but the repetition, one intolerable affront after another.

This was where I wanted specifically not to go. Awkward to write about and to read about, it stinks of truth and relies on sordidness as such subjects almost always do when introduced into fiction. Ah, but there is my remedy. It is fiction, isn't it, and you can never be sure how far to trust what you are reading. Narrators are unreliable. Writers lie. I do, certainly. Or at least we change details so that there is reasonable doubt, ladies and gentlemen of the jury, and from inferences and circumstantial evidence it is risky to leap to conclusions. Leaping is always risky, as the falling Wallendas demonstrated all too often. If the facts don't fit, you must acquit. O get a glove of a larger size. (Hundreds of dollars an hour for a jingle?)

I put it to you that my entire testimony is a tissue (rhymes with "miss you") of lies. But was I lying then or am I lying now? You must imagine Perry Mason's smug smirk and the bristling of his attack eyebrows. And Hamilton Berger, rubbing his furrowed face with his hand. They will, as is their wont. But consider, the writing of a text is a different activity altogether from the decision to print it out on paper and put it into an envelope to send out somewhere. Or, these days, to click on *send*. I can imagine an author writing such a cathartic piece for its cockamamie therapeutic effect (although I never feel much of that). But there is no need to publish it. What kind of therapy would that be?

"Pound on the facts, pound on the law, and if neither of those works, pound on the table." (Roscoe Pound, perhaps?) We have already established that nobody reads anything I write, no? My latest check from William Morris Entertainment, passed on from Oxford University Press UK was for $10.90, which represents $12.04 less commission. Is that better than nothing? I don't believe so. No one would send out a check for zero dollars, so there is no way I'd know what a publishing catastrophe I was. There would be no prompting for such gloomy contemplation. But here it was, printed out by a computer and mailed to me with 69¢ worth of postage—which, as you can see without doing the arithmetic, is more than half of their $1.14 commission. I am humiliated as I deposit my ridiculous check. If I were paranoid (all novelists are), I might think of the pleasure some pimply-faced kid took in the processing of the check, knowing how it would depress the recipient and enjoying his (my) distress. But it's all machines and they don't care. They just do what they have been programmed to do. As the pimply kid does, too.

So I needn't go to the trouble of assuming a pen name. My own name is sufficiently obscure. There are, as Nescio observed, members of my family who don't know who I am or what I do. It doesn't bother me (anymore) and I have learned to take some satisfaction in it. Do proctologists discuss their work at the dinner table? (They earn more and have far more prestige than writers do, so the temptation would be greater.)

Take it from me. (Please!) This is a fiction. Real persons' names were changed to protect the innocent author. And because his memory is increasingly unreliable. (Oddly, I couldn't tell the truth if I wanted to.) To the best of my knowledge and belief? I am not sure of anything and believe only in skepticism. So not only will I not swear, I won't even be able to affirm with a clear conscience. I sit in the witness box and make birdcalls and funny faces. Contempt of court? Who isn't guilty of that? Or rather what guilt is involved in it? In the old days, one could plead the fifth, but now it has to be the 750 milliliters, which doesn't have the right ring.

I have no idea what caused the estrangement between my sister and her daughter. I could ask, I suppose, but the risk is that my niece might tell me, in which case my anger at my sister would be ratcheted up even further. And there's no need for that. What I carry around with me is burdensome enough. Anyway, it doesn't really matter, because my sister was the parent and when parents deal with children they have to try to behave like grown-ups. Whatever happened then, it was my sister's fault that there wasn't a reconciliation in a few weeks or a few months. But twenty years? That's pride. That's stubbornness. That's bone-headedness.

Another lapse. "I do apologize for that," as all "advisors" say when you call them with some problem or other. That's the script they have to follow, and the executives who composed it were evidently under the impression that "I do apologize" is somehow stronger or more fervent than without the auxiliary verb. In fact, the effect is quite the opposite, because you know they're speaking from a script and don't mean a word they're saying. They have a job, however wretched. And it is not part of the job to care about what they're instructed to say. Time will pass and they will be able to take off their headsets, leave the Kafkaesque building, and hasten to the next whiskey bar (or I must die).

Svevo and Nescio self-published, which means they never got royalty statements or checks. The only money they ever made—or recouped—was from the sale of each book. Pseudonymous authors don't go selling their work door-to-door, so they must have found

bookstores that were willing to take a couple of copies on consign-
ment.

"Your book?" the manager asks.

"No. It's my friend's."

The manager nods and smiles, as one must do in the face of a face-
saving lie. The author smiles back in legitimate gratitude to the bookseller for accepting this fiction as well at the one between the covers of
the slender volume he holds in his hands. And then the author repairs
to a bar, or goes to a bar to repair himself with genever gin or grappa.

How often can they put themselves through this? Once a week?
Twice a month. The discipline this requires is greater than that needed for writing the books. Fortunately, there are only a finite number
of bookstores in Amsterdam or Trieste. But these poor guys have to
visit each of them and then go back to ask if the store can use any more
copies or wants to give back the copies it has on display. Or, rarely, to
collect money from sales of the book—half the cover price, let's say.
The bookseller is not running a charity and he has little patience with
these vanity press scribblers. (Pull down thy vanity presses, I say pull
down.)

Is that how it worked?

Nescio shakes his head. "I don't want to talk about it. I have been
trying to forget it, which should be easy because I'm dead, but the
bruise is still with me and every now and then I touch it to see if it still
hurts. Even in the dust it does. That is the outline of most Salinger
stories, isn't it?"

He's right about Salinger. I tell him that I'm sorry to have been
thoughtless.

"And you hold yourself out as such a thoughtful fellow," Svevo says
with a pained smile. (Do I?) "How little we know ourselves. But my
friend is right. This is, for both of us, a subject that requires some
delicacy. I remember some playwright telling me that the horrible
thing about his kind of work was that the audience was right there,
all together in one room. And together they laugh, or fail to laugh, or
laugh at the wrong places. I can't remember who it was, but it sounds
plausible and perfectly dreadful. With us, there are copies of a text
that people look at one at a time, one page at a time. If they look at all.
You must know that. If literature is like wine, theater is like cocaine.
It can kill you."

I tell him again that I'm sorry. He pays no attention but asks,
"Where in hell are we?"

Sorry, I say again. To them and to you. I forgot to specify a new
venue so we're sill in Sam 'n' Ella's up in Alberta somewhere. Etzikom,

I think. It's a bit primitive but both of the novelists find it picturesque. "*Affascinante*," Svevo says. "*Innemend*," Nescio agrees. Both of them are delighted by the idea of a tuna melt, which they cannot imagine. There are checkered tablecloths, red and white. Other than in movies, where do you see these anymore?

Aside from its windmill museum, Etzikom isn't much of a place. For serious shopping, one would have to go to Medicine Hat 42 miles away. The waitress overhears us. But, no, she isn't a waitress. She's Ella. And without having been asked she explains to us that Medicine Hat refers to the hat medicine men once wore with the eagle feathers. In the course of a battle with the Blackfeet (Blackfoots?), a retreating Cree medicine man lost his headdress in the South Saskatchewan River. The *pieds noir*s thought this was hilarious and called the place "of the medicine hat," which after a while lost its preposition and article. The town grew in size during World War II because nearby there was one of the largest POW camps in Canada. (Where would the prisoners escape to? Etzicom?)

Nescio and Svevo both order tuna melts. I ask for a fried egg sandwich, which is usually safe. And coffee all around—which is not so safe.

"However did you find this place?" Svevo asks. "Or dream it up?"

Stromsmoe introduced me to it.

"Whatever became of him?" Nescio inquires.

I don't know, I said, which is always pleasing when one is talking to Nescio.

It's none of my concern. I could have invented a life for him but that would have been tedious and novelistic. There are people we meet, some of them charming and entertaining, and we just lose track of them. They disappear into life's underbrush and, by the time we think about them, they're gone. *Disparu*. Dyspareunia (I do really and truly apologize for that.)

The coffee is not terrible and Ella refills our cups. She is cheerful and plump and reminds me a little of Shelley Winters, who was also plumpish and bosomy but spoke with a slight Brooklynese accent. She wasn't fat, but most leading ladies were thinner. Ms Winters could play a lead but it was usually a fallen or falling woman. Or a drowning one. I'd mention this to Ella but she may not remember the actress. Or if she does, she may not like the comparison. She is wearing a waitress's uniform, even though she is, I assume, half owner. There is an artificial corsage on her shoulder of the kind waitresses wore thirty or forty years ago. Now if a waitress says "corsage," she means "with onions," just as "Italian perfume" means "garlic." In the States that's true.

I'm not certain about Alberta. Come to think of it, I'm not absolutely certain that there is an Alberta. There was a Prince Albert, but he was in a can most of the time.

You are, as the ill-tempered doctor would say, losing patients. Me, too. It is difficult, once I've mentioned it, not to think about Belgium. Or Alberta. Or my sister. For most of the unpleasantness between us, I contrived to forgive her, more or less. I made excuses for her and then gradually allowed myself to be persuaded by them. So she wasn't a generous person. She wasn't a criminal or a liar. Or a drunk. She was presentable. She spent a great deal of energy presenting herself. She told me once that she never served dinner guests a meal that she'd made for them before. She was an okay cook, or even a good one, but she was arrogant about it, more interested in showing off to her guests than in pleasing them and relaxing a little. Some people are like that and can't change, even if they want to. And she didn't want to. She thought she was just fine. Perfect, in fact. But who needs four sizes of melon-ballers, carefully arranged on a rack?

Nescio interrupts my wandering: "A penny for your thoughts, as the English say."

I've always thought that comes from tuppence, which in French is very like *tu pense*. My mind was drifted off. I was thinking about . . . Shelley Winters.

They both make facial expressions announcing that the name means nothing to them. Or perhaps they mean it as a criticism: if I have conjured them up and brought them to this ludicrous place in Alberta, common courtesy would demand that I give them my attention. And they are right. *Je m' excuse.* Or *Je vous prie de m'excuser*, which is a little more graceful. Are they not grateful to be sitting here with their tuna melts and their coffee, and perhaps a piece of pie, rather than wisps floating amorphously in the literary ether? Evidently not.

Nescio wrote: "... there was no one, among the dead or among the living who showed that they had any idea of what the little poet felt in that poet's head he was dragging around with him to his inglorious grave." I tell him that it is one of the saddest sentences I have ever read and I thank him for it. His nod of acknowledgment is just barely perceptible. (Or up here it would probably be acknowledgement.)

Outside, we can see gently rolling hills, tilled fields, and open meadows. In the middle distance, there are trees among which the caribou wait for darkness when it will be safer to come out and graze. Also moose, pronghorns, longhorns, wolverines, and, to keep Stromsmoe happy, flying squirrels. Also the fisher, which is one of the few animals that eats porcupines, although I find it difficult to imagine how it does this. Perhaps after it eats another creature, it finishes off with a porcupine as a way of flossing? No, actually as the fishers figured out long ago, what they do is kill the porcupine (which is difficult) and then flip it over onto its back (also difficult), but then, where there are relatively few quills on its belly, the fishers begin their meal.

"Pie?" Ella asks. I am surprised that she is still here, that any of us are. It is a rare occurrence to wake from a dream, fall asleep again, and resume an earlier dream, as if it were a story and this is a second chapter. But once in a great while it can happen. Or the circumstances change but the main theme persists, and I am still looking for the luggage I lost in the earlier dream.

Svevo says, "Freud thought dreams were significant. Especially dreams that repeat themselves one way or another."

Did you know Dr. Freud?

"I never had the pleasure. But I have read much of what he wrote. And Jung, too."

I gathered that. Some of it is in *The Confessions of Zeno*. A great book, by the way. And now that time has gone by, that opinion is widely shared.

"A lot of good that does me."

It is good for Zeno.

"He is fictional, more or less."

At this point, so are you.

"The huckleberry is still warm from the oven," Ella informs us and we agree to have a piece of that to share. (Do dead people watch their weight? If they do it is only habit, which is a terrible thing to contemplate. Ghosts working out and keeping fit, counting calories, and conducting themselves as if they still had bodies is too depressing, which makes it all the more likely, doesn't it? What hell could be worse? But when Lazarus came back, did anyyone remark about what wonderful shape he was in? "You've lost weight!" "Corpses do.")

> Strawberry shortcake, huckleberry pie!
> I N A N I T Y!
> Do we have it? Well, I guess!
> (Your name here) High School, yes, yes, yes.

What was Joyce like? I ask Svevo.

"Depressed, I think. Withdrawn. But he was extremely kind to me."

"You get asked about him a lot," Nescio suggests.

Svevo nods yes.

"Do you think Joyce ever gets asked about you?"

Svevo laughs, a short bark of a laugh. "I've never thought about it. I shouldn't think so."

With a sly smile, Nescio asks, "And does that bother you?"

"Not until now."

What have I done? This is awkward. I am in some way responsible for these characters, and they are sniping at each other. But is that so surprising? To change the mood, I ask Svevo if he can remember anything in particular that Joyce ever said, some joke or a play on words, maybe.

He purses his lips. "It's silly, but I remember his asking once whether it was possible that Bohuslav Martinů had a brother named Tohuslav."

Silly, but profound, as word play can be. I feel enriched by knowing this. (Don't get excited, I made it up.)

We speak about being of two minds, but once we admit the plural there is no reason to limit ourselves to two. If Whitman's mind contains multitudes, aren't we all entitled to similar crowds, throngs, gangs, and flocks? He didn't say "my mind contains flocks" because it sounds just like my mind contains phlox, which is an absurdity beyond Whitman's reach. I like it, though. Even better, my mind contains lilacs. (Sounds rather French.) Anyway, a novelist is entitled to make up as many characters as he wants. Look at the first few pages of *War and Peace,* before the text begins. There's a list of characters that goes on forever, with an assemblage of princes, counts, generals, and their wives and daughters. Some editions have a bookmark you can stick in there so you can refer to the list when you forget which Russkie name belongs to whom. Better yet would be three bookmarks, one at the front for the characters and one at the back for the notes, unless you remember all the details of Napoleon's Iberian campaign. ("The siege of Cadiz has slipped your mind? *Pardonnez mo*i!") The third bookmark, of course, could be used in the usual way, to mark the place where you left off reading.

It crosses my mind that Svevo was a precursor of Nicholson Baker, who has a lovely novel about a guy going out to buy shoelaces during his lunch break (*The Mezzanine,* and that is the plot!). His book is an heir of *The Confessions of Zeno,* which you will remember is an account of the efforts of the eponymous protagonist to give up cigarettes. Tiny, tiny, but no less true. The entire world, if you look at it through the "wrong" end of a telescope appears to be tiny but preternaturally clear. That's the effect of both these books that are also lessons in how to pay closer attention. Cigarettes are the subject, too, of *Il segreto di Susanna* a silly opera by Ermanno Wolf-Ferrari. Susanna smokes (that's her secret), and the scent of tobacco in the house makes her husband suppose she has a lover. It is a farce and perhaps a little too self-consciously cute. (*Il Cigaretto di Susana?*) Generally we have nothing against farce. Seriously, I used to write seriously, but farce majeure... What can one do?

Svevo has one of the first unreliable narrators, so that it isn't what it seems, a novel with a narrative and characters, but rather a web of words. Language is the subject, as surely as paint is the subject of many of the abstract expressionists. (Or, if you want to be respectful, Abstract Expressionists.) The proof of Eliot's anti Semitism for many people is that he didn't give a majuscule to the "jew" who "squats on the window sill." Among his sins, though, this oversight seems *de minimus*. Even in that sentence there are worse and more obvious slurs. Apologists apologize, as is their habit, claiming that the poems don't actually mean what they say but are just language churning and churning in the hope that somehow butter will come. Betty Botter bought some butter, but she found the butter bitter, so Betty bought some better butter, and so to make her batter better, Betty decided to hell with it, she'd use margarine instead. And she went down to the superette and picked up some of that swell T. S. Oleo (with the picture of margarine in the cathedral on the label.)

Okay, okay. Why didn't we speak a word for twenty years (22 actually)? Because she was a shit. And I didn't talk to her. And because she was a shit, if I wasn't talking to her, then she wasn't talking to me. Sometimes I imagined that my silence reminded her how badly she had behaved. Or did she just put that out of her mind? I would have remembered committing any gross lapses in decency about which she might have been angry. But I don't think that was it. She was so self-centered that she could just drum me out of the planet as if I were a Venusian. ("Do you all have those antennae coming out of your foreheads?" "Yes, we do." "And those triangular ears?" "Yes, we do." "And those little round hats?" "Only the Orthodox.")

To review these details is tedious, but there is only a slight difference between tedium and Te Deum. Everybody knows that the devil is in the details, but so is God. Those tiresome routines we perform every day, washing our faces, brushing our teeth, taking our pills, and tying our shoes are repetitive exercises, of course, but look at those Buddhist monks spinning their prayer wheels or banging their drums while they iterate some mantra or other a thousand times, a hundred thousand times... This is one of the ways in which novels are persuasive. The plot isn't important, but the descriptions along the way of how a character, entirely unaware of what is about to happen to him, cracks open the soft-boiled egg in the eggcup before him and begins to eat it with one of those small spoons that can be used for demitasse coffee or, of course, soft boiled eggs. It has an initial on it, but not his. He picked it up for ten dollars at a flea market because he thought it was attractive and now he regularly has soft-boiled eggs for breakfast mostly so he can hold it in his hand.

Easy enough to do, but only a reader in a religious trance is likely to understand that the routine, repeated every morning, is a kind of prayer, not one that asks for anything or bores the deity with praises He has heard before, but just an assent to the world.

So, having touched on the subject of my sister and our estrangement I must either wash my hands or provide some of the circumstances--or else revert to my repression. It is hard to know which is more uncomfortable. You're a kid and your stomach is sending you dire messages. You are going to vomit or, maybe, if you just lie very still and try to think about something else, the nausea will pass. That's not the usual (pardon me) outcome but it can happen. It may take longer that way but it avoids the awfulness of throwing up, the terrible taste of vomit, the particles of partly digested food in the back of your nose, the smell, and, maybe worst of all, the helplessness. Not that, never that. And yet, you also know that if you go into the bathroom and heave, it will be over in a few minutes and, although you may feel shaky, you won't be nauseated anymore. If you can get through those five minutes, all the time beyond it will be better. At worst, you'll feel less terrible. At least the nausea will stop. The tiredness will help you fall asleep, which is what you're trying to do now. Which is worse? What difference does it make? (This would have made a much more interesting novel than the one Sartre published as *Nausea,* which isn't even about nausea but a general feeling of unsettledness.) Even as you carry on this internal debate, you know that the choice isn't yours to make. Your body will decide for you. You think you own it? No, sir, not hardly. It owns you. It is you. Just as Stromsmoe's owns him. You have always obeyed it, even though you mostly haven't realized this. But there comes a time when it asserts itself. It sickens, it ages, it slows down. The buffets of all those sunrises with the light beating down from the sky and battering you on your head at 186,000 miles per second per second have begun to take their toll and you are alerted to and then hounded by your finitude.

And the wisdom you are supposed to have acquired? It is not what you expected. You are less certain of things, not more. Doubts obscure your days and trouble your nights. How much of our quarrel was my fault? None? Really? Can there ever be a fight in which the fault is all on one side? Well, if I had been a saint, maybe I could have contrived to accept her slights or found some excuse for them. But I am not a saint. (That's one of the things about which I am absolutely sure.) And my feelings can be hurt. But it was more than hurt feelings. It was a defilement of everything I believed in, of everything we had learned from our parents and grandparents.

Listen. My mother's father, an immigrant, was a butcher. He had a shop down on the lower east side somewhere. And everybody back in the village in the old country knew that if they came to New York, they could go to my grandfather's shop and, if they needed to, sleep on the floor. Not just for one night, but until they got on their feet and could find a place to stay. He'd give them something to eat (butchers always have something) and a floor to sleep on. He was poor but they were poorer, and that's what a man does for a *Landsmann*.

In my parents' house—in our parents' house—that tradition continued. It no longer included everyone from that village in Poland but it did extend to relatives. Cousins, mostly, when they were going to college or law school, or were unable for some reason to live with their parents, would come and stay in the room across the hall from mine. For months sometimes. They would eat with us. And they would be treated as members of the family—which they were. Not to welcome any of them to join us would have been unthinkable.

I do not hold my grandfather or my parents up for special praise. I think—or hope—that this is how most families behave. Jewish, Christian, Moslem, Buddhist, atheist... It is more basic than religion, although every religion endorses such conduct. One doesn't even have to like the relative; it is the blood connection that entitles him or her to a bed and a place at the table.

That's background. The event itself was simple. Even trivial. Or, if you look at it the way I did, of enormous importance. I was in Washington, DC on some unavoidable business. The meeting ran longer than I had expected so I missed my plane home and was stranded. It happened to be the first night of Passover, and I would miss our Seder at home. But I had a sister in the District and I called her. She seemed a little stiffish at first. Then I understood why. She realized that this was the night of the Seder—when a Jew is supposed to invite even strangers to dinner. But she told me, her brother, "I'm afraid the table is full."

I was dumbfounded. I stared at the phone for a few seconds in the desperate hope that this was some kind of joke. She was teasing me. There would be a laugh and then an invitation to come over. Of course. But no. Just silence. I hung up as if the whole of the conversation had been some malfunction of the telephone. The table was full? The careful plans for a dinner party, the arrangement of the table settings... What in hell was she thinking about?

We hadn't been especially close but we weren't at odds either. There had never been any exchange of harsh words. It took me years to realize that it was her self-centeredness. I had presumed to come out of nowhere and, without warning, intrude upon her Seder. Or never mind Seder, her dinner party. The Haggadahs on the Minton plates were pro forma acknowledgements of what day it was. She was no more concerned about what Passover meant, what family meant, or what decency demanded than a cat would be.

I waited for days and then weeks for her to call and apologize. I couldn't believe that her obsession about a dinner party could be so intense that she forgot who we were and what we were heirs to. It wasn't merely that I had been insulted but our parents and their traditions had all been written off as if with her they counted for nothing. For their sakes as well as my own, I couldn't bring myself to forgive her. I tried, of course. I argued with myself that behavior of this degree of weirdness couldn't be that of a rational person. It was something mental, some defect in her vision that left her blind to what she was doing and had done. Could I not, then, overlook an action that was involuntary like a sneeze or a hiccup? Of course not. What serene bullshit. I was in a bad mood, your honor, and it was only for that reason that I murdered all my classmates, my teacher, the janitor, and two policemen before I surrendered. I had intended to shoot myself, too, but the gun jammed. And the judge, sorry to hear about my mood disorder, lets me off with a warning. I'm on parole for six months? My library privileges are suspended for a year?

Caribou cacca. She was in a bad mood? So was I. She could behave like a shit? So could I. And for far longer. I assumed that eventually she would try to make amends. On my birthday, maybe. A phone call or a card. But nothing. So on her birthday, which was five days after mine, no phone call, no card, nothing but a thought that became less and less angry and more and more sad. And after twenty years or so, she died. I was not notified about the funeral, which was fine with me. (My niece wasn't invited either but she went and no one had the nerve to throw her out.) As far as I was concerned the coffin could have been as empty as Saavreda's after he encountered his visa problems. The ceremony was terribly belated because our estrangement had become her monument as it went from terrestrial and corruptible to eternal and incorruptible.

I wasn't sad and I certainly wasn't happy. If anything I was re-lieved because she had already been dead to me and now was dead to everyone else as well. My fiction had morphed into reality, or say that one kind of truth had changed into another. The resolution of this dissonance marked the cessation of an annoyance. It hadn't been my sister who died or who refused to let me come and disturb the sym-metry of her table. She had turned into a person I didn't know and with whom I felt no connection. My loss if I had any was from years before on the night of the wise son, the wicked son, the simple son, and the idiotic son, who doesn't even know enough to ask what's go-ing on. That last one was me and it was during those moments on the telephone had I become aware of it.

You have seen through the mystery? You realize that it is much less upsetting to consider how fishers eat porcupines than to think about my sister. The ingeniousness of the fisher to have solved a problem that has baffled all other carnivores is comforting. Do fishers teach this knack to their offspring or is it hardwired into them so that they are born with it? And why don't the porcupines have this infor-mation? Or maybe they do but their quills have made them cocky and arrogant so that the caution any animal of that size ought to have soon disappears. Wolves, bears, and other beasts approach, get themselves impaled on the quills and hurry away. The mother protects the 'porcu-pettes' (seriously) until their quills come in and then she assumes that they are safe. They assume so, too. But like Achilles they have this one vulnerable place. They find out that they have been set up, tricked, betrayed. The world is not only unfair but wicked. (Or maybe they are born knowing this, too.) There are no epics about porcupines, or even fables that I know of. (It would be fun to write one but difficult to sell. Children's book editors work in that department usually because that is their reading level.)

That nature's randomness can produce so intricate a piece of drama is more of a wonder than Nescio's novels or Svevo's. Or mine. We are all human and can communicate in words. We have opposing thumbs and opposing souls with which to manipulate what little we can perceive of external reality, using it, distorting it, or ignoring it as we create another that is different if not better.

I have never been in Alberta. But I feel more of a connection to it than I do to Washington, DC. I can fill my lungs with its clear air with a balsamic tang from the fir and poplar trees and achieve an instant of peace. If there is air in heaven (if there is a heaven) it must smell like this. I can sit at a table at Sam 'n' Ella's and eat their huckleberry pie, and even if the name occurred to me as a joke, the place became less and less silly. I sip the coffee, take another forkful of the pie (the huck-leberry season is not very long and this is a delicacy) and before me on the red and white checkered tablecloth is a copy of *The Confessions of Zeno*. I am reading about the guilt Zeno feels at the death of his father and his helpless anger at the doctor, whose manner he finds insup-portable—although we know, as he does, too, that it is the death he can't stand. I feel for him. Which is better than trying to feel anything for myself. That part of me is dead. There is no place for it at the table.

For Amy

Made in the USA
San Bernardino, CA
24 October 2014